Café La Femme Book 3

KEEP CALM
—AND—
Kill the Chef

LIVIA DAY

d

by *deadlines*

www.twelfthplanetpress.com

First published by Deadlines, 2019
Copyright © 2019 by Livia Day
Edited by Alisa Krasnostein and Katharine Stubbs
Copyedited by Elizabeth Disney
Cover and text by Cathy Larsen Design

A catalogue record for this
book is available from the
National Library of Australia

For Alison and Heather
who like these books best

CAFÉ WARS POPS UP IN HOBART ...
Article by Lani Trendsetter

Remember *Café Wars*? YouTube sensation Cameron #ToffeeShark Crewe is about to make his internet comeback. Crewe's tea bar chain Teasperience hit the rocks last year with a series of calamities: a sexual harassment suit that cost 'bad boy' Crewe over $500,000 in legal costs and damages, arson attacks on two of their three Sydney outlets, and Crewe's legendary meltdown on live TV when his name was spelled wrong on a banner at the Melbourne Good Food Expo.

Now Cameron Crewe returns with a new series of his long-abandoned cult YouTube hit, in which he pits real cafés against each other in a series of elaborate challenges designed to drive the chefs, their employees and their customers into emotional breakdowns for the sake of cheesy clickbait.

After distancing himself from the #ToffeeShark label and his YouTube fandom when the first Teasperience bar opened its doors three years ago, Crewe appears to be climbing down off his profiterole tower to recharge his reputation as the angriest dessert chef in the business. Instead of pitting himself against the zillions of copycat shows based around Melbourne or Sydney food culture, he's heading for micro-city Hobart to set up a pop up Teasperience store and a brand new series of *Café Wars*.

Crewe's made a few smart choices this time around: Hobart has a reputation as a trendsetter location for cafés, art and culture, but we still rarely see it on mainstream TV. He has also pulled in the Queen of the Twitterverse, Kari Nagarra as host to give his new series some cred. Everyone's been wondering what Nagarra's next project would be after she made the shift from one hit wonder pop star and Indigenous affairs advocate to Young Australian of the Year and radio personality.

Is this too little, too late, to restore the #ToffeeShark to the top of the culinary food chain? Crewe launched the trend for Angry Dessert Chefs on Australian TV, but since he posted his last vid, our airwaves and band-width have filled with so-called food celebrities hurling pavlovas and hot toffee strands at their assistants. Short of inspiring actual homicide, how is Crewe going to raise the bar to prove he's still the maddest, baddest anti-cinnamon roll in the business?

We'll be watching.

WEEK ONE

The #ToffeeShark

vs

Hot Chocolate

= 1 =

Tabitha and the Terrible, Bad, No Good Idea
(before the murder)

'Hi, I'm Tabitha Darling of Café La Femme, and we're going to win *Café Wars*.'

Ever said the same words so many times that they spiral into nonsense syllables until it feels like you're saying 'engineer cupcake files, my Sharona, stat'?

Making a video for the internet is a lot like that. My smile is so bright it makes my cheeks ache, my sincerity is waning, and I've forgotten how to speak make good.

'Can you say it slightly less like you want to murder us all and turn us into lunch surprise?' asks Lara, from behind the camera.

'I was going for less murderous!' I protest. 'Yui, where are you going?'

One barista holds the iPad steady while arguing with me, and the other does her best to hide behind furniture. 'Do I have to be in shot?' Yui asks, embarrassed.

'It needs to look like I have actual staff,' I say sternly.

'Nin has threatened to quit if I put a camera in her face, the boy apprentice is visiting his probation officer, and Lara is holding the iPad. Also I really like what you did with your hair today.'

Yui is trapped somewhere between pleased and outraged, which is the balance I strive for with baristas. Keep 'em confused and they're less likely to apply for jobs elsewhere. I'm not even lying about the hair—she added aqua tufts to her usual shiny black locks that look arty and adorable.

'You can hold the iPad if you like, Yui,' says Lara generously. She gives me a dirty look. 'My hair also looks super cute today, thanks for noticing.'

'I never said it didn't.' The two of them swap places with far more hand-touching and secret-smiling than is required. They think they're so subtle about the enormous crushes they have on each other.

I grin until it hurts. 'Hi, I'm Tabitha Darling of Café La Femme, and we're going to win *Café Wars*.'

'Hey, Tabitha,' says the producer with a warm smile on her first visit to my café. 'I'm Kari Nagarra, and this is Tom, our camera operator.'

I smile back and shake hands with them both, trying not to squee too embarrassingly loud about Kari's celebrity status. We've emailed and texted over the last few weeks,

6

but seeing a famous face in person is a shock no matter how many emoticons you've shared.

Kari and Tom each have two scarves wrapped around their necks and giant puffy parkas, like they're about to set out for Antarctica. It's not even snowing on the mountain yet. *Mainlanders.*

'I'm looking forward to this,' I say as Tom sets up his equipment in a corner of the café. 'It's going to be fun.'

'Yeah, fun,' he mutters in an undertone.

My smile falters a little. 'I'm sorry?'

'Don't mind Tom,' says Kari quickly. 'He's jaded because of over-exposure to our celebrity chef. We've already filmed with the other two cafés today. Speaking of which, I have a checklist I like to go through for people who'll be working with Chef Crewe.'

'Okay, shoot,' I tell her. 'But FYI, one of my best friends used to date him. I am prepared for his personality.'

Kari raises a dark, perfectly plucked eyebrow. 'Have you met him?'

'No.'

'You're not fully prepared, then. Bear with me. Chef Crewe's brand is all about shock value, so don't hold back your reactions if he says something jaw-droppingly offensive.'

'When,' butts in Tom.

'Oh, yes, good point. *When* he says something jaw-droppingly offensive.'

7

'O-kay.'

'If it's extra horrendous, we probably won't air it. That doesn't mean that we can't use your reaction shot, so don't feel you have to laugh at his jokes or pretend everything's fine.'

'Righto.'

Kari leans in, her face deadly serious. 'No one expects you to laugh at his jokes. They're never funny.'

'Got it.'

'Please resist slapping him in the face, or engaging in any kind of physical contact, regardless of the provocation…'

'I'm not really a face-slapper.' Hair-puller, yes.

'Good for you. Still, the urge will be there. Fight it.' Is she trolling me now?

'I'll prepare myself,' I assure her.

'Not that it wouldn't make great footage, but he's successfully sued two previous contestants for unwarranted physical violence, and his lawyers are paid exceptionally well to define the word 'unwarranted' at a moment's notice.'

Youch. 'I'll keep that in mind.'

'I find it helpful to keep all stabby objects out of reach when he's talking.'

'Do cake pops count as stabby objects?'

'I wouldn't risk it.'

'I'm finding the lack of irony in your tone really distressing, just so you know.'

'Yes,' says Kari, sounding exhausted. 'I get that a lot.' Her phone beeps once. 'Okay, the man himself's on his way. We should get the intro out of the way before he gets here. Rolling, Tom?'

'Got it,' says Tom, looming up out of his corner with a large camera fixed to his face.

I jump. 'Oh, we're doing this now?' Where have Lara and Yui disappeared to, the traitors? I turn to the kitchen door and catch them both peering at me through the little glass window. 'Nice,' I say pointedly.

Kari steps in front of me, all smiles and charisma. 'I'm Kari Nagarra, and you are watching a brand new series of *Café Wars*. Legendary Australian dessert chef Cameron Crewe is challenging three of Hobart's best cafés to test themselves on the barista battlefield. Today we're here at Café La Femme, in the heart of the little city that could. Say hello to Tabitha Darling.'

She steps out of my way faster than I'm expecting, leaving me to smile at the camera and do an awkward finger wave. 'Hi. Welcome to Café La Femme.'

Kari leans back against the counter like we'd practised this a dozen times. 'Café La Femme is also known as the murder mystery café. Famous for killer milkshakes, and poisonous tea parties.'

My smile freezes on my mouth. 'That's not our thing. Who told you that was our thing?'

9

'Café La Femme has a police station at its beck and call, a detective agency upstairs...'

'Blame my landlord for that one,' I interrupt, because really? Murder mystery café, that's my brand now? Do I not get a say in this?

'There's been many a corpse found in this very building,' continues the presenter, not picking up on my frantic 'do not go there' vibes—or perhaps enjoying them a little too much. Apparently I've been selected for the show because of my past troubles as much as (more than?) my awesome skills with gateaux. *Café Wars* wants a story—and like all the reporters and bloggers and nosy parkers who've sniffed around my café before them, they want *that* story.

Tabitha Darling, cake-baking detective.

'*One* corpse has been found in this building, and it was years ago,' I say, more sharply than I mean to. 'Mysterious deaths are not our theme. Cake is our theme. Cake hardly ever gets people murdered.'

'So Tabitha,' Kari goes on smoothly. 'What's the secret to your killer milkshakes?

I regretted letting Nin call them that almost as soon as I agreed to it.

Kari's trying to rattle me, so I stare straight down the lens of the camera and give them my most deadpan tone. 'My killer milkshakes have three secrets. You can fit a lot more ice-cream in a hipster jar than you think you can,

Nutella is best served in giant scoops … and I don't murder the customers I like.'

———————

Five minutes after we're done, Cameron Crewe walks into my café like he owns the place. I guess that's how he walks into most places.

He really is stupidly handsome. My bloke is also stupidly handsome, so you'd think I would be immune to it, but there's something about Cameron Crewe. He has a TV Famous Glow about him. Maybe it's his teeth that make the overall look so disconcerting. He has Hollywood teeth, and eyes too bright to be real. Basically, he's a cartoon character in a nice suit.

'Tabitha Darling,' he says, adding more rrrs to my name than required. 'I've heard all about you.'

We're still on camera, and he knows it. Does he even exist when the camera's turned off?

Yeah, I bet you have. Somewhere in the back of my head is a repeated mantra of 'I told you so, I told you so.' It sounds a lot like my BFF Xanthippe, who once dated and dumped this shiny slab of celebrity.

'Thanks for choosing our café,' I say with the warmest of smiles. Faking warmth is the first thing you learn in the service industry.

'For Week One, Café La Femme takes on the hot chocolate

challenge,' purrs Cameron. 'Lucky last, as our other contenders put up a very impressive first showing. What have you got for me, little lady?'

'Hot chocolate challenge for Chef Crewe!' I call to the kitchen, hoping they aren't slacking off back there. Yui pushes the door open and holds it for Lara, who carries the tray we had prepped earlier.

Unlike ninety-five percent of food served during TV cooking shows, it's piping hot.

'Chef Crewe, I know you're a fan of taking something classically brilliant and turning it into a dish that's over-complicated and difficult to consume,' I announce cheerfully. 'So I've made you hot chocolate sliders. That's four different types of hot chocolate—raspberry white, chilli dark, pure milk and marshmallow melt—served in cups too tiny to be practical.'

For my presentation, I chose 1950s egg cups shaped like cartoon sailing ships. I have a tall, dark dreamboat in my bed most nights, but vintage egg cups are the true love of my life.

'Aces,' says Cameron Crewe, regarding my ocean blue tea tray, and the bright white sailing ship cups filled with chocolate deliciousness. 'What's this garnish?' he asks, stabbing a finger at the sugar sculpture balanced over the froth of each cup.

'They're shark fins,' I say with my sweetest smile. 'Made

out of toffee.'

His eyes are flinty, gleaming like shards of melted caramel. 'You know, love, no one ever actually calls me that nickname to my face.'

Kari Nagarra, out of shot, has a frantic 'back away and call emergency services' look on her face.

'That's a shame,' I tell him, leaning in over the counter. 'It's a great nickname. If I had one like that, I'd put it on t-shirts and sell them. Oh wait, that shell company you set up totally does that.'

'And what do they call you around here, sweetheart?' Crewe asks, looming so far over me I can practically smell the smarm on his skin.

I don't flinch. 'They call me Tabitha. Politely. Because I'm the boss.'

2

Xanthippe and The Wildly Inappropriate Birthday Present

We all have regrets. Here's an exciting assortment of mine for you to sort through at your leisure:

I regret that I kept my papa's last name, even though he fucked off when I was twelve and he doesn't deserve that kind of acknowledgement.

I regret that I gave my mum hell for most of my teen years, when she was doing the best she could.

I regret that I fought my brother Leo every step of the way, whenever he tried to act like we're family. I still do it.

I regret that one time I tried to fake a murder and nearly ended up an accessory to a real one.

I regret that I never told anyone that I was in love with Carly Denver, even after she disappeared when we were sixteen and never, ever came back.

I regret that I've screwed up every relationship, every friendship, every challenge, because I'm always looking over my shoulder, waiting for the other shoe to drop.

I regret that I didn't figure out what I wanted to do as a job until I was twenty-seven years old, and only then because my stupid rich ex handed it to me on a plate.

This is how it happened.

Back in January, a call came up on my phone from my ex-boyfriend Darrow, who appears in my contacts list as Don'tCallHim. 'What do you want now?' I snapped, continuing a conversation from months earlier.

'Carides, don't hang up.'

I huffed a sigh into the phone. 'I forgave you for the car thing. We're done.'

'I was thinking about your birthday.'

'My birthday is three months away.'

'I know. I was wondering if there was anything you needed.'

This was embarrassing. For both of us. You wouldn't think an enthusiastic ex-boyfriend with too much money on his hands was a problem, but I didn't have to be an amateur detective to suspect he was after more than friendly gratitude. 'Don't buy me anything. Especially not something that has to be planned three months in advance.'

'I want to do something special for you!'

'You're forgiven, okay? You can stop with the grand gestures.'

Replacing my beloved vintage sports car after crashing it was fair and reasonable. I still mourned my Lotus. Some day when I could bear to, I'd paw through the wreckage and rebuild her from the ground up all over again. But he made up for it with the Spider. And I was so. Over. Having to reassure him that we were square. Every single time we talked. His guilt was exhausting.

Darrow also gave me shares in the café he and Tabitha owned, and I let him because it was funny how much it annoyed her. I shouldn't have.

'Fine,' said Darrow, and now he was the one acting huffy. 'How's Café La Femme?'

'Tabitha is sick of me, the baristas hate me, the coffee machine is actively trying to kill me, and I still can't make a decent cup of tea. Apparently. Like water temperature is some kind of science or something, I don't know.'

'It's not working out?' His tone of voice was that of a man who gave me a cute puppy in a basket, only for me to drop a piano on it.

'Darrow, it's fine. Everything's fine. I'm ... looking for something new, that's all. The café business was never going to work for me.' My pathological dislike of cooking and being polite did not mix well with Tabitha's 'everything can be fixed with pancakes' philosophy, or the service industry as a whole.

'I have an idea.'

This was bad. Darrow with ideas was terrible, because he had the resources to carry them out without stopping to think, and that was how things like smashed sports cars happened in the first place. 'Darrow, no. Listen to me very, very carefully. NO. Do I need to spell it out? N—'

The line was dead. I stared at my phone like it was a bomb about to go off.

In three months' time, possibly. For my birthday. Oh, hell.

———————

In early April, I received a key stuffed into a retro birthday card that declared 'All Men Are Stupid'. The address printed on the back of the card was one of his buildings, of course … one I knew all too well. It was the same address as Café La Femme, two floors up.

I knew that flat. It once housed a glam rock band I did some PR work for. It was also the site of a murder, and no one had lived there—as far as I knew—for nearly a year.

I made my way up the stairs slowly and suspiciously, waiting for a giant whoopee cushion to appear under my feet, or balloons and streamers to pour down from the ceiling.

Instead, I found a new door with smoky glass panels and a shiny brass panel that announced: Xanthippe Carides, Private Detective.

My life. I can't even.

I reached out and brushed my fingertips against the nameplate for a moment before stepping inside the office.

I hadn't known this was something that I wanted, really wanted, until now.

How did Darrow figure it out when I didn't know myself? There is no quality more irritating in an ex than telepathy. (To be honest, he has so many irritating qualities that his unerring ability to tell what I'm thinking gets lost in the crush.)

This one time, he got it exactly right, and I couldn't even be pissed off about it.

You're never going to sleep with him again, remember that, no matter how many doors he writes your name on, you really don't want to…

The main room was empty, for the most part—polished wooden floorboards and blank walls. A black and white poster of *The Big Sleep* pinned to a corkboard.

Darrow had provided a large, sturdy wooden desk, an honest-to-god typewriter that must have come from the tip shop, and a bottle of whiskey with a fifth missing. No drinking glasses, because real detectives don't share. There was a telephone, an old fashioned one with a proper receiver, though when I looked closer it turned out to be a novelty mobile charger.

A battered, antique fedora hung on a wooden hat-stand in the far corner.

'You're an idiot,' I said aloud, in the echoing office. But I was smiling, damn it.

———————

'Holy hell,' said Tabitha, after she ran up the four flights of stairs in response to my frantic texts. I'm not normally a 'say it with emoticons' person, but it was that kind of day.

She found me slouching back into my chair, boots on the desk, hat pulled down over my eyes. 'I know, right?' I drawled.

'Most exes don't even send flowers.' Tabitha gazed around the office, lost in a black and white movie marathon inside her own head. 'This does explain why he asked me if it was possible to make a Humphrey Bogart cake.'

'Oh, is there cake?'

'No, I thought he was kidding. Should have known better.' Tabitha came over and sat on the desk. 'Is this something you want to discuss, Zee? Is this what it takes to get you to girltalk?'

'I don't do girltalk,' I said firmly.

'Not even on your birthday?'

'Especially not on my birthday.' I removed the fedora. 'He's filed the paperwork. I can do this for real, if I want to.'

Private detective. I was so up for it. I could find missing teenagers (and check they wanted to be found before I reunited them with their families), prove shithead husbands were cheating on their wives (photographic evidence costs extra!) and make my own hours. It had to be better than working in PR or suffering at the hands of a coffee machine that bears a grudge.

'I'm jealous,' Tabitha said lightly. 'I'm the one who trips over accidental murder mysteries all the time, and you get the detective office?'

She'd only done that like two and a half times, and she hated it, so I don't know what her problem was. 'Hey, if you want to get your Veronica Mars on, we can make this a partnership,' I threatened. 'Anytime.'

The words came out of my mouth before I could stop them. It wasn't the world's worst idea. When it came to people skills, Tabitha has my share and then some.

For a moment, Tabitha looked like she was seriously considering it, then she shook her head and smiled. 'As a detective, I make a great barista. Speaking of which—'

'Oh, I'm totally quitting the café. Rolling back to silent partner.'

Tabitha looked relieved. 'Good, because you were terrible at cake-slinging, and you've had one foot out the door since you arrived. But that wasn't what I was going to ask.'

'Oh. Go on, then.'

'I've been invited to enter the café in a — well, a sort of competition.' She bit idly at her lower lip.

Tabitha and I have known each other since high school. She's super cute, and a genuinely nice person (with enough sarcasm and snark that I can stand to be around her most days) but she has this one terrible habit. When she is about to pitch a truly terrible idea, her eyes get wide, she nibbles on her lower lip, and her voice takes on this 'softening you up with cupcakes' tone that is like chalk up a blackboard for me.

Tabitha has almost as many terrible ideas as Darrow, but she doesn't have the money to put most of them into action. Just, you know, endless stores of energy, pastry recipes and a massive network of friends who'd lie in front of a tram if she asked sweetly.

Tasmania doesn't even have trams.

'What's the catch?' I asked. Guilt was pouring off Tabitha like cinnamon steam from an apple pie.

'It's a reality TV show,' she said, about thirty seconds away from twirling a braid. I swear, if she twirled her hair, I was going to reach for the scissors. 'On YouTube. Not a huge commitment, maybe a day's filming once a week, and we can fit it around café hours… It doesn't even affect you if you're going silent partner on me.'

A reality TV thing. On YouTube. I frowned harder. 'Something like *Café Wars*?'

Tabitha lifted her chin defiantly. 'It *is* *Café Wars*,' she admitted.

I slammed my boots to the ground. Panic isn't a thing I do, most of the time, but breathing was suddenly very difficult indeed. 'Oh, Tish, no,' I spluttered. Not that. Anything but that.

Tabitha was distressed by my reaction—my face must be appropriately murderous, then, good to know. 'I know you have history with Chef Crewe...'

'Yeah, and not the happy fluffy revisionist history they teach in primary schools. Think crashing, burning, betrayal, siege warfare.' The thought of it made me sick to my stomach. Cameron Crewe. Here. In Hobart. 'I used to work for that arsehole, I know what I'm talking about.'

I had slept with him a total of six times and I wish I could take back every single one of them. He's the biggest epic fail bullet point in my list of professional and personal disasters. I can't even access memories of why my self-esteem was so fucking low that I allowed myself to get swept up in his ego and bullshit.

'It's only for eight weeks—'

'Lives can be destroyed in eight weeks, Tabitha. I've seen it happen. We're talking *plagues of locusts*. Even you can't match the right cup of coffee to plagues of locusts.'

Tabitha backed away slowly. 'This is over-dramatic even for you.'

'I'm not over anything,' I ground out. 'Cameron Crewe is *poison*. He's the toxic foam on a cappuccino of solid gold bastard. He'll cause havoc with your staff, he'll belittle and alienate your customers, and the worst part is you'll probably end up hooking up with him, and then my brother will shoot him in the face and we'll all end up in prison.'

'So,' said Tabitha, sounding wan. 'You're saying I shouldn't have signed the contract.'

I let my head fall to the desk with a thump. It was reassuringly solid. Darrow's contractors did good work. 'Why do you ask my advice after you've committed yourself to the thing you were going to do no matter what I said?'

'To create the illusion of teamwork?' Tabitha gave me a very small, cheeky smile. 'Look on the bright side. If Cameron Crewe drives me to murder, I've got a brand new private detective on my side. You can bail me out when I inevitably murder him!'

'That's so much less reassuring than you think it is,' I growled.

Living in Tasmania, you get used to coincidence. Cameron Crewe choosing Hobart, Tasmania as the backdrop for his YouTube comeback … tapping one of my oldest friends to be a contestant on his show, with a café I partly own?

None of that is out of the realms of possibility for a big fat coincidence.

And yet.

If he knew I was here, if I factored even slightly into his choice to be here, then what came next would be as much my responsibility as anyone else's… If Tabitha was involved, I would be helping to clean up the mess no matter what.

———

Between April and May, I moved out of the share house where I'd been living with Tabitha, Ceege and the boy apprentice. Nothing personal, but my new office came with a futon in the back room, blissfully silent evenings to myself, and a power shower. As a bonus, I wouldn't be up close and personal for the inevitable *Café Wars* disaster zone.

May did indeed bring an exciting variety of disasters to Tabitha and the café, but because I was doing everything in my power to keep away from Cameron Crewe and his latest vanity project, I didn't realise how bad it was until it was far too late to help.

With a lot of things, as it turned out.

———

June arrived. As winter settled over the city, the shit hit the fan. Winter in Hobart is a combination of all possible winter weathers, thrown in a blender to rotate at high frequency. This year was especially frosty.

There was snow on the mountain, a chill in the air, and my phone was ringing.

I awoke slowly. Yes, I was in the back room of my detective agency (officially official now, I'd been handling cases and everything) and yes, I was getting too old to sleep on a futon.

It was time to commit to real furniture, since the 'being

a grown up thing' was working so well.

The bright white screen of my phone informed me that it was 4AM, and the police station was calling. That was…

Yeah, there was no way that was going to be good news.

'Carides,' I said into the phone, thinking it had to be about my brother. *Leo, you'd better not have done something stupid and got yourself shot in the line of duty.*

I wasn't expecting Tabitha. Tabitha, sounding quiet and frightened and altogether not herself. 'Zee? I need your help.'

'Help how? Help with what? Is this a Leo thing?' Too late, I remembered that Leo and Tabitha were officially Not Together any more (I mentioned how disastrous May had been right?), so what the hell was this? 'Tish, it's stupid o'clock, use small words.'

'I need you to bail me out,' said Tabitha with a heavy sigh, sounding miserable. 'From the actual police station. Well, not bail. Metaphorical bail. Non metaphorical police station.'

I sat up, fully awake now. 'More words than that!'

'Cameron Crewe was found dead yesterday evening,' Tabitha said, her voice shaking only a little. 'On his own kitchen floor. With a toffee shard knife stuck in his chest.'

Not as surprising as it should have been. This was not the time for *I told you so*. 'Who found him?'

'I did.'

'Are you a suspect?' I managed not to ask the question 'did you kill him' and was proud of myself for not going there. Not yet.

'They didn't charge me with anything.'

'That doesn't entirely answer my question.'

'I have … motive. And the knife was mine.'

I groaned. This sort of shit could only happen to Tabitha Darling. 'Tish, you need a lawyer.'

'No,' said my friend—my squishy-centred, soft-hearted, emotionally raw oldest best friend. 'It's worse than that, Zee. I need a private detective.'

≡ 3 ≡

Xanthippe and the Scones of Evidence

Tabitha looked terrible, her long honey-coloured hair jammed under a hand knit beanie, and her shoulders hunched in her vintage coat. She didn't speak a word when I picked her up from the police station.

Well, she spoke one word, and that word was 'tea.' Only it came out more as a plaintive 'teeeeeaaaa.'

'Café?' I asked, steering Tabitha towards the car park.

'No, not the café!' said Tabitha in alarm.

'Home, then.'

'Too many boys.'

She wasn't wrong there. Since I moved out, Tabitha's housemates consisted of Ceege the former engie student, and Jase the apprentice chef who towed a swarm of teen boyfriends around him at all times. The house was wall-to-wall X-Box and guyliner.

'I have a kettle in the detective agency,' I offered. Nothing Tabitha would consider proper tea, but desperate times and all that. I had some Dilmah bags and more than one cup. (Sometimes detectives do share.)

'The beach,' said Tabitha. She lurched off across the street in the direction of my beautiful cherry-red Spider. 'I need to go to the beach, no particular reason, don't judge me.'

'Does the beach serve tea?' I asked carefully. Being in the police lockup overnight had obviously broken Tabitha.

All I got in response was half a shrug and a mumbled, 'I dunno, maybe.'

As it turned out, yes, the beach served tea. Tabitha slid out of the car, shuffling her way towards a brightly striped canvas tent and a series of battered vintage couches.

My first thought was that someone was having a garage sale, but then I saw the chalked blackboard of a menu leaning against the striped canvas, the trestle table covered in teacups, and the sign above the tent with a hashtag instead of a name.

#Sconebros

'Why does that sound familiar?' I wondered aloud. Tabitha sprawled out on a venom-green couch near a table made from a beanbag, several upcycled vinyl records and a rough length of corrugated iron. The tension in her shoulders eased.

Eh. If I was the one who had to be bailed out of the police station at the arse-end of the morning (and I admit nothing, but let's just say it wouldn't be the first time) I would also claim the privilege of picking the breakfast spot.

Tabitha detected food trends like zombies sniffed out fresh brains.

A white guy with a massive, gravity-defying beard and a green apron with an artfully-scattered pattern of flour across it (seriously, had they used a stencil, that flour was actually in the shape of a teacup) came out of the tent to take our order.

'I'll have the #Sconebros combo with the marjoram scone and chocolate salt,' said Tabitha, not even looking at the menu. 'Cheers, Bruce.'

My eyes narrowed.

'Preferred tea blend?' asked Bruce, sporting a New Zealand accent along with his mighty beard. Seriously. I think he curled and waxed his sideburns. Barista beards are getting out of control in this city.

'Cornflake,' said Tabitha.

I waited a beat, realised that Tabitha was not in fact joking, and met the bearded #Sconebro's eyes with my calmest smile. 'What's the best thing on the menu?' I asked.

'The Parmesan cookie cup, but they/we only make those on Thursdays,' Tabitha and the barista said, practically in unison.

'I'll have a long black.'

'Is that … ironic, bro?' asked Bruce. I could not take my

eyes off his beard. Had it eaten all the hipster beards in the area to create a Mighty Steampunk Emperor of Beards? There were beads in it. And a hint of glitter.

'They don't do coffee,' Tabitha explained to me.

Wow. Cafés were now too cool to serve coffee. I got out of the PR game at the right time. 'Surprise me,' I said, waving Bruce away.

I waited for him and his artisan beard to amble back to whatever they were using as a kitchen in that tent before putting my cards on the table. 'Okay, I'm all for style over substance, that's been my business model for most of my life, but why are you cheating on your own café with this cornflake-drinking Kiwi hashtag zone? And while we're asking the difficult questions, how did you find Cameron Crewe's dead body?'

'It's a long story,' said Tabitha in a small voice.

'Tish, I have time,' I assured her. 'My least-favourite exes don't get murdered every day of the week around here. Let's call it a special occasion.'

Tabitha gave me a frantic look. 'Should I be more sensitive to your grieving process?'

'No, you should share faster. I'm not crying in my non-existent coffee cup over that arsehole's tragic demise, but I am worried about whether or not I'm going to have to visit you in prison!' Any feelings I might have about Crewe's demise could be squashed down safely and saved for

32

another time.

'That's almost sweet.'

'Talk, Tabitha.'

'When I have tea,' she said, plaintively enough that I relented, for the moment.

———————

Our breakfast arrived. Tabitha was soon sipping a cup of tea that smelled of cornflakes.

My surprise was a pumpkin scone flavoured tea blend and a pumpkin scone infused with tea. It was the most meta food I had ever experienced, but it came with quince salt and crabapple jelly, so I wasn't going to make a song and dance about it.

I had no idea whether pumpkin scone tea required milk or not. When I reached for the milk jug on Tabitha's end of the vinyl record coffee table, Bruce behind the counter twitched in mild agony, which suggested milk was not recommended.

I added the milk. His distress made the tea taste sweeter.

'How are your tea levels?' I asked Tabitha after a few moments had passed.

'Sufficient,' she sighed, inhaling the steam from her cup.

'So,' I said in my best 'leading questions' voice.

'So...' said Tabitha.

'Cameron Crewe.'

'So dead.'

'Did you bang him?'

Tabitha was offended. 'The police asked that too. More than once. They were very invested in the idea, which was super gross.'

'That's not an answer, Tish. Look, I'm not judging you or shaming you. I'm trying to help.' She looked about as embarrassed as I felt, and I *never* get embarrassed. 'Things have been weird lately.' I guessed. (This was a safe bet, with Tabitha.)

'You mean since your brother broke up with me, and Stewart was stolen by adorable elderly lesbians?'

'Since—all this *Café Wars* business started.' We talked less these days. Maybe because I didn't work at the café any more, or because I moved out, or because of the Leo thing. In retrospect, it was probably something I should feel guilty about. I hadn't been paying attention to Tabitha, and her life fell apart long before the murder raised its head.

'I didn't have sex with Cameron Crewe,' Tabitha growled. 'And it would be irrelevant if I had.'

'Not in a murder investigation.'

'I quit solving murder mysteries!' She spread her arms wide. 'Eighteen months clean.'

'That's not how it works when you're a suspect. No one's asking you to solve the mystery, Tabitha. You want me to help clear your name. That means not getting in my way.

And that means…'

'Answer your questions without being a bitch about it,' she said sullenly.

'Bingo.'

She slumped back against the venom green couch. It was a great couch. If I wasn't sure Tabitha would dob me in, I might nick it for my new office. 'Can you imagine if I did bang him? Ugh.'

I didn't bat an eyelash. 'Because he's dead?'

'Because he's an arsehole. Who is also dead. And your ex. Worst rebound ever.'

I could have told her that. Oh wait, I did.

Still, that's not what a friend would say. A friend would say: 'Hey, at least you didn't rebound with someone who has genuine feelings for you, thereby ruining your friend-ship forever.' But for all I knew, she had done that too—it had been a busy couple of months.

Tabitha managed to sulk and glare at the same time. 'I preferred it when you were asking me deeply embarrassing personal questions.'

A cue if ever I heard one! 'Okay, I'll start out easy. What do they have on you? They didn't charge you, Tabitha, but it sounds like they're treating you as a suspect, not a witness. You. Daughter of a former superintendent. What evidence is floating around that police station that we have to worry about?'

She gave me a wary look.

I pulled out my spiral notebook. Clients feel more reassured if I appear to be making notes while they talk. '*You* called *me*, babe.'

'The knife,' she said reluctantly. 'When I found him, he had a toffee knife sticking out of his chest. It's mine, so it would be a miracle if it didn't have my fingerprints all over it.'

'This isn't Poirot,' I pointed out. 'Fingerprints are circumstantial, especially if you have witnesses to support that you made the knife in the first place. How did the knife get to Crewe?' Really, what I wanted to ask was, how does one make a toffee shard knife? But I didn't have time for a diversion into exotic confectionary technique.

'It was part of the Week Six challenge. I made a—' and she took a deep breath before saying the rest '—I made a freaking murder scene, okay? Out of confectionary. The theme was Coffee to Die For. I made toffee murder weapons and fake syrup blood to arrange around my trio of pastries—espresso éclair, cappuccino crème brulèe, and a cornetto alla marmaletta made with mocha marmalade ...'

I was going to need more than a pumpkin scone for breakfast at this rate. 'Are we absolutely certain he didn't die of diabetes?'

Tabitha gave me a filthy look. 'The filming of the segment went fine yesterday, in the early evening. The knife I made, the other leftovers from my display, and some of my favourite fondant tools were all in a plastic container in the Teasperience pop up bar. I should have taken them home with me, but I was distracted and I forgot.' She took a deep breath and let it out in a rush. 'Last night, at around nine, I got a text from an unknown number, that I thought was from someone in production, reminding me to grab my stuff. The light was still on in the kitchen. I went in and found Crewe dead on the floor.'

'Tell me about the knife. Who knew it was yours, that it would have your fingerprints on it?'

'Anyone who was there yesterday, when we were filming,' Tabitha said reluctantly. 'Crewe, Kari Nagarra, Tom the camera operator. My baristas—Lara and Yui. Nin, though she's been keeping clear of anything to do with *Café Wars*. Anyone who's been in and out of the Café La Femme kitchen, the last few days. Stewart and his new aunties. I don't know. It wasn't a secret.'

I drew a stick figure with a knife sticking out of it. 'So what do the police think—that you grabbed the toffee knife and stuck it in Chef Crewe as some kind of, ugh, crime of passion?'

'Of course I didn't!' Tabitha looked exasperated. 'How tough do you think toffee is? You can't stab someone with it. It would break on his ribs. It would break on his *apron*.'

'Then what are we even talking about?'

'Someone stabbed him with a real knife,' she said impatiently. 'Then replaced the real knife with my toffee decoration. For, I don't know, flourish? So the police are, I reckon, looking for a suspect who likes cakes and/or murders to look pretty.'

'Any other reason why they suspect you?'

Bruce emerged again, his notebook at the ready and his teacup stencil freshly re-floured. 'The new scount will emerge at six am,' he reported. 'It's a pepperberry base with elderflower creme and a bush honey crumble.'

'We'll wait,' said Tabitha, as if his words made perfect sense to her.

'Tea top up, bro?'

'Please.'

'Do you have anything with bacon on your breakfast menu?' I asked. All this talk of coffee eclairs and the stability of toffee had me craving salt.

The #Sconebro tipped his head at me in something like wonder. 'I'm enjoying your ironic questions.'

'She's good, isn't she?' agreed Tabitha. 'Feel free to share them on Twitter. More tea for both of us, please. And two scounts when they're ready.'

Even if this had nothing to do with the murder, I still had to know. 'Explain scount.' My question was to Tabitha, not Bruce, who was already seeing to our order with startling efficiency for this early in the morning.

Tabitha brightened like we weren't here to discuss a murder. 'You know how a cronut is like a doughnut made out of croissant?'

'Let's just say for argument's sake that I do.' I had been out of the café biz for two months, and this happened? To be honest, though, this could be old news. Whenever Tabitha talks food trends, I zone out and run imaginary taekwondo forms in my head instead of listening to her.

'A sconut is half donut, half croissant, half scone.'

'There's something terribly wrong with your maths.'

Tabitha sighed happily. 'They design a new flavour every Tuesday, and only bake one hundred, no repeats. The only way to get one is to be here before the pre-work rush.'

I gave her my filthiest of filthy looks. 'Tish, did you bring me here to sit on a couch on a beach at 5:30AM on a weekday after picking you up from a police station because you wanted to try a *limited edition scone*?'

Tabitha rolled her eyes at me. 'No, I brought you here because I'm suspected of murder and I need a private detective to clear my name. Keep up.'

In the time it took for the #Sconebro bread artisans to perfect the bushberry sconut, Tabitha admitted to more evidence of her involvement in Crewe's death. She had not only found the body, but was caught on security camera driving into the nearby car park a full twenty minutes before she reported the murder.

I considered beating my head against the vinyl record coffee table.

'I was going to go in straight away,' Tabitha said miserably. 'But I sat in my car thinking about my crappy life choices for a while, and how much I hated working with that bastard, and then I got the reminder text, and *then* I went inside and found the body.'

'So you had the motive, the opportunity and there's a time-stamped video showing that you had plenty of time to kill and decorate him at your leisure.'

'To be fair,' Tabitha pointed out. 'Everyone who's ever met Cameron Crewe had a motive for killing him.'

Well, yeah. She wasn't wrong.

I turned my notebook to a new page. 'Remember how I told you that signing up for *Café Wars* was going to be a total disaster, and I didn't want to hear anything about it?'

'Sounds familiar,' said Tabitha sourly.

'I think it's time you tell me *everything* I've missed over the last six weeks. And I will hold back from saying I told you so.'

'Do you promise?'

'No.'

4

Tabitha Gets Judged
(before the murder)

The thing about a YouTube show, as opposed to real television, is you don't have to wait three months before you and your loved ones see it broadcast.

Or, you know, have a perfectly sensible early night (some of us have to be up at six for café prep) interrupted by the sound of your flatmates howling with laughter.

I stomp downstairs in my kimono and ugg boots to glare at the usual suspects filling my living room:

1) Ceege, currently rocking a real job that requires him to wear a suit and tie on weekdays. He makes up for it in his leisure hours by hibernating back into his former uniform of ACDC t-shirts, ripped jeans, ballgowns and body glitter.

2) Jase, my boy apprentice, currently serving the tail end of a suspended sentence for manslaughter (it's a long story) and studying to be a chef at hospitality school. Beautiful cinnamon roll, too good for this world.

3) Jase's entourage: Mate A who has a hipster beard and a massive crush on Jase, Mate B who looks like an extra from *Home and Away* only with more hair product, and has a massive crush on Mate A. Jase's massive crush, of course, is on Mate B. Fucking love triangles. I wouldn't go back to being nineteen if you paid me.

4) Stewart, my Scottish BFF. We aren't speaking right now because he's a filthy traitor who broke my coffee machine's heart.

5) My cat, Kinky Boots, sitting on Stewart's lap, purring.

There are too many men in my life. Thank goodness the lipgloss balances out the testosterone, or I wouldn't be able to cope.

'What the hell?' I flap at them. 'Keep the noise down. You know I'm doing all the early shifts this week. No one is allowed to have fun in this house after ten PM.'

'Sorry, Tabs,' says Ceege.

'In our defence,' says Jase. 'We were laughing at you.'

'Nice one,' Stewart says sarcastically to him. 'Verra smooth.'

'Look,' says Ceege, who has lived with me long enough to know there are some situations where only a shiny distraction will do. 'Your video is up.' He spins his laptop on the coffee table, so I can see the screen. 'They left in the part where Cameron Crewe looked like he wanted to murder you.'

'I bring that out in a lot of chefs,' I say modestly.

'Your hair looks really good in the video,' notes Mate B, my favourite of Jase's entourage. I might bother to learn his name someday.

'Okay,' I sigh. I'm awake now. 'Play it again and you can *all* tell me how great my hair looks.'

The vid isn't too bad. The editing team treads a fine line between showing what an arsehole Cameron Crewe is, while still making him look clever and talented enough to be worth the attention.

Also my hair does look exceptionally great.

'Are the other introduction vids up yet?' I ask. 'Who are the other contestants?' If it's the Eclair Witch Project from the eastern shore, I might have to start taking this more seriously.

'The #Sconebros one is up,' says Ceege.

'Do I know them?' I'm out of touch with who's hot and edible here in Hobart ... too busy keeping my own customers to worry about the competition. If they're not in the CBD, I probably haven't stalked them lately.

Wow I really haven't been getting out much.

'They're new,' says Jase. 'Kiwi bakers—students, I think, or they started out that way. They move around every month or two—like a food truck, but working out of a circus tent. They know their shit when it comes to social media and their tea is epic.'

'Sconuts,' says Mate A, nodding with approval.

'So good,' agrees Mate B.

Huh, I am totally going to have to espionage myself some tea and scones. Sco-nuts. Okay then.

'How about the other café?' I ask. 'The third contestant. Anyone we know?'

Everyone avoids my eyes, gazing at random strips of wallpaper, each other, and the carpet.

'You know, I've gotta,' says Ceege, levering himself up.

'Yeah, we should,' says Jase, catapulting himself off the back of the couch.

In thirty seconds, they all ninja out of the living room, leaving me with a warm laptop, a purring cat ... and Stewart, pinned to the couch by Kinky Boots and her convenient claws.

So much for not talking to him. 'Something you want to tell me, McTavish?'

'See, I knew ye were going to overreact,' he says, which for the record is not what a sensible person should ever say to me.

'It's those adorable elderly lesbians,' I say between gritted teeth.

'They have names,' he protests.

'Is that why you're here? Bad enough that you ditched me for the competition—'

'That is no' a fair description of events.'

44

'Are you seriously telling me that The Chocolate freaking Teapot is my competitor?' I narrow my eyes at him. 'Did you put them up to it? How did they even hear about it? Little old ladies with quaint bakery kitchens do not become YouTube stars all on their own.'

'Tabitha, they're no' cave people, they use the internet. Dot tweets more than you do, and Daisy is all about the Instagram.'

Dot and Daisy. How freaking cute. 'Is that why they sent you over here, to spy on me?' That's going too far, I know it. Sometimes my mouth and my temper don't connect to the sensible part of my brain that has no insecurities and designs awesome salads.

'Are ye still angry I took a job wi' them?' Stewart demands incredulously.

Well, duh. Was he not paying attention?

'I offered you a job,' I retort.

Until recently, Stewart was a professional blogger as well as a romance novelist. When *Sandstone City* lost their government funding, he looked for casual work to supplement his writing income, and it turned out the one thing he had going for him was barista training and experience.

Only, you know, my café wasn't good enough for him. Despite the fact that he has been flirting with our coffee machine for the last couple of years, and is actually the person who understands her best in all the world.

'Is this why you've been avoiding me lately?' Stewart sounds genuinely gobsmacked.

'I thought it was obvious.' Do I have to send out a memo every time I was mad at him? That seems like a waste of resources.

'We talked about it. Ye said it was fine.'

'Not the kind of fine that's *actually* fine. The kind where I want to set fire to everything you own.'

'How am I supposed to know the difference?'

'Listen harder.' I pick up Ceege's laptop and prepare to sweep upstairs with it, so as to spy on the competition in private.

'Tabitha,' says Stewart slowly. 'Can ye really no' see why us working together might be a slight strain on the friend-ship?'

'Don't use logic when I'm flouncing!'

I'm in mid-flounce, hair swishing behind me, when I hear his voice, sharp and cutting, add, 'Congratulations, by the way. On the engagement.'

The ring on my finger feels extra tight. It does that, whenever someone calls attention to it. So yes. The engage-ment thing. I've been trying not to think about it.

I turn back to Stewart. He's regarding me thoughtfully. The ladies of The Chocolate Teapot obviously like their baristas tidy. He's always clean-shaven and nicely combed these days. Not nearly as scruffy as when he first crashed into my life with an intriguing smile and a complicated backstory.

'Obviously,' he goes on now, eyes holding mine. 'I was waiting for the right time. To congratulate you.'

I swallow. 'Good choice.' When in doubt, sarcasm.

'Happy for ye both.'

'Me too, we're wonderful people.'

'So...' he says, deepening his voice slightly, to emphasise the accent. Bastard knows how much I love his accent. 'How long are ye going to be mad about this Chocolate Teapot business? Ballpark figure.'

'I don't know,' I say, looking anywhere but directly into his eyes. I guess ... it depends ... on who wins the next couple of challenges.'

He gasps. 'Tabitha Darling, are ye suggesting I sabotage my adorable elderly employers?'

Well, if he puts it like that...

'Yep,' I tell him, setting the laptop down again and joining him on the couch. 'You're dead to me until the health inspectors—or the cameras—find a rat in their lasagne. I'll settle for an old sock, or a large wodge of fingernail.'

Stewart scrunches his nose at me. 'Not lasagne. It's more, miniature *croque monsieurs* and charming cottage pies served on lace doilies.'

I lean my head on his shoulder. 'You won't put a dead rat in their charming cottage pies? Not even for me?'

Stewart boops me on the nose with his thumb. 'Not even for you, Tabitha Darling.'

'There are no true friends left in the world,' I lament. But I don't move my head from his shoulder.

Everything feels a whole lot better than when we started this conversation.

————————

The judging video goes up on Friday night. The Chocolate Teapot win the Week One Challenge, their classic cup of Belgian hot chocolate taking out my sarcastic shark sliders, and the chocolate tea with cinnamon crumb served up by #Sconebros. I throw a small cream cake at Stewart's face in retaliation. He's such a good friend that he doesn't even duck.

[Cut to: exterior shot of Teasperience Hobart]

KARI NAGARRA: Time to meet the Judge, Jury and General of Café Wars, here in the Teasperience pop up store in the Hobart mall. It's Chef Cameron Crewe! What are you making, Chef?

[Chef Crewe presents a frozen tea cube on a miniature plate, decorated with a small blue flower.]

CHEF CREWE: I have perfected the Tea-freeze, a delicious artistic take on the traditional iced tea. The Hobart Teasperience will present a different custom-made flavour every week, never to be repeated.

KARI: You know it's nearly winter, right, Cameron?

CHEF: It's never too cold for an excellent teasperience.

KARI: Seriously, it's actually snowing on the mountain right now.

CHEF: This Tea-freeze is a rose and lemon sphere, encased in powdered Lady Grey tea dust, placed on a charred caramel smear, with a sugared borage flower.

KARI: Damn, that looks good.

CHEF: I know.

KARI: So what are you hoping for with the new series of Café Wars?

CHEF: I want fabulous food, fierce coffee, and a team of excellent kitchen professionals driven to the brink of desperation because they'll never be as good as me.

KARI: At least he's honest about it.

CHEF: I enjoy it when they cry on camera.

5

Xanthippe is a Good Bro
(after the murder)

Nothing with a name like 'sconut' should smell this good. Clearly a conspiracy to ruin my tastebuds for all future pastry.

Game over, nothing but vegemite sandwiches from now on. Why even bother with dessert?

Tabitha still looked small and miserable as she ate hers, but she was making squeaky happy noises that she possibly wasn't even aware of, so at least part of her was revived by the experience.

A large van with the #Sconebros logo pulled up nearby, and a huge Maori bloke got out and started unloading boxes.

'That's Maaka,' said Tabitha, not looking up from the remains of her delicious sconut.

'Should that mean something to me?' I asked, glancing at him over my shoulder. He saw me looking and gave me an appreciative glance back.

51

'He used to work with Cameron Crewe, back in Sydney,' Tabitha said in a low voice. 'Which puts him in the top ten people who hated his guts.'

Now, that was interesting. The most effective way to get Tabitha off the hook for this murder would be to find a more enticing suspect. Could Maaka be that person?

Maaka disappeared into the circus tent and came out again a little while later, sporting a dark green apron with a flour stencil depicting a teapot. 'Hey, Tabs. What's up?'

'Hi, Maaka,' she said gravely. 'I need to tell you something about Cameron.'

His expression changed from casual cheer to tense suspicion, held mostly in his wide, muscular shoulders. 'What's that arsehole done to you now?'

'Got himself murdered,' sighed Tabitha.

Maaka was unsurprised. 'Fucking typical, bro.'

'Do you have an alibi for yesterday evening?'

I blinked at Tabitha, surprised at her giving him the head's up so blatantly.

'Sure,' Maaka said easily. 'I was with Niko and Ani. Bruce came over for a feed too. Good night.'

'You're right then. No worries.' She relaxed and smiled at him.

'Sweet as,' he replied, as if it hadn't occurred to him to be bothered.

Ugh, Tabitha was the worst murder suspect ever. Far too

nice, and friends with everyone.

'So you're going to go around telling everyone they need an alibi?' I asked in front of Maaka. 'Police are going to love that, Tish. The murder hasn't even hit Twitter yet. There must be a reason they're keeping the news under wraps.'

Tabitha pulled a pair of giant movie star sunglasses out of her handbag and put them on, pouting behind them. 'I don't work for the police.'

'Any suspects?' Maaka asked. 'Except, you know...'

'Everyone he's ever met?' I said dryly.

He pointed his finger at me. 'I like you. Have we met before?'

If Maaka had worked with Cameron Crewe in the past, we might have crossed paths. 'Sydney, maybe? I did some work around the restaurant scene, a few years back.'

'You're local, though?'

'Tasmanians always come home to roost.'

'Back to me,' said Tabitha. 'I'm the main suspect, Maaka. I found the body.'

'Nah, tiny little thing like you?' He smirked at her. 'Can't see you taking a carving knife to a celebrity chef, not even on a bad day. A frying pan to the head, maybe.'

'How do you know he was stabbed?' I asked, smooth as you like. Look at me, private detective.

Maaka was credibly shocked. 'Shit, really? I was kidding,

bro. Everyone who worked for Cameron Crewe joked about stabbing him at least twice a week.'

That was true.

'At least,' Tabitha agreed. 'Maaka, I'm gonna need another sconut to make it through today.'

'Nope,' he said. 'One per customer. No exceptions.'

She lifted her giant sunglasses to gape at him. 'Seriously, bro?'

'Rules are rules, Tabs. If I break them for one murder suspect, where will it end?'

We headed to the café next, because Tabitha refused to accept 'no sleep last night' as a reason to take the day off. Turned out, there was a welcome committee.

Or, not a welcome committee so much as a 'concerned and cranky' committee.

Tabitha's staff was gathered in the kitchen along with Ceege, and the filming team from *Café Wars*: Kari Nagarra and Camera Bloke. They all exploded into noise and fuss as we entered. This. This was why I had removed myself from the service industry.

'Tabitha, were you *arrested*?' Lara demanded, while the others buzzed around, asking variations of the same thing.

Tabitha held up a hand to silence them all. 'I wasn't arrested. Though if Inspector Fitzgerald stays on the case, it might not be long.' She darted a quick look at me, her eyes troubled. 'It was basic witness-at-the-scene questions at first, until he came in and started—looming over me.'

'Do we know a Fitzgerald?' I asked. I hadn't heard of him.

Tabitha shook her head quickly. 'Nope. Once he got involved, I didn't see any friendly faces, not until Inspector Bobby turned up about 3AM and pressured Fitzgerald to let me go.'

Ah, good old Inspector Bobby, he had a soft spot for Tabitha ever since her dad was his boss. 'Hasn't he retired yet?'

'His wife won't let him.' Tabitha glanced around at the troubled faces. 'Stop looking at me like I burned the biscuits! I'm fine, no one has arrested me, it's all good. Apart from, you know, the whole dead body fiasco. At least it wasn't in my building.' This time.

Ceege pounced for a hug. Nin made a soothing pot of tea. Yui blinked back tears. Jase stood against the cupboards, looking brittle and stressed, probably having flashbacks to his own arrest trauma.

Kari and Camera Bloke stayed out of it. Promising. I needed a few cool heads to bounce ideas off. I caught Kari's eye and nodded towards the main room of the café. She followed me, her offsider trailing in her wake with a camera still hooked around his wrist.

'I take it this isn't going to feature in the next episode of the series?' I said pointedly.

'Sorry.' He unclipped it, setting the camera aside on the cake display counter. 'Forgot I had that on.'

'What series?' Kari said bitterly. 'It's all over now. I can't believe he's actually dead.'

'Can't believe no one's thought to arrest us yet,' said Camera Bloke.

She blinked and stared at him. 'What are you talking about, Tom?'

'Come on, Kari. We've been in Crewe's pockets for the last two months. Who's most likely to have snapped and hit him over the head with a coffee press?'

Tom the Camera Bloke's imagination was even more vivid than that of Maaka the #Sconebro.

'Can I pose a theoretical?' I interrupted.

They both looked at me.

'Like what?' Kari asked.

'Everyone's assuming a crime of passion—or pissed-off-ness. But if we eliminate all the people who might have impulsively killed Cameron Crewe for his personality, what do we have left?'

'You mean motive?' put in Camera Bloke. 'Beyond the obvious.'

'If it's the obvious, the police will sort it easily enough,' I decided. 'Impulsive acts of violence and murder don't come with precise scene-cleaning skills. There will be evidence aplenty if one of his colleagues or a *Café Wars* contestant snapped in the moment...'

'You want to know if anyone wanted to kill him, in a planned and prepared sort of way,' Kari put in, connecting the dots. I guess they don't let stupid people become Young Australian of the Year. 'I'll think about it, let you know if I come up with anything.'

'Cheers.'

'He was getting a lot of calls from Sydney,' Kari added. 'Trying to hook up the next TV deal. We—*Café Wars*—were a stop gap along the way to his real comeback.'

'Any names?'

She shook her head. 'Nothing I can remember right now. Sorry.'

If I wanted anything useful, I was going to have to get hold of his phone. Which was probably in an evidence drawer already.

I turned my attention on—hell, what was his name? 'Tad,' I ventured, making it half a question.

'Tom,' he said, not annoyed. I guess he was used to being a wallflower.

'Tom,' I said with my patented 'sexy enough to confuse you' smile. 'You snorted when Kari used the phrase 'hook up.' Got anything to add?'

'What—no I didn't.'

I let my smile warm up, all the way to my eyes. 'Now that we've established it probably wasn't a crime of passion, who was Cameron Crewe hooking up with?'

Tom's eyes flicked to Kari's, and they both hesitated for long enough to tell me there was something I was missing.

'Hey, Tabitha's making hot chocolate,' announced Jason, pushing his way through the swinging door to the kitchen. 'Seriously, she's melting four kinds of chocolate for this, it's a work of freaking art.'

Kari and Tom both took the excuse to join the others in the kitchen.

I raised my eyebrows at Jason the boy wonder, suspicious about his bad timing.

'Detective Carides,' he said in a deep voice, only slightly sarcastic. Oh, this was adorable. Baby cub trying to protect his mumma!

'Teen interloper,' I replied, deepening my own voice. The kid was turning twenty in a few weeks so being called a teenager made his whole face twitch. Hilarious. 'How's my room?'

'Covered in boy band posters.'

'Exactly as I left it, then? Nice.'

Jason took a couple of steps towards me. Since Tabitha brought him into her little misfit family, he'd grown about a foot, most of it in confidence and hair gel. 'I know Tabitha thinks you're on her side.'

That was bloody rich. 'I am *always* on her side,' I hissed. 'I was on her side when you were—' Don't do the maths, it will make you feel old, '—playing LEGO or whatever toddlers like to chew on.'

'You ditched Café La Femme,' he said stubbornly.

Preserve me from judgmental infants. 'I was a terrible barista!'

That got through to him. 'You were pretty terrible,' he agreed.

'Can we get on with the keeping Tabitha out of jail part of our day, then?' I went for the low blow. 'She did as much for you, if you recall.'

Anger blazed in Jason's face. 'Fuck you.'

'Short temper you've got there, Skippy,' I observed. 'Must have been fun to hold back when you were working for the Toffee Shark.'

'I never worked for him—'

'You did, though,' I reminded him patiently. 'Didn't you? There was a challenge where each of the cafés sent a staff member to Teasperience.' I needed to catch up on the show on YouTube. All I remembered right now was from the occasional complaints that wafted up the stairway in our building every time Tabitha stomped up to vent about something, only to realise halfway up that Stewart didn't work on the first floor any more.

At least seventy-five percent of her visits to my detective

office have been for that reason—she hates admitting her mistakes.

Stewart. I'd have to put him on my list to check in with. I was surprised not to see him now in the kitchen of support crew, though I guess he counted as the enemy these days.

Oh, Tish. So much stubborn wrapped in so many vintage frocks.

Jason was regarding me warily. 'Week Two,' he admitted. 'Soup kitchen. Mostly frozen beets and extract of basil oil crushed on a cheeseboard and inhaled, arty food wank like that.'

'What happened during that week that you don't want to tell me about?' It was a shot in the dark.

Jason immediately looked like he wanted to murder me. (Manslaughter was more his thing.)

A thought crossed my mind. 'Hey, you weren't the one sleeping with Cameron Crewe, were you?'

I knew enough about Crewe to be sure he was shagging someone around town, probably multiple someones.

A look of abject horror crossed Jason's face. 'No I bloody wasn't,' he said, when he recovered. 'He is so beyond not my type it's not even funny.'

It was a little funny.

'And he's straight,' he added. 'Total homophobe, I almost punched him the first day because he kept making stupid

KEEP CALM AND *Kill* THE *Chef*

gay jokes.'

Love the way Jason had already forgotten why we were having this conversation, enough to confess to violent thoughts against the victim. 'I thought all celebrities were bisexual these days.'

'Yeah, not so much.'

One of the more charming facts I only found out about Cameron Crewe after we slept together was his habit of hitting on anything female within a small radius—female staff being his favourite targets. Hence all the sexual harassment suits. 'Did you see him with anyone—flirting, groping, making assignations?'

'Who says assignations in this century?' complained Jason, all grossed out. 'His staff are one hundred percent male because he's sexist as well as being a gay-hating douchebag so yeah, he keeps his hands to himself. Except Ani—the staff member borrowed from #Sconebros for the Week Two challenge. Chef Crewe learned pretty sharpish to stop patting her bum after the second time she 'accidentally' dropped a rolling pin on his foot. Made sure she bombed out in the challenge too. Bastard was vindictive.'

'Yes,' I muttered. 'That I knew about him.'

Add Ani to my list. 'Who did The Chocolate Teapot send along as their representative for that soup week?'

Jason hesitated for a moment.

'Stewart, then,' I said, making a note of it. 'What else can you tell me? Anything you overheard? Anyone out to get some special attention from Crewe?'

Who was he sleeping with? I wanted to ask again, but it wasn't like that information would stay hidden if it were important. The best and worst thing about this city is the way that gossip lays so lightly across it. Everyone hears everything sooner or later, even if they'd rather not.

'You really are helping her,' Jason blurted out. 'I mean, you're going to keep her out of jail, right?'

I blew at my hair impatiently, pushing it back out of my face. 'Trust me on this one, kid. I'll keep her out of jail even if she did it.'

What has the law ever done for me, except keep my brother gainfully employed for the last decade? I owe Tabitha a lot more than that.

Speaking of my brother...

'Go watch Tabitha melt things,' I told Jason. 'And let me know if you think of anything helpful.'

He nodded, and lurched forward on his feet as if he was maybe going to go for a hug. We exchanged mutually horrified expressions at the very idea of it, and he spun around and went back into the kitchen for the hot chocolate love fest.

I made a call, though all I got was Leo's messagebank. Even his voice is stuffy and law-abiding.

'This is Leo Bishop's phone. I'll get back to you when I can.'

'This is your friendly local private detective,' I said brightly. 'Two things, I'll be quick. I picked up Tabitha from jail this morning, where she was being questioned on suspicion of murdering a celebrity chef. They don't have enough evidence to charge her.' I was really proud of not adding a cynical 'yet' to that sentence. 'What do we know about an Inspector Fitzgerald? He's keen to pin this on her. Also, I know I said I never needed to know any details about why you two broke up. I think I was wrong. Call me back, mate. We have to talk.'

WEEK TWO

The #ToffeeShark

vs

Hot Chocolate

[Cut to: exterior shot of Café La Femme]

KARI: So, Tabitha, tell me more about yourself. Are you really engaged to a police officer?

TABITHA: What? Um. Yes. I'm doing the bride thing, it's all completely fine and not a problem.

[Tabitha flashes ring finger, realises ring finger is empty, looks panicked, hides hand in pocket]

KARI: Wow, way to sell the romance to the audience.

TABITHA: Sorry, can we start again?

KARI: It's fine. Does your police officer fiancé approve of you solving murder mysteries in your spare time?

TABITHA: I don't do that anymore. It wasn't even a phase, more a strange series of events—can't we go back to talking about my killer milkshakes?

KARI: We've met your waitresses, the adorable Lara and Yui...

TABITHA: I have to call them baristas now, because they got their proper certificates and they're really terrible at handing food to people.

KARI: And your Head Chef isn't keen to talk to us...

TABITHA: She's a vampire, so she doesn't show up on camera.

KARI: But there's one staff member we haven't met yet!

[Camera pans out to show Jase—a good-looking nineteen-year-old with spiky gelled hair and five piercings in one ear.]

JASE: Yo.

TABITHA: Really, that's what you're going with? Were you even

67

alive when 'yo' was a thing people said?

JASE: I'm bringing it back. [does fingerguns]

KARI: Jason, you're an apprentice here at Café La Femme while you're studying to be a chef at hospitality college. How did you and Tabitha meet?

[Jase grins fixedly at the camera. Tabitha looks like she wants to strangle somebody.]

JASE [still grinning]: Should I lie?

TABITHA: That's always worked out well for us.

JASE: I can never tell when you're being sarcastic.

TABITHA: Assume I'm always being sarcastic.

JASE: I don't know, do I?

TABITHA: You'll edit this, right?

KARI: Are you kidding? This is my favourite thing I've filmed all week.

TABITHA: I have a burning need to talk about soup. Soup is this week's special subject.

JASE: We met when I was suspected of murder this one time.

TABITHA: Damn it, Jase.

JASE: She's really good at solving murder mysteries. I was hardly even convicted.

TABITHA: I don't do that any more. Shush.

6

Tabitha is a Good ~~Girlfriend~~ Fiancée
(before the murder)

'Are you sure about this?' I ask Jase. It's time for the Week Two challenge, and I'm walking him to the lion's den like it's his first day of primary school. I'm worried the big kids might be mean to him in the playground.

He gives me an impatient look. 'Dude, it's a job, I get to work with a famous chef, it will look great on my resume.'

'I'm not a dude, Jasonicus, don't make me pour tapioca in your gym bag.'

'I know you hate repeating yourself.'

I'm protective of Jase. He's had a rough time over the last few years, and he deserves better than being shouted at by an egocentric celebrity. On the other hand he genuinely wants to be a fancy chef and that means I have to let him out occasionally from under Nin's cozy apron strings into the big, nasty world of professional culinary power-stress.

The challenge for Week Two is Soup Kitchen—a super tacky title to use if you're not feeding the homeless—and each of the cafés have to send one staff member in to work for the Teasperience pop up store for a week.

Jase looks strange in the industrial grey scrubs of a Teasperience employee. There are green tea leaves embroidered on his cuffs.

'You can't go,' I decide as we cross into the brick-lined alley behind the cafés and restaurants of the Hobart mall. 'He's going to ruin you, Jase. You'll come back smelling like freeze-dried vanilla pods and quinoa.'

'Leave the lad alone. I'm sure he can defend himself against the villainous hordes o' vanilla pods.' Stewart is leaning against the outside wall of the restaurant in grey scrubs that match Jase's, waiting for us. His accent washes over me, making my stomach all warm and happy before I remember that I'm still a bit mad at him. A tiny bit.

I pat Jase's hand. 'Don't let the bad man force you to temper chocolate before you're ready. Make good choices.' Then I look up, to meet Stewart McTavish's steady gaze.

Jason, craven beast that he is, scampers inside to start his work day without further input from me. Kids these days.

Stewart looks good. Suspiciously good, even in the Teasperience scrubs. His new haircut suits him, and his shave is closer than he bothered with when he was a professional blogger working upstairs from my coffee machine. I resist the urge to touch his chin. That would be weird.

'Aren't you well turned out?' I coo instead. 'The dress

code *is* rather smart over at the Lady Hatter's Tea Party. I'm surprised they don't have you in a twin set and pearls.'

'We save that for casual Fridays,' says Stewart. His smile is warm and genuine, which is totally not fair. 'How are ye, Tabitha?'

'Oh that's right, I haven't seen you in ages, because of all that fraternising with the enemy you've been doing.'

He rolled his eyes at me, leaning against the nearest red brick wall. 'It's been a week. Get over yourself. Make coffee, not war, Tabitha.'

I make a wild, emphatic gesticulation in the direction of the large blackboard sign that shouts CAFÉ WARS! FILMING TODAY! 'Look! We can do both!'

That only makes Stewart grin wider, his eyes blazing with genuine goodwill. So annoying. 'A reality TV show isnae worth drawing battle lines over,' he chides me.

'I was cranky at you before your precious chocolatiers even joined the show,' I mutter.

'I know that *now*,' he says. 'Mind if I go to work?'

'I'm not stopping you.'

He pats me on the shoulder. 'It is good to see ye, Tabitha.'

'You too, shut up, whatever.' I'm blushing, which is not okay in any sense of the word. 'Keep an eye on Jase? He's young and susceptible to food trends.'

Stewart crosses his fingers solemnly. 'If I see anyone making artisan toast, I'll wrap the lad in a blanket and throw him out the nearest window.'

'That's all I ask.'

———————

So I'm a fiancée now. Still. Assuming that … well, I'm not going to get into that now.

My current status, romantically, is fiancée.

Things Fiancées Do that Casual Girlfriends and/or Sex Buddies Mostly Don't #25: pick your man up at the airport.

Can you believe that the police have conferences? I guess everyone has conferences these days. Anyway, Tall Dark and Law-Abiding is on the fast track to another promotion, which means a lot of flying to different states and talking to other police officers about how clever he is.

At least, I assume that's what they do at conferences. I've been a bit distracted lately, and I don't always listen when he talks. He has stopped pretending to be interested when I go into one of my side salad rants, so it evens out.

There he is now, at baggage control. Leo Bishop, my teenage crush turned proper grown up ~~boyfriend~~ fiancé, all smouldering in a 'one haircut away from a Jane Austen hero' kind of way. I wait for him to get past the sniffer dogs (I know they're only trained to go after specific drugs and/or illicitly imported fruits and veggies, but I always smell like delicious food, so no point in risking it) before I throw myself at him.

I think before I act, these days.

'You're here!' says Bishop, sounding surprised.

'I said I would be.'

'I always assume you'll be waylaid by cupcakes.'

I hang on to his manly shoulders while rolling my eyes at him. 'What decade do you think we're in? No one gets waylaid by cupcakes any more. The world barely even cares about macarons.'

It was a sad day when we had to drive macarons out to the cupcake graveyard. Just because a trend is tired doesn't mean it's not tasty.

'So what did I miss?' Bishop asks after we collect his suitcase. We head out to the airport car park.

'I'm a reality TV star now,' I admit.

'My relatives called to inform me. You're the reason my Nonna now knows what 'the Youtube' is.'

'You're welcome?'

He frowns as he loads his suitcase into the boot of my battered blue Renault. 'You recovered your ring, I see.'

I show him my hand, pointedly. 'All in one piece.' If anything, it's shinier than when he went away. Turns out, dropping it in pumpkin puree is not a bad thing for diamonds. 'Funny story,' I add.

'Is it a bread dough related funny story like the last three times you lost it?'

'Think soupier.'

'Maybe you shouldn't wear it at all,' he suggests. 'I mean, when you're working,' he adds quickly. I must have let a flash of hurt show on my face.

'No, fair point. Nin said much the same thing. Only she suggested I wear it all the time, but don't come into the kitchen any more.'

'Seems extreme.'

'I know, right? It's not like all the soup servings had unexpected diamonds in them...'

I start the engine, and head out of the maze that is the local airport car park. 'Never mind my hijinks. How was your police tweeting workshop?'

'Policework in Digital Landscapes? Mostly not about tweeting.'

I nod sympathetically. 'It's okay, maybe next time.'

My phone rings as I pull on to the highway. Other people have fancy buttons they can tap to make their calls go to Bluetooth. I flap a hand at my ~~boyfriend~~ fiancé until he accepts the call, hits speaker, and holds it in the air near my face.

'Tabs, you picked up Sergeant Hotstuff yet?' asks Jase, way too loud.

'Present,' says Bishop in a low thrum of a voice.

Awkward pause!

'He won't arrest you for sexual harassment if I distract him with muffins,' I assure Jase.

'Is that a—'

'No, that's not a euphemism. Did you really call me to make sex jokes about food, because I don't think they cover that in hospitality college till final year.'

'Nope, this is gossip about celebrity chefs. You got time?'

'Always!' I blow a kiss to Bishop without taking either hand off the wheel, because I'm classy like that. 'What have you got for me?'

'Cameron Crewe is some kind of psychopath. I think he ordered all his assistants from the same Nordic catalogue, or possibly a robot factory.'

I remember that from my research on the guy. 'It's an aesthetic, yes?'

'Hella creepy aesthetic—maybe he rolled them all out of cookie dough. I would not put it past him, Tabs. I am surrounded by cloned kitchen assistants who smell like pie crust and bergamot. Their names are Earl and Grey and Lief.'

'Hang in there, kid. Maybe you'll learn something.'

'Like how to appreciate that my real boss is so much saner than this temporary maniac?'

'At the very least!'

'I mean Nin, clearly, not you.'

After Jase hangs up, Bishop and I drive in silence for a while, along the main road back toward the river, and the city on the other side of the bridge.

'I wish you'd never said yes to this TV series,' he says after a long silence. 'I hate the idea of you being anywhere near a creep like Cameron Crewe.'

'I know what I'm doing,' I say firmly, which we both know is a lie.

My best work always comes from making it up as I go along.

The engagement ring rubs uncomfortably against the steering wheel, and I try to pretend it's not bothering me.

We got engaged at Christmas, a year after deciding that we could totally do casual. Turns out that while Leo Bishop and I are both bad at committing time to a relationship, we're equally bad at doing anything casually.

Being engaged made some kind of sense at the time, but when our couples counsellor pointed out I was a lot more enthusiastic about that than the option of living together … well. She wasn't entirely wrong. When he found out I signed up for *Café Wars*, Bishop said we should break up. I panicked, and he panicked, and he took it back, but…

Is that something you can take back?

He got a promotion at work recently, a new unit, and now all these conferences. It's great for him. *Café Wars* is going to be great for me.

Eventually we'll figure out something that's great for *us*, other than our sex life and occasional Sunday morning brunches. All I have to do in the meantime is keep my engagement ring out of the soup.

And probably start telling him my secrets.

'So, uh,' I say.

'Uh oh,' Bishop says automatically. He gets me.

'I should tell you, I didn't just sign up to *Café Wars* to promote my café. Though that is a legit side effect I am hoping for!'

Bishop sighs. 'You surprise me,' he says in a voice that makes it clear I really, really didn't.

'You knew?'

'I knew there was something. Come on, then, Tish. What are you up to that's so dodgy you took this long to admit it to me?'

'That's—' Unfair. 'Uncomfortably accurate. So.' I take a deep breath. Here we go. 'Cameron Crewe is a monster, and someone has to stop him.'

KARI NAGARRA: *Each of our competing cafés sacrificed a soldier to the Teasperience kitchen this week. Jason, Stewart and Ani have spent five days learning how to craft the perfect Teasperience menu. Here we have Earl and Lief, two of Cameron Crewe's regular assistants, to give us some insight into what the last week was like for our contestants.*

EARL: *Hell on wheels.*

LIEF: *Hell on wheels with sugar on top.*

EARL: *Chef Crewe is a perfectionist, and he likes to throw fresh meat in at the deep end.*

KARI NAGARRA: *Is that how he got the name, the Toffee Shark?*

LIEF: *Sure. If you like.*

EARL: *You don't make an omelette without breaking heads.*

LIEF: *Eggs.*

EARL: *Also eggs. We can't complain. Chef Crewe is tough but fair.*

LIEF: *Can we go now? We only get a ten minute break.*

KARI NAGARRA: *The three of you have been swimming with the Toffee Shark for six days—how was the experience?*

ANI: *We learned a lot.*

STEWART: *Aye, I'll never look at soup the same way again.*

JASON: *Everyone who works for Chef Crewe wants to kill him. His regular assistants are about twelve hours and one bad batch of deconstructed croissants away from a major psychological breakdown. But my knife skills have improved.*

[Awkward pause]

STEWART: He's no' wrong.

ANI: I have more incentive to improve my knife skills than ever before.

KARI: With this new knowledge under your belt, each of you returned to your own café and had twenty-four hours to work with your team to perfect an original soup recipe to pitch to Chef Crewe for the Teasperience menu. What have you got for us?

ANI: The #Sconebros brand is all about taking fresh, local produce, whether we're in New Zealand or Tassie. We looked at what was missing from the current Teasperience menu and we came up with a soup to honour iconic Tasmanian ingredients. So here we have chilled salmon chowder with dill and wasabi, served in a shot glass.

STEWART: The weather's turned cold this month with snow on the mountain—well, cold by Australian standards. The Chocolate Teapot has always been about comfort food, so we cooked up a classic French Onion soup served in a vintage gravy boat, with a cranberry-brie muffin top.

JASON: Teasperience means fusion and surprises, so the Café La Femme team worked together on a savoury lemon meringue soup. We were going to serve it as a glaze on a Portugese tile and then we decided that was a load of old bull so we put it in a soup bowl instead.

STEWART: Brave.

JASON: I know, right? Sometimes you've got to respect the crockery.

KARI NAGARRA: Here's Chef Crewe with his official verdict on the super soups!

[Cameron Crewe walks past the bench. He doesn't even look at #Sconebros Ani, but swipes at her dish on his way past, so the shot glass smashes on the floor. Ani's face does not flicker.

CREWE: That one's rubbish.

[Crewe stops at Stewart's gravy boat, and tastes the sample.]

CREWE: Flavour's good, but serving's too generous, Teasperience is all about minimalist grandeur.

[Crewe tastes the lemon meringue soup at Jason's station.]

CREWE: Not bad. Yeah. This one is less shit than the others. [Walks away, making no eye contact with anyone]

KARI NAGARRA: So that's a win for Café La Femme in the soup kitchen challenge!

[Jason and Stewart both turn to Ani, who looks at the wall. Uncomfortable pause.]

= 7 =

Xanthippe in Chocolateland
(after the murder)

'Everyone not actually working in this café can leave right now,' Tabitha declared. She'd been kneading bread dough for the last fifteen minutes. It had a restorative effect on her confidence.

'Are you sure that's a good idea—' I started to say.

'Tried that,' Nin interrupted. 'Café's open, she's staying. The rest of you can leave if you're not rostered on for this morning's shift.'

I knew when I was beaten, and made a strategic exit out the café entrance, along with Kari Nagarra and Tom the Camera Bloke.

'Don't suppose we can convince you to do a short interview for our YouTube channel?' Kari asked thoughtfully.

Had to hand it to her, the woman was a fair dinkum professional.

'See the thing about private detectives is, it's much easier to do our job when we're not featured prominently in a reality cooking show that is about to go viral thanks to a horrible murder,' I said, giving them both a speculative look as the words came out of my mouth because hello, motive. 'Which I guess is a good scenario for the two of you?'

'You're kidding, right?' said Tom. 'Our contracts are shit if the show doesn't get finished. Without Crewe alive to be a dick on camera for the next two weeks, we're both stuffed.'

'Speaking of which,' said Kari. 'We have sponsors to call and a production team to keep in the loop. See you later.'

'Sure,' I said, and watched them head off down Davey Street before I went to reclaim my own car from the nearby meter.

Thanks to Tabitha's fetish for doughnut-flavoured scones (or scone-flavoured doughnuts), I had already managed to check out one of the cafés that she was competing against. Time to track down the other.

———————

The Chocolate Teapot was adorable. I don't use that word lightly. It was a restored brick cottage on a Sandy Bay street, with white furniture on a pale pine verandah out front, a fairytale mural on the outside wall, and a window full of gingerbread wombats and vintage china.

I could imagine Tabitha running a place like this in forty years time. Maybe that was what had her so cranky about its very existence.

(Though honestly, I knew why she was cranky at them, and it had nothing to do with The Chocolate Teapot's mint green 1950s saucer collection that matched at least two frocks in her wardrobe)

Inside, the adorableness ratcheted up by a factor of ten without maxing out. From the retro fittings to the furniture, this café was a sugar-coated nursery rhyme shabby chic paradise.

And coffee, thank god, I could smell it along with the shortbread and the tea leaves and the cherry jam. No irony or too-hipster-for-caffeine bullshit to be found in this cocoa-frosted neck of the woods.

The barista was a clean-cut man in his late twenties, hair trimmed too short to suit him, wearing a tie under his shirt and apron like something out of a 1950s milk bar.

When he saw me, he slumped slightly to the counter. 'Don't even, Xanthippe. It's been a rough week.'

'You have no idea, sunshine.' I strolled over and patted Stewart's head. 'So your new career is professional time traveller? Nice one.'

'Also I make good coffee.'

'Let's put that to the test, shall we? I need an espresso to make up for being denied coffee at fuck off o'clock this morning, and a macchiato because I like saying the word out loud.'

Mac-chiato. It makes the world a better place.

Stewart set to work at the chrome-and-candy-pink espresso machine, while I took another turn around the café. There were only a couple of customers in the window, plus more on the verandah out the front. They all looked happy and relaxed, like being here made their day a little better.

Yep, I was starting to see why Tabitha might hold a grudge.

'Can I get ye anything to eat?' asked Stewart, interrupting my perusal of the enormous pine colonial-style dresser that took up most of one wall. It was covered in a collection of porcelain chocolate pots and tea cups, many of them hand-painted or antiques.

'I'll have a pumpkin scone with a cornflake crumb and a side order of Let's Make Scones Arty and Complicated,' I said, and was rewarded by his low laugh.

'We don't use the 'scone' word around here,' he warned me. 'My employers suspect the #Sconebros nicked a recipe or two of theirs.'

'Sounds serious,' I said. No one knows better than me how cutthroat the café industry really can get.

He set the two coffees on the counter for me, side by side. 'How's Tabitha doing?'

'You know she was arrested last night?' I asked. On the one hand, how could he not know, but on the other hand, nothing had been 'normal' between those two lately.

'Ceege texted me to give me a head's up,' said Stewart, serving up my second coffee.

I blew on the first cup to cool it until I could knock the shot back, then held on to the macchiato to savour its possibilities while the espresso seared its way down my throat. 'You weren't at the consolation party, though?' I made it sound like a question but we both knew there was another question underneath that one.

'It's awkward,' he informed me, which wasn't exactly helpful.

'When are things not awkward with you and Tabitha?'

'It's especially awkward at the moment, and no I'm not going to tell ye why.'

'It might be relevant to the case.'

'It might get me killed.'

'Fine,' I said, huffing. I could do so many more productive things than parse out the details of Tabitha's complicated love life and friendship circles. If not for the murder thing I would opt out of this bullshit entirely (oh wait, that's what I'd been doing for months now). 'Tell me about Cameron Crewe.'

'Ye mean, do I want to confess to his murder?'

I blinked. '*Do* you want to confess to his murder?'

'Not today, thanks.'

'This isn't a joke, McTavish.'

'I'm well aware,' he shot at me. 'I don't have an alibi, thanks for asking.'

'Do you need one?'

'Does Tabitha?'

I gave him a very stern look. 'Please. Promise me no one will be faking an alibi for anyone else. This job is hard enough without random outbursts of Agatha Christie tropes. Tabitha didn't do anything. There's barely a fragment of evidence against her. She's going to be fine.' I waved an airy hand. 'I'm asking a few questions to make her feel better, that's all.'

'I'm no' so sure,' Stewart said, like there was something he wanted to get off his chest.

Before he could blurt out any more grand revelations, the door to the kitchen opened and one of the most stylish elderly ladies I've ever seen came bustling out with a tray of spectacular chocolate eclairs.

'Hello, my dear, now you do look familiar,' she said as Stewart took the tray off her like the gentleman he is, loading up the glass display cabinet. 'Do I know your mother?'

'This is Xanthippe Carides,' said Stewart, a little too quickly. 'Zee, this is Daisy, one of the owners of The Chocolate Teapot.'

Daisy, who wore a pale pink silk rose pinned into her silver hair, with a matching blouse and a long tapestry skirt like something out of *Bohemian Glamour* magazine, was utterly delighted to meet me. You can't fake that kind of enthusiasm. 'Is this your young lady?'

'No!' Stewart and I both said with equal emphasis.

I got offended faster. 'Hey!'

'Nothing personal, Xanthippe,' he assured me. 'But I find ye terrifying.'

Fair.

'That is my favourite effect I have on people,' I conceded. I turned to Daisy with deep curiosity. 'Does he have a young lady? Can you send him to the kitchen so we can gossip about him behind his back?'

'That sounds like an excellent idea!' Daisy pronounced, thereby making her my favourite. 'Stewart, run along and sweep something.'

'This is harassment in the workplace,' he noted, and pointed a finger at me before obeying like the good lad he was. 'Promise me the conversation will mostly be about murder.'

'Ninety percent,' I vowed. 'Okay, maybe eighty.'

Muttering something unchivalrous beneath his breath, he disappeared out back.

'I'm going to show you my chocolate pots,' said Daisy, which I assumed was a sign of her new trust and affection for me, possibly leading to my imminent adoption as her new granddaughter.

'I'd really like that,' I assured her.

———

Within an hour, I was thoroughly embraced by The Chocolate Teapot family. I had eaten a Battenburg slice, an Eccles cake and something called Parkin that tasted of treacle and the apocalypse. I had tasted three different kinds of tea, while chatting to Daisy about her travels in Europe, and what Carnaby Street was really like in 1966.

I was introduced to Dot, Daisy's dapper wife, who was responsible for most of the cooking and also for forcing Stewart into his recent haircut. I also met Zandra, Dot's punk rock great-niece, who shared barista duties with Stewart and had the best Joan Jett tattoo I had ever seen in my life.

Oh, and I managed (finally) to pull the conversation on to Cameron Crewe, because I am a freaking professional.

Unfortunately, in Daisy and Dot, I had finally found two people who thought Cameron Crewe was the bees knees. So disturbing.

'Such a nice young man, and so successful,' said Daisy. 'You have to admire that entrepreneurial spirit. A tragic loss to the restaurant industry.'

'I got the impression he was more of a—' Don't say dick in front of the sweet old ladies, don't say dick in front of the... 'difficult soul.'

We have achieved tact!

Stewart looked like he was about to burst out laughing, and Zandra looked like she was eating a lemon.

'Oh, that circus act of his was all for the cameras,' Daisy said, dismissing all of Cameron Crewe's character faults with a flick of her perfect manicure. 'No one wants to watch a polite chef any more, especially on the YouTube where it's all about hits and bitemarks.'

'Soundbites,' corrected Zandra, who couldn't help herself.

Daisy smiled sweetly. Oh, she was doing it deliberately. Nice. I do admire an old person who fully commits herself to trolling the younger generation.

'Can't have been easy,' remarked Dot, who rarely added much to the conversation, but watched everyone with a considering expression. 'He had a lot to be troubled about. The custody battle.'

'The death threats,' Daisy agreed.

Custody battle? That was news to me. 'I didn't know Crewe had children.'

'Recent development,' said Zandra curtly.

'That's right, it was last week that he came over to check on our Earl Grey crème brulée for the teacup challenge,' said Daisy. He sat down and simply poured his heart out to us. I'll admit I hadn't much time for the poor boy before that—'

'Understatement,' said Zandra under her breath.

'But I couldn't help but see him in a new light.'

'People love talking to Daisy,' said Dot fondly. 'She serves them tea and they spill their guts like there's no tomorrow.'

I glanced at Stewart, who looked like he had been hit

over the head. Had he not noticed before now that his new employer was a vision of Tabitha's twilight years? I met his eyes and he gave me a crooked, embarrassed smile.

8

Xanthippe Finally Acquires a Suspect (other than Tabitha) (after the murder)

I emerged from the haze of elegant affection and spiced patisserie that was The Chocolate Teapot, weighed down by more questions, and more shortbread than a human person should consume if they ever want to fit into a cat-suit again. I caught sight of Jason lurking further down the street. Before I could call out to him, a voice right behind me made me jump.

'Don't listen to my aunts.'

I spun around to find Zandra standing there, an unlit cigarette in one hand.

'Daisy and Dot seem trustworthy,' I said, which was not untrue, but that didn't mean I believed a word that came out of their mouths.

'They're very trusting,' she corrected. 'And suckers for a sob story. They hired Stewart because they thought he had sad eyes.'

'That was mostly his old haircut.' Also his habit of pining

over unavailable women, and his default fashion aesthetic: 'homeless band groupie'.

'Anyway,' Zandra said impatiently, ruffling her pink hair at me. 'Of course they liked Cameron Crewe—they ate up all his bullshit with a spoon.'

Disturbing image.

'What part should I not listen to? The part about his custody battle or the part about the death threats?'

Zandra's mouth made a thin line, disappearing behind a slash of dark cherry lipstick. 'Any of it. He was good at telling people what they wanted to hear, anything to make them sympathise with him, so he could get away with—'

'Murder?'

She gave me an impatient look. 'He's not the victim here.'

Apart from the minor detail of him technically being the murder victim. 'So where were you when he was killed?'

'Having sex with my boyfriend,' she said sharply.

'Thanks for sharing.'

'He deserved everything that came to him and more,' she added, then whirled away, back to The Chocolate Teapot.

I shook my head, and headed across the road to where Tabitha's favourite teen sidekick was pretending to be a telegraph pole. 'Boy band,' I greeted him.

'You wish you had my way with hair product,' said Jason.

'I do all right.' I frowned at him. If he was here, that

meant trouble, right? Had Tabitha been arrested again? 'What's wrong?'

'Nothing,' he said hastily. 'Nothing new, anyway. I want to help.'

'You're Tabitha's apprentice, not mine.'

'Can't I be both?'

'I'm not hiring.' But I wasn't idiot enough to turn him away, not when he obviously knew something.

'Tabs was playing detective when I met her,' he tried.

'And what, you imprinted on her hobby like a baby duckling?'

'Stranger things have happened.' Jason gave one of those all-body shrugs of his. He was still growing, and the rest of him hadn't caught up to his shoulders. 'Tabitha kept me out of jail. Let me help return the favour, yeah?'

We were only a few blocks from the house.

'I'll walk you home and you can tell me what else you know on the way,' I suggested. 'Helping is fine. But don't shell out cash for a trench coat any time soon. Very few of us can pull that look off.'

He nodded, and then managed to be silent for at least a block and a half. 'Trouble is,' he burst out suddenly. 'I'm sympathetic. You know. To whoever offed Chef Crewe.'

'Tabitha could end up taking the rap for them,' I reminded him. 'Also, murder is wrong,' I added, possibly a beat later than I should have done.

Ethics, why do you have to be so hard?

'He was such an arsehole,' Jason muttered.

'Sadly that is a human right which does not come with the death penalty—in this country, anyway.' I nudged him with my hip as we walked along. 'Come on. You worked in his kitchen for a week. You must have a suspect or two. Who did he really piss off?'

'Women, mostly. Total sleazebag. He'd do this thing where he'd like … compliment customers or delivery people or whatever, and be just short of creepy. If anyone called him on it, he'd act like they were crazy.'

'Sexual harassment and gaslighting, classic combination,' I noted.

'I've been thinking about Ani.'

'Do I know an Ani?'

'From #Sconebros. She was their rep for the soup kitchen challenge.'

Oh, I'd watched that vid this morning, before I headed to The Chocolate Teapot. The combination of cheesy cheerfulness and the Cameron Crewe cringe factor meant I couldn't bear to watch more than one episode at a time, and even then I probably wasn't paying close enough attention to excavate all possible clues.

'She's the one with the salmon chowder that he smashed,' I remembered. 'What was the story there?'

'I dunno,' Jason said. Then, a moment later. 'I mean,

I noticed, right? He made comments now and then—brushing up against her, not quite anything obvious enough to make a thing about. She didn't react, so I didn't know how bad it was or I would have stood up for her.'

'Okay, so now we've got your male pride out of the way...?'

'We still had to work another day in the Teasperience kitchen after he smashed her soup, and once we were finally done with that bullshit, Stewart suggested we take her to Café La Femme to celebrate. Thought we could cheer her up.'

'You took her to Tabitha,' I said thoughtfully. Sneaky boys.

'You know what Tabitha's like. Took one look at Ani's face, whipped out the beetroot brownies, and the whole story came out. Crewe was trying to get her alone the whole time, even spun her this line about extra tutoring, and getting her work in Sydney. When she realised he was cracking on to her, she said no and ... he took it out on her on camera.'

'Starting to see why his kitchen assistants are all male,' I said.

'Yeah, no kidding, his production line of sous-clones. I said we should do something, but Ani wasn't having it. Didn't want to make a drama, just told Maaka she wouldn't be in the show any more.'

95

Add 'talk to Ani at #Sconebros' to my task list. Anything to procrastinate watching the rest of those vids. 'You think she might be a suspect?'

'Dunno really. But if not her—she can't be the only one, can she? Must be a long line of chicks who had a reason to, you know.'

He wasn't wrong. If one thing was certain about this whole mess, it was that many people had good reason to stick a knife into Cameron Crewe.

'What did Tabitha think about the business with Ani?' I asked as we turned into the familiar street, to the house Jason shared with Tabitha and Ceege.

If Tabitha wasn't home, I could take the opportunity to raid her wardrobe and liberate clothes she had stolen from me while I was living there.

'She said,' and Jason trailed off, not wanting to finish the sentence.

'She said...'

'She said she was going to kill him. But not in a threatening way,' he added hastily. 'More a sort of—Tabitha being dramatic way. I think she was sort of—amped up because that was around the time of the Break Up, you know, so she was threatening to kill almost anyone who pissed her off, it wasn't like he was special, or...'

'Jase?'

'Yeah?'

'Stop talking. Be especially not talking when the police are around, yeah?'

'Yeah,' he agreed. 'Fair call.'

[Exterior shot of The Chocolate Teapot]

KARI NAGARRA: Were you disappointed about losing this week's challenge?

DAISY: Oh no, dear, we are proud of our French Onion soup. When your only criticism is that the portions are generous, there's not much to complain about!

DOT: We were disappointed in that man's behaviour, though.

KARI NAGARRA: You mean Cameron Crewe?

DOT: Yes I do!

DAISY: Ani is a sweet girl, and he didn't need to be so cruel to her.

KARI NAGARRA: Stewart and Zandra, what did you think of Café La Femme winning with their lemon meringue soup?

ZANDRA: I think they're taking the—[stops herself] I think the Café La Femme team is good at predicting what Chef Crewe will like, but they're moving forward in the competition without being authentic to their own café's personal style.

STEWART: Hey now, that's not fair. Café La Femme has always had a touch of the wacky. I don't think Tabitha's soup was all that different from an everyday special.

ZANDRA: I highly doubt that.

STEWART: As a veteran of the summer of bouillabaise cupcakes, I respectfully disagree.

[Camera frames a closer shot of Stewart]

KARI NAGARRA: You and Tabitha have a history, don't you?

STEWART: We've been friends for years, aye.

KARI NAGARRA: So you made up from your fight?

STEWART [genuinely confused]: What fight?

KARI NAGARRA: Hang on...

[Kari pulls up her phone and calls up part of a Week One episode]

TABITHA [Offscreen]: Stewart McTavish is a traitor, and we're not on speaking terms right now. He knows what he did.

[Camera zooms in on tight close-up of Stewart as he literally face-palms]

9

Tabitha's Toffee Massacre
(before the murder)

Stewart always finds me at the worst possible moment. That's a pattern in our friendship. He's seen more ugly crying and random freak-outs than any person should.

Our timing is always awful.

My café is closed, Kate Bush is playing out of every speaker I own, and I'm up to my elbows in molten toffee—not literally, though I have it flecked in my eyelashes and smeared on my apron, so

I'm not ugly crying yet, but this cooking isn't pretty. I could say I'm here right now because I have a recipe to perfect. That wouldn't be a lie in any technical sense... Except, I'm here this late in the café because my ~~boyfriend~~ fiancé is waiting for me at home, and I don't want to hear what he has to say.

Bishop's not happy with me.

We've been fighting a lot lately, about this whole Cameron Crewe business and ... well. It's amazing how many things you find to fight about once you get started. Tonight, he wants to talk. He wants to talk, so I'm here, making toffee clouds dance in the air.

There's something cathartic about spinning sugar—the caramel is so hot that it might scald you at any moment, but you flick and spin and twist, and the sugar flies out into a wild cloud of nearly-nothing. Sugar-flavoured air. Gourmet fairy floss.

Today, my sugar is ruby red, like the shiny toffee apples you used to be able to buy at the supermarket but now you only find on vintage-style cake stalls at markets and school fairs. As I spin and flick, I create wild, twisty droplets of what look like blood.

It's a work in progress.

'This is either a thing of beauty or a cry for help,' Stewart observes from the doorway.

Damn it, did I not lock that door? I spin in the wrong direction, overreacting even though I know it's him and I trust him more than almost anyone. His lovely accent is programmed deep into my bones.

Definite miscalculation. The toffee twists and un-spins. Instead of my neat ball of airy sugar strands, it tangles around me. In an instant, I'm the victim of a candy assassin with a sticky sense of humour, and the assassin is me.

'Don't laugh, I'm perfecting my craft,' I huff at him. Damn it all. 'A little help, here?'

'No idea where to start.' He comes forward and dutifully unwinds me from my glorious, messy creation. 'What's all this, then?'

'I'm going to deconstruct the toffee apple, and revolutionise cake design. Also I have some sugar sculptures planned for later in the competition.' I have a sudden thought, and jerk away from him before he can peel the last of the sugar cloud off my hair. 'No, wait. Is this you being an industrial spy? You're not allowed to take my secrets back to your adorable love nest of octogenarian, Chanel-wearing teapot collectors.'

'You'll like them,' he protests and, oh. Are we having this conversation now, right now, with my emotions all over the place and my distraction toffee clumping across my face like I'm a guest star in a stop motion animated horror movie? Stewart gives me the sternest of stern looks. 'I hear we're not on speaking terms still. Which is news to me...'

'Anything I might say on YouTube about being still mad at you is ... probably just for the show and not something you should take seriously.'

'So ... you're not still mad at me?'

'Of course I'm mad at you, don't you watch the show?'

He looks shifty. 'I thought ye got over me taking the job.'

'When have you ever known me to get over anything?'

'Daisy and Dot are great, Tabitha. They're good bosses, they're nice ladies, and I'm happy working for them.

How is this still a problem?'

'It's not a problem, everything's fine,' I snap, moving out of range as he tries to help me with my toffee massacre hair. 'It's fine, leave it. I'll start a trend.'

Stewart steps back, looking at me with that cute, baffled expression I so often inspire in him. 'Do ye not think it's time to forgive me?'

'I have a coffee machine. I needed a new barista and I hate training people,' I sulk. 'You were looking for exactly that kind of work after your blog lost its funding. What's so wrong with Café La Femme?' *What's so wrong with me?*

He laughs, actually laughs at me, like he can't feel the laser bolts drilling into him from my eyes.

Okay, I don't have laser vision, but there's cooling toffee in the pot near my elbow.

'Tabitha, no offence,' he says when he has recovered himself. (No good sentence has ever started with the words 'no offence' but I allow him the benefit of the doubt.) 'But that's a terrible idea.'

'Why, because I'd be such an awful boss? Xanthippe clearly thinks so too, she cleared out the second she got a better offer.' I'm working really hard not to burst into tears, which is awful and ridiculous.

Stewart looks at me, really looks at me, no longer distracted by the toffee. 'Tabitha, what's wrong?'

'Nothing's wrong, I'm fine, and if you want to see other

cafés, I'm not going to stop you.' I want it to sound all tough and mean, but it comes out soft instead. Ugh. 'I'm such a mess right now.' I could be talking about the toffee. But I'm not.

He hugs me then, his long limbs folding around me. It's a comfort I didn't even know I needed until it was right there, being kind to me.

'I like your mess,' Stewart says gently.

Oh wow, now I am going to cry.

'You just don't want to deal with it every day,' I say acidly. There we are. Mean girl Tabitha is back.

His face grazes gently against my cheek. 'Tabitha. I didnae go anywhere. I'm *not* going anywhere. And your mess is better than anyone else's ... anything.'

Oh. That. That makes it very difficult to end this hug.

'I hope you aren't letting your fine coffee skills go to waste, surrounded by all those vintage teapots,' I mumble at him.

'Truce, then?'

'Don't pretend like you were even pulling your weight in this fight,' I complain into his neck.

'The fights we have entirely inside your head are my favourites,' Stewart assures me, pulling back from the hug. 'So. Anything else ye need to tell me?'

I should tell him everything about Cameron Crewe, and my plan. I know I should. Stewart's always had my back.

But I have to save some emotional energy for the conversation waiting at home for me.

'I'll tell you,' I promised him. 'If things get worse.'

Stewart looks guilty.

I blink at him. 'Unless you *already know*.'

'Jase has a big mouth,' he confesses all in a rush.

'Bloody hell.' I'm not on the brink of tears any more, but I might be about to collapse in giggles. 'That worm. Seriously. You're in this, all the way? After I was so mean to you?'

Stewart gives me an impatient look. 'I told ye. I never went away.'

Kissing him would be deeply inappropriate right now. 'Tea,' I say quickly. 'Tea, and no more questions.'

'Coffee,' says Stewart, sounding plaintive. 'And uh. Jase wants you to meet Ani from #Sconebros? He thinks ye might be able to convince her that not all professional kitchens are made of brimstone and bitchiness.'

'Is he bringing her here? When?'

'In about ten minutes.' His puppy eyes are ... large and entreating.

I should go home. This is ... a completely unnecessary indulgence. This doesn't count as a legit reason to work late, not by any stretch of the imagination. 'Fine,' I say in a long-suffering voice. 'I might have fresh brownies.'

'And coffee?' Stewart actually flutters his eyelashes at me. He only flirts when coffee is on the line.

'Do you deserve coffee?' I wonder aloud. 'After heart-lessly abandoning our beautiful coffee machine for some vintage model? She holds a grudge, you know.'

Never has a man looked so pathetic.

'Fine,' I grumble. 'One cup. To remind you what you've been missing.'

———

One coffee and a plate of brownies turns into—well, a makeshift Tabitha counselling session. Once I finally send Ani and Stewart away, I make Jase help me clean the kitchen, so he doesn't get too big for his boots. I send him home ahead of me, though.

I have thinking to do. A lot of thinking. Ani's story isn't unique. It adds more fuel to the fire. Our plan is important. Something has to be done about Cameron Crewe.

Thanks to the resistance of toffee to traditional cleaning products, it's nearly midnight by the time I get home—bad form for a café owner rostered on to open tomorrow morning. Worse form when I told my significant other I'd be home as early as I could, because *talking*.

I let myself into the house, exchange vague vowel sounds with Ceege (we have been living together so long that consonants are unnecessary) and put a blanket over Jase who still forgets that he has Xanthippe's old room now, and doesn't need to crash on the couch.

Then I go upstairs, take off my typewriter key earrings and my jelly wedges, and brace myself to deal with the beautiful man sitting on my bed.

As soon as I see his face I know exactly why I've been putting off this conversation, and I know that he knows it, too. Part of me hoped he would give up on me and head home. Or he'd be asleep by now. Not this.

Leo Bishop, love of my life so far: built out of loyalty and stubbornness. He is waiting for me, and he is not happy. 'So,' I say with false cheer. 'Is this the part where you ask me for the ring back?'

'That depends on you,' he replies, steady as a rock.

I think about Ani's tear-stained face tonight, and Cameron Crewe's arrogance—his assumption that he can get away with anything because he has money and fame and an endless capacity to hire assistants and treat them like crap.

'I'm doing the right thing,' I insist. 'I can't stop now. I believe in what I'm doing.'

'Yeah.' Leo Bishop stands up, walks towards me and kisses me on the forehead. It feels like goodbye. 'That's what I thought you'd say.'

Ultimatums are the worst. Once spoken aloud, they're out there, eating away at your relationship. No one wins. Not unless the person who was idiot enough to put the ultimatum out there changes his mind, takes it back, and allows room for compromise.

I wait, but he doesn't take it back.

So.

I guess this one's a deal-breaker.

WEEK THREE

Cake in a Jar

vs

The Sister Detective

[Camera shot on The Chocolate Teapot]

KARI NAGARRA: I don't know about the rest of you, but I'm excited about this week's challenge. We're talking cake. In a jar. The twenty-first century looked at cake, and decided that the only way to improve it was to make it portable, and store it in recycled glass containers. Daisy, Dot, what do you have for us?

DAISY: Well, dear, the important thing about constructing jar cakes is to make the most of the see-through glass by forming distinct layers, and plenty of fun textures. We've created our own version of the classic banana split, using a red velvet cupcake as the base, with fresh banana, crème anglaise and our own secret four-chocolate sauce.

KARI: So I'm just going to take a few jars of this home with me...

[Cut to: camera shot on Café La Femme]

TABITHA: We've used Nin's secret special beetroot brownie, baked into the jar with a melting chocolate fondant centre. Normally I'd add strawberries, but this is the one time of year in Tasmania when you can't get good ones, so I've gone for a pear crumble layer with plenty of space at the top to pipe in spiced custard. Well, it was going to be spiced custard, but I slipped and fell and somehow it's limoncello marscapone.

LARA: This cake tastes like an angel died to make it happen. [Tabitha looks concerned] I mean in a good way. No joke.

KARI: Tabitha, the viewers want to know more about the mind behind the menu. I can't help noticing...

TABITHA: Oh, that.

KARI: *You're not wearing the ring.*

TABITHA: *So I'm not engaged anymore, still friends, no one's fault, can we stop talking about it? Back to the cake.*

[Camera lingers on her face.]

TABITHA: *Seriously, let's move on. I have so much more to tell you about why limoncello marscapone is the best possible substance to pipe into a jar.*

[Cut to: camera shot on #Sconebros exterior.

[Cut to: Maaka at the counter]

MAAKA: *Scone in a jar, bro! Raspberry jam, whipped cream. Sorted.*

[Maaka makes fistbump explosion directly into the lens]

═ **10** ═

As a Sister, Xanthippe makes a Good Detective. (after the murder)

My brother. Let me tell you about him.

Leonidas Bishop is a surly thirty-something macho throwback who would have been better off being a policeman in the 1950s, or possibly the 1850s, if the descendants of Greek immigrants were allowed to wear the uniform in Australia back then. Did Australia have cops in the 1850s? Anyway, moving on.

Leo doesn't respond well to the following circumstances:

1. Change
2. Trends
3. Emotions
4. The 21st Century
5. Shenanigans

Against my better judgement, I chose #Sconebros for our familial interrogation.

This had nothing to do with my desire to further investigate the concept of 'sconut', (though they were horribly delicious) and everything to do with me wanting to see his reaction when a scone technician bro informed him that this place did not serve coffee, ironic or otherwise.

I was disappointed when Leo barked 'long black', barely turning a hair at my request for sunflower seed crumble with the tea of the day (salt and vinegar). The bearded #Sconebro promptly went away and returned with a legit cup of coffee.

'This place doesn't do coffee,' I accused the #Sconebro, feeling betrayed.

Leo sipped his long black and gave me his patented 'are you high' expression. 'Everybody serves coffee.'

'We have it for the kitchen staff, and for members of Tasmania Police,' said the #Sconebro.

I gave him a filthy look. 'Maybe I'm working undercover.'

Our server was unimpressed. 'Better not blow your cover then,' he said over his shoulder as he walked away.

'So I'm here,' said Leo, half a silent long black later. 'I'm not sure why I'm here...'

'The murder of Cameron Crewe,' I said calmly.

'No.'

'But I—'

'No.'

'Are they even looking for a suspect other than Tabitha? This whole mess makes no sense.'

Leo was thunderous. 'This is not my case, Xanthippe.

I can't comment. Can't discuss it. Can most definitely not discuss my ex's role as a suspect.'

'She's either about to get swallowed up by a miscarriage of justice, or she's actively being framed. Do you not care about this?'

'I can't care about this,' Leo growled. 'It's not my case. I can't help her as a boyfriend because we broke up a month ago. And I can't help her in the job because they won't let me near this.'

'Fiancé.'

'What?'

'Not boyfriend. *Fiancé*. That was your official status before you demoted yourself, right?'

His face closed over. 'I'm only going to say this once. Stay out of it.'

That was so bloody unfair. I had spent a month staying out of it. I'd given them both their space to deal with their break up. But that was May and this was June, and I was over treating them both like they were made of glass. 'I need to ask questions.'

'Because you're a detective now. Despite having no training, or anyone to answer to but yourself. You're going to crack the case all by yourself.' I could hear the sarcasm oozing out of Leo's pores.

'Are you pissed off at me?' I was more curious than angry. We had not yet had the conversation about my recent career change. I knew he wouldn't approve, but there was something else going on here—anger behind his eyes that maybe wasn't entirely about me.

Leo banged his cup down. 'Damn straight I am. If you want to solve crimes—and if it's something you're going to stick at for more than a year, unlike every other job you've flirted with—then get some qualifications. Join the police.'

I laughed at that, because me? A police officer? 'I'm sorry, have you met my issues with authority?'

Leo leaned in, eyes very dark. 'If you're not prepared to take it seriously, you shouldn't be doing it at all.'

'You know that most of my work is cases that the police can't or won't touch, right? Small stuff. Helping the underdog.'

'Spying on people for divorces and minor accident fraud?' he scoffed. 'You're contributing so much to society.'

I chose not to share that I spent a good part of last month helping a single mum prove that it was her bastard neighbour and not herself who should be evicted for noise violations. When Leo has a steam up about something, it never helps to offer facts or logic.

'Fine,' I said flatly. 'Tell me Tabitha is going to be okay, and the system will protect her. Tell me that with hand on heart, and I'll back off.'

My brother glared at me. Stubbornness runs hot on both sides of our family.

'Fine,' he said after a moment. 'Be a detective, if you must. Solve the case, and save Tabitha from her web of bullshit. But that doesn't mean you get a post-relationship debrief from me.'

A female #Sconebro executive with curly black hair delivered my food and tea on a tray. I leaned over the arm of the feral tapestry couch on which we were seated. 'Are you Ani?'

She looked startled. 'No, I'm Soph. They hired me when Ani quit.'

'When did Ani quit?'

'Few weeks back. She didn't even give her notice, just walked away.'

As Soph returned to the counter, Leo made an impatient face at me.

'You're jealous of my multi-tasking,' I informed him.

'Yeah, that's what it is.' He stared at the dregs of his cup. 'I don't think this is real coffee after all.'

'Poor baby. Did they serve you something squeezed out of a dandelion?'

I lifted my own teapot for one, and a perfectly brewed stream of espresso poured out of the spout and into the teacup. 'Okay, they're definitely screwing with us.'

———

It was a long day. Interrogating people in cafés had left me completely uninterested in further food, tea or coffee. The sunflower seed crumble didn't change my mind on that, which would teach me to order the funniest thing on the menu instead of something that sounded like food.

When Maaka relieved Soph at the counter, I left my sulky brother with my over-caffeinated teapot while I deepened my investigation.

'Hey, I was here with Tabitha earlier...'

'Yeah,' Maaka said warily. 'I remember you.'

'You know I'm trying to find out what happened, since the official murder investigation is trying to pin Tabitha as a suspect?'

He gave me a broad grin. 'I hear everything, bro.'

'I was hoping to talk to Ani about an incident that happened on *Café Wars*.'

The smile fell off Maaka's face. 'Yeah, nah. She's gone.'

'Gone for the day, gone from the job...?'

'Gone back to New Zealand.' The flat line of his mouth made it clear this was a sore subject.

Considering my ability to poke and prod at a sore subject, it's amazing I didn't become a private detective years ago.

'Because of what happened?'

'Nah, think she had family stuff to sort out. Or visa problems.' Lying liar who was lying.

'Can you give me a number or an email address to get in touch with her?'

'Sure,' he said, and dug around behind the counter as if

he wasn't trying to come up with a bunch of reasons to turn down my perfectly reasonable request.

While I waited, a couple of trendy teenagers came up to pay their bill, and I saw that one of them had a *Café Wars* sticker on her phone. They weren't buzzing with frantic excitement, so either the news about Crewe's murder hadn't leaked to social media yet, or kids today don't care about murder. According to my sources, the police were holding a press conference tomorrow morning. I'd already texted Tabitha that we needed to be there to learn what narrative they were spinning. Like wild horses would have kept her away.

'Has *Café Wars* been good for business?' I asked casually after the kids were gone.

'Too right it has,' said Maaka. 'I guess all that's over now, though.'

It was hard to imagine them continuing the show without Crewe, but stranger things had happened. A mysterious murder was likely to bring the customers in at a high lick, at any rate.

'You might need to invest in a few more couches,' I suggested. 'Do you have that contact number for Ani?'

'Yeah, nah, I can't find it,' he said apologetically, as if he had ever intended to give it to me. 'Give us your number and I'll text you when it turns up.' He handed me his phone.

'You do that,' I said, typing in my number with the name

Ace Detective.

'Choice. You don't know any Kiwis looking for work, do you? I could do with a new #Sconebro.'

'You only hire New Zealanders? No locals?'

Now I wasn't pressing him about Ani, Maaka treated me to another of his beautiful smiles. 'Gotta support my people. Besides, everyone knows Australians can't bake decent scones.'

Ouch, could I have a Band-aid for that burn?

'I'm Australian, you tool!' yelled Soph from the kitchen.

Maaka looked alarmed. 'Can I fire you for that?'

'No!'

'Have you been faking the accent?'

'Yes!'

'Do you … know any other Aussies who can fake the accent that well? Got to protect the brand, bro.'

As I headed back to the couch where my brother was frowning at his own phone, I caught sight of Jason lingering nearby. Were interns usually this proactive? Apprenticing to Nin and her eyebrows had obviously instilled some kind of work ethic in him.

Jason was chatting to the teenagers who had just been here, the *Café Wars* fans, and I finally saw what was scrawled on the backs of their shirts.

I leaned over Leo, stealing one of his toffee crumb scones because he'd barely touched it. 'Am I imagining things, or are those kids wearing shirts with the word McTabitha printed on them?'

'You are not imagining things,' Leo said calmly. 'And you forgot to pronounce the hashtag.'

I made a hashtag with my fingers, as sarcastically as possible, and gave him the finger to finish. 'Does that mean what I think it means?'

'None of my business.'

'Tabitha didn't cheat on you?' It didn't seem like her style, unless you counted her deep and monogamous relationship with her café, which would always come before any men in her life.

Leo gave me a long-suffering look. 'No. She did not.'

'But you're still not going to—'

'Still none of your business.'

'Worst brother ever.'

'I try my best.'

I let him go after that, because he was giving me nothing, and he was miserable company. Plus, something called paperwork he had to get on with? Ugh, working for the man. He could keep the police service, and leave me to my beautiful empty office with a lockable door.

As soon as Leo was gone, Jason ran across the grass and vaulted into the couch beside me. 'How's the investigating, boss?'

'Riveting as ever. Three murder suspects tried to shoot

me this morning. Same old, same old.' I gave Jason a piercing look as he chomped through Leo's last remaining scone like it was his last meal on earth. 'Do you really want to help?'

'Sure,' he said with a shrug. I assume in teenager speak that meant: *yes, I am deeply committed to helping you solve this murder and save Tabitha.*

'Get me an introduction to Cameron Crewe's kitchen staff.'

'No problem, do you speak robot?'

I blinked. 'The what now?'

'Haven't you noticed how creepily similar they all are? I swear, he trains them into conformity. They finish each other's sentences. The second day I was there learning soup wankery, he fired Lief, right? And the next day he came in like usual, only I realised round about lunchtime that it totally wasn't him. It was some other bloke, same basic build, slightly Nordic look.'

'That's...'

'Creepy as, right?'

'Yes. Yes it is.' I raised an eyebrow at him. 'I need an introduction to Crewe's current and former kitchen staff, including both Liefs. Think you can swing that?'

'No problem,' said my sidekick-in-training, pulling out his phone.

'Do you know why my brother and Tabitha called it a

day?' I added, only half-thinking that I might catch him unawares enough to spill more than he meant to.

Jason caught on to me, and flicked his eyes up with a smirk. 'Nah,' he said after a long pause, now texting without looking at his keys. 'But I reckon I know how to find out.' He made a 'duh' face at me.

Oh, right. I could ask Tabitha. Like a real person.

———————

When I got back to the café, it was nearly closing time. Tabitha was still busy in her natural habitat, and I didn't want to get talked into helping out with anything, so I slipped up to my office to finish off a report.

One of the first clients I took on as a detective was a Sydney-based woman who bought a couple of cottages in Battery Point sight unseen and asked me to set up some camera surveillance—not to protect her investment, as I originally believed, but because she was pretty sure her renovation team were slacking off on the job.

Spoiler: they weren't, but it turned out her neighbour was sabotaging the renovations because he was pissed off her new multi-million dollar greenhouse was going to spoil the view from his bathroom window. Also, the kid they had hired as their assistant was knocking boots with said neighbour's hot wife, which I left out of my original report despite it livening up the story considerably.

Anyway, this month's surveillance was much less interesting to type up, but I do enjoy the warm fuzzy sound of an invoice being emailed into the void, so I got on with the paperwork.

My phone pinged with a text from a number that hadn't exactly been running hot since I made my break from the café. Nin, Tabitha's assistant chef, rules that kitchen with an iron eyebrow. We never got along when I was working there because she doesn't believe I should be allowed anywhere near a kitchen, a coffee machine, or customers. Also, she thinks I'm a bad influence on Tabitha. All reasonable grounds for dislike, though maybe she would hate me less now she didn't have to trip over me in her kitchen.

Nin's message said:

Code Lamington

There were so many things that could mean, but I couldn't think of any. I typed back

WTF

Sigh

I'm sorry, did you type the word 'sigh' at me, because I've had a long day, and I don't feel that is deserved.

Code Lamington = Tabitha is poring through CWA cookbooks in a manner suggestive of a near future baking-related emotional meltdown.

Every piece of information Nin added only inspired further questions. Quite a lot of questions. Like:

Why me? Who do you usually send these codes to? Is there a code book?

There was a long-ish pause, and then I received the following:

She doesn't have a boyf any more. She and Stewart are on and off and I can't be bothered to check if they're currently talking to each other. Ceege refuses to involve himself in baking interventions cos he's selfish and likes the extra cake. Jason has a hot date. I need to sleep if I'm going to open tomorrow. Which I'm doing, by the way, so Tabitha can go to the murder press conference that YOU thought would be a good idea.

This was the longest and most detailed conversation that I had ever had with Nin.

Am I last on the phone tree?

Yes.

Not even a hint of irony.

Seriously? You have a Tabitha emotional meltdown baking phone tree, and I'm SIXTH?

I didn't know whether to be insulted or relieved.

After you, we're scraping the bottom of the barrel with that glittery dude who works in the morgue, or her hippie absentee mother. Please.

So this was what desperation looked like.

I'll be right down.

Your blood's worth bottling,

Nin typed as her sign off which was, hands down, the

nicest thing she'd ever said to anyone in my presence. Possibly I could be friends with text-Nin. Stranger things have happened.

[Unaired Café Wars footage]

[Camera resting on counter in Teasperience kitchen, captures Chef Crewe and his assistants Earl, Grey and Lief as they walk past, preparing food, apparently unaware of the filming. Kari Nagarra is also present, out of visual range of the camera]

CAMERON CREWE [off camera]: Fucking cakes in jars. What the hell am I paying you for? What is this, the Women's fucking Weekly? Are we running a fucking bake sale?

KARI NAGARRA [off camera]: Your fans voted via online poll to select the food trends they wanted represented on the show. We agreed to that format…

CREWE: So everything's out of date! I create food trends, I don't follow them. This whole shitshow is going to make me look like a washed up has-been.

[Muffled sound from camera operator]

[Crewe stalks towards camera]

CREWE: You got something to say, funny guy? Something to laugh about?

TOM [off camera]: No, Chef.

CREWE: You want to get anywhere in this industry, you'd better not piss me off. Right?

TOM: Um, what was the question?

[Crewe leans in, the camera shot captures his apron and neck, close up]

CREWE: You want to get anywhere in television, dickhead?

KARI: Don't bully him. You have enough lawsuits to deal with.

CREWE: *I'll get to you in a minute, chickie. You. Dickhead. You want to get anywhere in television?*

TOM: *Yes, sir. Chef. Yes, I do.*

[Crewe leans down further, grinning directly into the camera lens]

CREWE: *Well, then. Better make me look good.*

WEEK FOUR

Comfort Food

vs

Tabitha's Feelings

vs

Pie

KARI NAGARRA: So it's Week Four and that means comfort food—Tabitha, what's your concept?

TABITHA DARLING: It's all about the pie, Kari. There's nothing more heartwarming to the Australian palette than the crunch and heat of a savoury meat pie, and I'm channelling my own childhood with these little darlings.

KARI: They are the most adorable pies I have ever seen in my life! Why do they look so round?

TABITHA: They're hand-shaped to get that soft, spherical shape, with gumleaf pastry detailing, inspired by the epic artwork of May Gibbs.

KARI: OMG, they're—

TABITHA: Snugglepies. Yes they are.

KARI: I can't even—I want to bite into this right now!

TABITHA: No one's stopping you. Careful, though, the gravy's super hot.

[Kari bites carefully into one of the snugglepies, making happy noises as steam pours out of the pastry]

TABITHA: That's locally sourced lamb, flavoured with bush pepper and rosemary, a classic combination with a bit of a kick to it. I slow cooked the lamb for two days, which means the pie is eighty percent gravy.

KARI: Excuse me, I think the pie and I need some time to be alone together.

TABITHA: I designed a killer milkshake to drink with it, but that might be over egging the pudding.

LIVIA DAY

KARI: What flavour milkshake?

TABITHA: Pavlova.

[Kari whimpers]

= 11 =

Tabitha Darling is Open to Adoption
(before the murder)

By the time we get to Week Four, I've forgotten what it's like to not be on a reality TV show. I guess that's how they suck you into revealing all your squishy feels on screen.

Luckily, my deepest emotions have always been wrapped up in food, so when it's announced that the Week Four theme is rebooting the concept of comfort food for my café (and 100,000 people on YouTube), I'm spoiled for choice.

If it takes burying myself to the elbows in delicious, lardy pastry to forget my personal dramas, so be it.

When I was a kid, my mum always said no day was so bad it couldn't be improved by a steak and mushroom pie. Her pastry was so more-ish that when she retired from the police canteen and ran off to a tie-dyed lentil-soaked incense-burning ocarina-blowing artist colony somewhere on the North-West Coast, I found myself besieged by her former customers.

After my dad died, I couldn't bring myself to even roll

out the crust, so I inflicted a year's worth of salads and bok choy on Tasmania Police instead.

Now, I'm making up for lost time.

Bishop and I are done. Time to move on.

I have three slow cookers lined up on the counter of my kitchen at home, testing out different fillings. I'm banking on the lamb as a winner, but my slow curried chicken is edging up behind it as another favourite, and the third cooker contains steaming meatballs in case I decided to go for Italian meatball pies, full of sticky mozzarella strands and sweet roasted garlic.

Ceege, who had trouble fitting into his fancy Real Job suits for a while there, leaves the house in a huff because the scents are too glorious and it interferes with his new policy of eating raw vegetables and hating himself.

'So it's true,' says a voice from the doorway. 'Tabitha Darling is secretly Sweeney Todd. I always suspected it. *She puts people in the pies.*'

I smile without looking up. This. I need this. 'The postman gave me a funny look this morning. He was basically asking to be turned into stroganoff.'

When I glance around, I see Stewart leaning in the doorway, watching me. I'm not fighting with him any more, hooray. That was exhausting.

He's heard about the breakup, I'm sure. With the way our friend circle works, he likely heard about it before I did.

Two years ago, I made a choice between two kisses, two possible futures. It could easily have been Stewart and I breaking up right now.

That's a horrible thought.

'Too much thinking,' says Stewart, laughing at me. At least my inner turmoil is entertaining to others. I'd hate to think it's entirely without value. 'When do we eat?'

'Not for another twenty-four hours,' I pronounce, putting the last lid on the last slow cooker.

His face falls, which is flattering. 'You're kidding.'

'So not kidding.' Huh. I took the day off to prep for tomorrow's *Café Wars* filming. But it's not even noon, and I've done all my jobs. 'Oh hell. I have nothing to do.' Nothing but wallow in my poor life choices, surrounded by the tantalising scents of something no one can eat until tomorrow. 'This is bad.'

'Where are we in the breakup recovery list?' asks Stewart. We've seen Ceege through two major breakups in the last eighteen months, and Jason through about forty-seven.

'Somewhere between the Jimmy Stewart movie marathon, and baking a Bombe Alaska.'

'That sounds fun, let's do that last one,' Stewart grins.

I throw a tea towel at him. 'It's nearly June! Bombe Alaska can only be made at the height of summer, or in an outdoor tent, or it's cheating. Also, ice cream will make me cry right now. We'd better save it for a last resort.'

Stewart tucks the tea towel into my apron. 'I'll give ye a choice. We start a new tradition with *The Thin Man* movies, because Jimmy Stewart is highly overrated, or we go on an outing.'

'Outing, please,' I say quickly because if I don't get out of the house soon, I'm going to explode. Also, he is extremely wrong about Jimmy Stewart, and I don't have the energy to fight with him about it.

Stewart twirls a finger in a circle. 'Frock up. Something suitable for a tea party.'

I eye his indie rock t-shirt and paint-flecked jeans. 'Are you also making an effort for this hypothetical tea party?'

'Away wi' ye, woman, get changed before I remember that days off are for hobbies and sleeping in.'

It's too cold to wear adorable retro sundresses, which is always a rough transition for me to make as winter closes in around Hobart.

On the other hand, I own patterned tights with vanilla beans on them, which look great matched with a chocolate-brown tweed skirt (I'm flirting with 'retro librarian' as a fashion genre right now) and a rose-pink polka dot cardigan over a high-buttoned cream blouse.

'Neapolitan,' says Stewart when he sees me. 'Thought there was no ice cream in the game plan.'

'I don't know what you're talking about,' I say haughtily while adding strawberry clips to my hair. 'Ice cream is overrated as an emotional coping tool.'

One pair of stompy brown Doc Martens later, I am ready to face whatever Stewart thinks is a good distraction.

———

I'm glad I made an effort. Stewart brings me to The Chocolate Teapot.

'You're not trying to convince me to betray my own café, are you?' I ask, not entirely seriously.

Stewart looks oddly nervous. 'I think ye should get to know each other, that's all.'

I sigh loudly. 'This smells like a set up. Is it a set up? Do your new adopted grandmothers have some nice boy they want to matchmake me with, to console me in my heartbreak?' Too late, it occurs to me that the nice boy in question might be standing right next to me. 'Um, I mean. You know what I mean.'

'I should warn ye…'

That's exactly what you want to hear coming out of someone's mouth when you're in a fragile emotional state. 'What is it?'

He picks nervously at the soft paint on his jeans. It looks fresh, though he's capable of wearing the same pair for a week even after a messy major painting project.

I realise the source of his guilt. 'Oh, *hell no*.'

'It meant nothing.'

'You painted them a mural?'

'It was good money.'

I'm stunned for a moment and yes, jealous. First they take Stewart, and now this?

My mural is sacred. It marks the cornerstone of our friendship, and it makes my café look like the most fabulous place on earth (which is accurate). I can see why he held this particular detail back when defending his right to seek employment somewhere other than Café La Femme.

'It better not be as good as mine,' I warn him.

'It's rubbish,' he promises me. 'I barely even coloured within the lines.'

———————

Stewart didn't put Wonder Woman or Audrey Hepburn in The Chocolate Teapot mural, so mine was naturally superior. Instead, he painted one of the outside walls of their cottage café with a delicious nursery rhyme/fairy tale mash up, featuring a large chocolate teapot (with frosted doors and windows like a gingerbread house, or possibly the shoe that the old woman had to fill with her ungrateful, bratty children) and a whole bunch of mice in sweet little costumes.

It's so cute I'm surprised anyone ever gets as far as order-

KEEP CALM AND *Kill* THE *Chef*

ing the chocolate drinks and desserts in this place.

'What do you think?' Stewart asks, deliberately casual.

'Aww,' I tease. 'Did you bring me here to show off your pretty picture? Do you care about my opinion, Stewart?'

'No,' he grumbles. 'I brought ye here to be sarcastic about it, which is every artist's dream.'

I smile beautifully at him. 'I'm glad it's not as pretty as mine.'

Stewart narrows his eyes at me. 'Worst. Friend. Ever.'

'I try my best,' I say modestly. 'Come on, Hansel. Time to introduce me to the wicked witches.'

He mutters something that might have been 'see who gets pushed in an oven first, aye,' but I choose not to hear his exact phrasing, for the sake of inter-café diplomacy.

I can so too be diplomatic!

———————

So. What is there to say about The Chocolate Teapot? I want to hate it. Obviously I want to hate it. I barely even watched their appearances in the show so far because I've been so cranky about Stewart joining their den of fairy tale wonders.

As we cross the verandah and head inside, I notice so many darling little touches, like the vintage pattern on the curtains, and the squeaky pine door, and the iced petit fours spilling out of teacups in the window display ... even so, I steel myself to not fall for it. Have some pride, Tabitha!

We step into the cozy space, and come face to face with the most elegant old lady I've ever seen in my life. She wears a pale pink Chanel suit under a butcher's apron with wide green and white stripes, and she's slicing her way through a tray of bright fuschia zwetschgenkuchen.

I utter a squee so shrill that only dogs and other chefs can hear it.

'Tabitha, ye all right there?' asks Stewart, baffled at my elbow.

'Mr McTavish,' says Daisy of The Chocolate Teapot with a knowing smile. 'Did you finally bring Miss Darling to meet us?'

Stewart gives her a distressed look that I barely even pay attention to, my eyes locked on the glorious cake.

'But where did you get the plums?' I burst out. Real European prune plums, the Empress variety that turn a spectacular beetroot colour when you cook them.

'Oh,' says Daisy, pleased. 'We have a little man out at Woodbridge who grows special varieties for us. He ran a Kickstarter last year to develop a wider range of historical fruit. Have you had this before? It's—'

'Zwetschgenkuchen,' I say reverently.

Her smile widens even further. 'Miss Darling, I just knew we'd get along. Would you care for a little Kaffee und Kuchen?'

'Omigod,' I say, smacking Stewart on the elbow. 'You didn't tell me they were escapees from the Chalet School books. I'd have been here months ago!'

'Miss Darling,' says Daisy with a stern look. 'If I was ever granted my wish to live inside the Chalet School books, I would never escape.'

And that, dear reader, is how I fell in love with Daisy Ann Beckenbauer, and adopted her as my honorary grandmother.

Best break up present ever.

= 12 =

Tabitha Tells It All
(before the murder)

Stewart looks way too pleased with himself. Daisy slices the delicious plum cake that I have never been able to properly replicate after the winter I spent baking in Bavaria.

Daisy orders Stewart around happily, insisting that he grind her favourite coffee beans and locate the special teaspoons, while we settle in at a table near the fireplace.

'This is your offering for the comfort food challenge?' I ask, digging in deeply with my fork and inhaling the rich, sweet plummy smell. 'Good choice. I went for savoury.'

'I don't think meat can ever be quite as comforting as cake,' says Daisy, patting my hand. 'But I'm sure you did your best, dear.'

Even when she's patronising me, she's stylish and extraordinary. I want to wear her like a coat.

It's the perfect afternoon. Dot, Daisy's wife (they got married in at least three other countries before Australia allowed them to do it here) shows me the epic herb garden they've built in the yard behind The Chocolate Teapot. Daisy makes me try her freshly-set basil toffees, which come close to killing me dead with sweet envy.

I also witness Dot arguing with Stewart about whether the restaurant industry has reached 'peak salted caramel' and that gives me a great idea for a killer milkshake—food fashions that have peaked! Let me pile a macaron and a cupcake on top of your mountain of salted caramel froyo...

The best part is, I'm surrounded by people who would get the joke. This place is Disneyland for Tabithas.

Stewart is right (shush), this is exactly what I need—a breath of deep coffee fumes, far away from my own kitchen surfaces. He knows me so well.

The vibration of my phone, tucked away in a pocket of my ironic Harris Tweed handbag, is the only thing that disturbs my contentment. Every now and then it buzzes with a text message, and I ignore it.

Bishop texted me that morning, something innocuous and friendly, and I haven't brought myself to unlock my phone ever since. Whoever this is can wait.

Stewart sits nearer to my bag than me. At one point, he catches my eye and mouths the words, 'Do you need to get that?'

I shake my head firmly, and he doesn't push.

Finally, it's time to go home. I refuse Stewart's offer to walk me, *only* because I live a half a suburb away, and not at all because I was worried that in my post-relationship vulnerable state, I might pin him to a wall and rebound his brains out.

I let Daisy and Dot pack a basket of goodies like I'm freaking Red Riding Hood (I'm not going to say no, especially when a massive slab of zwetschgenkuchen goes into the Tupperware container, I'm only human) and I leave Stewart in their capable hands.

Yeah, yeah. They're good for him. Somehow he's managed to find yet another little family to make sure he's eating his vegetables, and not living on coffee alone.

I have no doubt that Daisy and Dot regularly Skype Stewart's mother back in Scotland, keeping her updated on his life.

It's one hundred percent adorable.

Out on the verandah, before I lose my nerve, I scrabble for my phone to check whether the messages I've been ignoring are from Bishop.

Huh. Apparently not. All four of the messages are from a private number. Slowly, I set my basket down on the verandah and scroll through.

Two minutes later, I turn around, go back into the café and inform Stewart that yes, actually, I will take up his offer to walk me home. Let no one say I don't learn from past mistakes.

I don't miss the secretly delighted expressions that Daisy

and Dot exchange as we leave together. Oh dear. I'd better let them down gently.

Stewart and I … I'm pretty sure we missed our moment to be anything other than friends. As long as I keep resisting any catastrophic rebound-related impulses, it can stay that way forever.

Friends stick around longer than boyfriends or fiancés, anyway—that's the story of my life, and I'm not willing to test the theory yet again, not with the Bishop Disaster still stinging my pride.

'What's all this about?' Stewart asks, picking up my basket as we set off down the street.

'I don't really want to—' We pass a group of giggling girls in matching glittery t-shirts. They give us very pointed looks on their way to The Chocolate Teapot.

Stewart has gone white. I know he's British and all, but that colour cannot be healthy. 'Keep walking, don't look back,' he mutters.

I let him steer me along the street, and around the corner. If anything, the giggling gets louder as we walk faster. 'What was that?' I ask, once we're out of sight.

'Don't ask.'

'Did those t-shirts have my name on them?'

'Not exactly.'

No, it hadn't been… 'Hashtag McTabitha,' I say thoughtfully. 'Is that a thing now?' Kids these days.

'You would have been better off not knowing!' I've never seen him so embarrassed.

It clicks. 'They're fans of the show!' I've been getting a lot of Looks since the episodes started airing, but didn't pay attention to it. It doesn't take much to get famous (or infamous) around Hobart, and I've been there a few times before.

'They're fans of *us*,' Stewart says grimly. 'You and me. As a, ugh. Celebrity couple, oh god, is this my life?'

'Are we Brangelina? Are we *Stucky*?' I gaze at him in awe. 'Is there fanfic?'

'Don't Google it,' he says too quickly.

I pull out my phone, forgetting what else is on it for a moment. 'I can answer that question right the heck now!'

'Please no,' he begs. 'It was—that vid a couple of weeks back, when I defended your soup and Kari got me to admit we were friends. There were comments on the YouTube page.'

'Never read the comments, Stewart.'

'That's how I went nearly two weeks without knowing there are people shipping us, merch and all.'

'I can't believe Ceege didn't clue me into this,' I muse. 'He's let his gossip standards drop since he got a real person job.'

'Can we stop talking about this now?' Stewart is roughly the colour of zwetschgenkuchen.

But this is great. I mean, it's embarrassing and squicky, and I can't help wondering if Bishop knows about it (not that anything would have made things worse by the time we reached the point of no return) but it's at least a silly distraction from the unpleasant feeling that has been living in my stomach since I read those horrible texts on my phone.

I KNOW WHAT YOU'RE UP TO WITH CAMERON CREWE

CALL IT OFF NOW, OR YOU'LL BE IN A WORLD OF PAIN

AND YOU WON'T BE THE LAST

Yeah, I'm going to have to do something about that. But not today. Today, I have a basket of treats, a Stewart to tease, and I don't have to walk home alone shortly after being texted a bunch of violent anonymous threats.

Things could be worse.

'So,' says Stewart after a moment. 'What don't I know?'

I unlock my phone and pass it over to him, so he can see the recent messages. 'I've forgotten what you know and what you don't,' I confess.

Stewart reads quietly. When he emerges from my phone he looks serious and worried, but not grumpy or judgy. I'll take it. 'Start at the beginning,' he says. 'If you're still talking when we reach your place, ye owe me coffee and cake.'

I smile at him, feeling better already. 'We literally just had coffee and cake.'

'More coffee, more cake.' He hooks his arm in mine,

KEEP CALM AND *Kill* THE *Chef*

like we are Hansel and Gretel escaping the Gingerbread House. 'Talk it through, from the top. Go.'

I take a deep breath, and tell him the story so far.

KARI NAGARRA: Why comfort food as this week's theme? Don't people associate the Teasperience menu with innovation and drama rather than comfort?

CHEF CREWE: Any chef who only considers the look and taste of the food is an idiot. Most chefs are idiots. Actually, most people are idiots, which is why they go to the same [bleeped out] place every day and order the same [bleeped out] meal. Customers are sheep, and sheep don't want to try something new when they've already got their arsegroove dug into a couch that's halfway decent.

KARI NAGARRA: So what are you saying about the restaurant industry?

CHEF CREWE: Any wanker can create an artistic experience and sell it as food. Price it at four times what it's worth, and the sheep come running to buy it, Instagram it, tell their friends about it—doesn't even matter how it [bleeped out] tastes. You can make a name on that, found a reputation on it. But making food that people actually want to eat all the time, every day, the food they'll crawl over broken glass for? The food that reminds them of their [bleeped out] granny, or their childhood, or that one time they scraped up the dough to go to Paris? That's the real shit, right there.

KARI NAGARRA: That's ... almost poetic of you, Chef.

CHEF CREWE: And that's when you can really start screwing the money out of them.

152

= **13** =

Xanthippe Gives Good Intervention
(after the murder)

Tabitha was indulging in the pie factory method of concealing stress. When I let myself into the café, I was almost knocked out the door again by the overwhelming scent of sweet apples, cinnamon, and blind-baked crusts.

The stovetop was covered in bubbling pots of berries and rhubarb and enough apples to relaunch the Tasmanian orchard industry. There was so much hot sugar in the air my eyelashes were sticky.

And the pastry, oh the pastry. Warm brown crusts cooling on the counter, new crusts baking in the oven, and she was still rolling pastry like a champ: elbows smeared with butter, her hair pinned up in a random assortment of ladybird-themed grips, slides and the occasional paperclip, to keep strands of hair from getting in the way.

I knew without even looking that the fridge was chockas with five different flavours of chilled custard.

'The apocalypse called and you volunteered to bring pie,'

I announced from the doorway.

'I'd say screw you, but you're not wrong, and also I'm not sure how to stop myself right now,' said Tabitha Darling, café owner and pie goddess from outer space. 'Are you here to bring me more ceramic baking beads, because I sent a mental cry for help into the universe fifteen minutes ago.'

'Tabitha,' I said in a heavy voice. 'This is a cry for help.'

'Sure, but that's not solving the baking beads crisis.'

I found a nearby stool and sat on it. Sitting down in this kitchen was normally a crime akin to supermarket-bought sponge cake, but I was a tourist now, not a worker bee, and I do what I want. 'If I stay too long, will I need to eat my way out of here?'

'Could be worse. After Leo and I nearly broke up the first time, I made nothing but borscht for three days. Ceege is still peeing purple.' Tabitha gave me a wary look. 'If you're here to stop me making pies, I will cry at you until you go away.'

'As if I'd stand in the way of your craft.' I was with Ceege on this one—eating Tabitha's pain is a terrible duty but also delicious. There are no ethics when pie is in the oven. 'I have to ask you something deeply sensitive. I could have Googled it, but I think your personal response will be more significant.'

'Shoot,' said Tabitha, picking up a—I'm not even kidding about this—rolling pin with a houndstooth pattern engraved into the wood.

'McTabitha,' I said.

She stilled for a moment, and then kept rolling. 'I don't know what you're talking about.'

'Of course you know. It involves people and Hobart and social media hashtags and *you and Stewart*. Enlighten me, or I'm going to start guessing, and you won't like any of my guesses.'

'It's embarrassing,' she admitted.

I grinned at her, completely unashamed. 'I'd be disappointed if it wasn't.'

'Stewart and I have a fandom, shut up, because of this one time he said something nice about me on camera, shut up, and the internet is insane because it's full of people who have too much time on their hands, and seriously, Zee, if you don't stop laughing, I'm going to hit you with my rolling pin.'

When I recovered enough to speak, the first thing I asked was, 'Is there fanfic?'

'I choose not to answer that question on the grounds that it might incriminate the universe,' Tabitha wailed. 'You would not think this was funny if it happened to you.'

I wiped my eyes. 'Tish, the best thing about this situation is that it would never happen to me. Your life is a special snowflake.'

She glared at me from under her pastry-flecked eyelashes.

'I thought you'd be pissed off. You know. Because of Leo. Bros before besties, and that sort of thing.'

'Tell me why you broke up,' I said impulsively. We didn't girltalk, Tabitha and I, but maybe it was time we figured out how.

She stared at me, her eyes wide and her hair starting to wisp out from under the Cookie Monster beanie she always wore when she was baking. 'Can't.'

I frowned at her. 'You do want me to keep you out of jail, yes? The easiest way to do that is to figure out who killed Cameron Crewe and fling that person at the police.'

'I'm pretty sure Leo didn't do it,' Tabitha said in an attempt at humour, and turned back to her baking.

Hmm.

I knew better than to push, right now, when she was obviously on the edge of exhaustion and stress. But there was only so long I was going to let her get away from keeping important shit from me.

———

After Tabitha's piemaking frenzy, I led her back to the house rather than trust her to drive herself in a haze of sleeplessness and crusty sugar.

I slept over on the couch despite Jason's vague attempts to be a gentleman about it, which was something of a relief to the pretty boy he brought home with him sometime after midnight.

By seven-thirty the next morning I was up, dressed, and wading my way through the sea of ballgowns on Tabitha Darling's bedroom floor.

I swear, she purchases these vintage frocks mostly for insulation.

For a moment, I wondered how my brother coped with sleeping over regularly in Zsa Zsa Gabor's boudoir, then I decided never to think about that again.

'Not going,' Tabitha muttered into her pillow. She hurled a plush panda half-heartedly in my direction, and it disappeared with a soft 'whump' into a heap of tangled fancy dress costumes.

'I'll drag you if I have to.'

'You are the meanest girl I know.'

'I worked hard for that title.'

She lifted her head slightly, all honey-coloured fuzz and pillow-creased skin, and peered at me. 'Are you in disguise?'

My usual work wardrobe as a private detective is similar to what I wore as a barista, a PR expert, and all my other jobs before that—black, form-fitting, basic garments teamed with 'fuck off' sunglasses and flat-soled shoes. Also, the occasional leather jacket which hadn't been stolen by people currently in this room.

Still, I've learned there are times when playing pretend pays off nicely. Today I was pretending that I was a business casual person, all soft white blouse with a job-interview grey jacket, low heels and lip gloss.

It was a work in progress.

'If your mother could see you now,' Tabitha said in wonder, so amazed at the sight of me looking respectable that she forgot she didn't want to wake up.

'Leave my mother out of this,' I said sharply. 'Up, dressed. Wouldn't hurt you to throw on a little normal person cosplay either.'

'I don't want to commit fraud and add to my possible jail time,' Tabitha muttered. 'Go and kitchen. I'll be down in a minute. See?' She stuck a bare leg out from under her doona. 'I'm up.'

Downstairs, I found Stewart and Ceege pouring coffee. Stewart had scrubbed up more than usual, wearing a t-shirt with no holes in it, and his least artistic jeans. Ceege was dressed for work, in a shirt and tie. Talk about real person cosplay—it was odd to see him behaving like a grown up. I was surprised Tabitha still allowed him in the house.

'You're coming?' I asked Stewart.

'Of course,' he replied, as if it was obvious.

'Are you press gallery?' I had not missed the large camera slung around his neck.

Stewart gave me a dry look. 'No more blog, remember? This is for my private collection.' To prove it, he took a snap of me. I visualised his violent death, and let it show all over my face.

He took a step back, so I hadn't lost my touch.

'We're all coming,' said Jason, coming through from the living room in a too-large for him suit, with Tabitha who had decided to dress like Grace Kelly in 50s pastels, with a giant handbag and retro sunglasses to hide behind.

'It's not a trial or anything,' she huffed. 'It's a press conference. I don't even have to be there. I don't require moral support.'

'You always need moral support and also, shut up,' said Jason. 'Maybe I'm not even coming along for you. Maybe I'm interning with Xanthippe as a pee-rivate dee-tective.'

Tabitha's head whipped around, catching me in mid-gesture as I mimed to him to cut that shit right out. 'Oh really?' she asked, growling her rrrrs.

'I didn't steal him,' I said quickly. 'It's not my fault. If you don't overwork your sidekicks, they're going to start looking for new people to treat them terribly and take them for granted while paying them nothing.'

'Should I be insulted?' Jason wondered aloud.

'I'm wondering if *I* should be insulted,' Stewart considered.

'I need to know what they're saying about Crewe and the show and me,' said Tabitha, talking over all of us. 'You can all stay here.'

'Nope,' we said in unison.

Ceege shrugged. 'I'm going to work, babes. But call me if you need me.'

'I won't need anyone!' Tabitha insisted. 'I hardly even got arrested. I'm *fine*.'

———————

'Tabitha!' called a voice as we approached the town hall. Tabitha jumped like the Feds were after her, but it was Kari Nagarra, bright eyed and excited, pushing through the crowd.

'There you are,' she said breathlessly. 'I lost Tom, he's doing crowd shots. Can you believe all this?'

'Well, murder is a great way to grab public attention,' I said sarcastically.

'I need to talk to you after,' Kari said to Tabitha, ignoring me. 'To all of the contestants, about the future of *Café Wars*.'

Tabitha almost dropped her over-sized handbag. 'You're continuing the show?'

'How can we not? Our hits have tripled since the news leaked about Cameron's death.'

Hmm I wonder how it 'leaked'.

'Isn't that kind of tacky?' Tabitha asked.

'Cameron was a tacky bloke,' said Kari. 'Look, I'm not going to pretend to be cut up about what happened to him. It was a shock and all, but he was a horrendous person.

Meanwhile, I have dynamite footage of all the things he said that were too outrageous to edit in at the time—and we have a contract to put out regular episodes for another two weeks. We can create something good out of this.'

They looked at each other, like there was a conversation going on that had nothing to do with the words Kari had said aloud.

I wondered for a moment if Kari had just leaped on top of Tabitha's suspect list like she had on mine. Tabitha batted her eyelashes at Kari and turned on her bright and breezy armour like her life depended on it. 'Okay, let's do this! I'll talk to you after, for sure.'

As soon as Kari turned away, Tabitha glanced at me and mimed pulling a fedora down low on her face, with a suspicious frown. That's my girl.

Over the last twelve hours, the online alerts I set up to track the phrase 'Cameron Crewe murder' went wild.

It wasn't the first time Cameron Crewe had been announced as 'dead', though the last time was a false rumour leaked to coincide with a legal case, distracting his followers just long enough to get him a wave of media sympathy.

This week's rumours were enough to put a bunch of mainland reporters on planes and get them here, when normally they wouldn't spit on Hobart if it was on fire.

I couldn't help wondering about the delay. Did the police deliberately set it up so the media had twenty-four hours to construct their version of the story, before facts got in the way? Why would they even care?

'Why doesn't it start,' Tabitha moaned beside me. Stewart, on her other side, patted her arm. He hadn't made a move to do anything with that camera of his, which was suspicious, even if he wasn't working as a photo journalist any more. How could he resist getting these shots—the police milling about near the podium, the crowd gathering?

I saw familiar faces among the police and the journalists as well as the observers. There were Daisy and Dot in discreet lavender-and cream ensembles, tasteful as ever. There was Maaka with his #Sconebros entourage.

It was so loud in here I could hardly hear myself think. A uniformed officer walked past us, heading for the stage, and Tabitha pounced. 'Heather!'

The senior constable—I knew her too, she worked with my brother— turned and looked at Tabitha, her face deliberately blank. 'I can't talk to you right now.'

'Yes, that's what you said when I was arrested,' Tabitha said, sounding betrayed. 'Can you at least tell me who's in charge of the investigation?'

Tabitha knew the local police even better than I did, thanks to the jobs of both her parents growing up, and more recently her relationship with my brother. She knew most of them by name.

When Heather reluctantly said 'Fitzgerald,' Tabitha was shocked.

'I'm still a suspect, then,' she said quietly.

Heather said nothing more, turned and headed for the podium.

'What makes you say that?' I asked in a low voice.

'Fitzgerald is new, he's maybe the highest ranked officer in the south of the state who doesn't know me,' Tabitha hissed. 'Also, he took lead on questioning me, the night of the murder. He's the reason I was there for hours, and he made it pretty bloody clear that he thought I was dodgy.'

'Doesn't mean they're going to charge you with anything,' I whispered back. 'We know there's little evidence to go on. They're just making sure no one can accuse them of bias later on, when they arrest the actual murderer.'

'Sure,' said Tabitha, but she looked frightened.

'Unless there's anything you haven't told me,' I said in an undertone. 'Any important information you've left out?'

Tabitha shook her head quickly and impatiently, her lips pressed shut.

Jason, who had got taller than her somehow, hooked an arm around Tabitha's neck, and she let him lean into her.

That was when I realised Stewart and that camera of his had disappeared.

'What are you two up to?' I asked Tabitha. Stewart wouldn't leave her side at a time like this unless she told him to.

She shrugged innocently at me.

Worst client ever.

The microphones screeched, and Heather stepped forward. 'Good morning, and thank you for joining us. I am Senior Constable Heather Richards, and I am joined here by Detective Inspector Cliff Fitzgerald, who will be speaking to you about an ongoing case involving a suspicious death on the premises of the Teasperience restaurant in central Hobart.'

An excited buzz rose up in response to the name of the restaurant.

Detective Inspector Fitzgerald looked like the Grim Reaper, all angles and grey hair. Not much witty banter likely to come from this one.

'Good morning all,' he said stiffly. 'The body of a deceased male, early forties, was discovered in a restaurant kitchen in the Hobart mall on the night of the fifteenth of June, by a local chef.'

I glanced across at Tabitha who mouthed the words 'local chef' thoughtfully.

'The deceased was formally identified today by family members as the television personality Cameron Crewe,' Fitzgerald went on, managing to pronounce the words 'television personality' with the same tone he might reserve for 'playground paedophile'. 'Tasmania Police do have reason to suspect foul play, and we ask at this time that anyone who has information as to the movements of Mr Crewe on the fifteenth of June, or information on how he met his death, to please contact the police directly. We would also like to request on behalf of the family that anyone with information about Mr Crewe's death not discuss it with anyone outside the official channels of the police.'

He had to mean the flock of journalists when he said that, but I could have sworn that he looked directly at me as the words came out of his mouth. Well, that wasn't going to make things any easier for me to clear Tabitha's name.

I noted down the information that he was making public— no mention of the murder weapon, or the toffee knife, and nothing that identified Tabitha directly as the person who had found the body or the first suspect they had interrogated.

Questions flew back and forth—how did Chef Crewe die, who found the body, do they have any suspects, are they close to an arrest—but Fitzgerald refused to divulge any more information. Anyone would think the man disapproved of press conferences.

'We are releasing no further details at this time,' he said gruffly, stemming the questions. 'However, Mr Crewe's wife would like to make a public appeal.' He sat down quickly, in a cloud of shrill questions and shouting.

I glanced at Tabitha. 'Did we know Crewe was married?'

She shook her head quickly. 'Look at the journos, they're wetting themselves. *No one knew.*' A celebrity gossip exclusive, then. Dynamite material for the evening news. People might even start reading newspapers again, with a reveal like this. Trust Cameron bloody Crewe to cause a media frenzy after his death.

$=$ **14** $=$

Xanthippe Does Not Mime
(after the murder)

A woman stepped up behind Inspector Fitzgerald and took the microphone from him. She was beautiful—dark curly hair, olive skin, a bosom that wouldn't quit, and a designer black dress that hugged her perfectly shaped baby bump.

'Holy fuck,' hissed Tabitha beside me.

Crewe's supposed wife looked familiar, but only in that way that all famous, outrageously beautiful women look familiar. Was she a soap star? A newsreader? I must have seen her on TV, or on the covers of supermarket magazines. The journos were all shouting questions now, howling over each other, but the exquisite woman merely stood there and let their demands wash over her, and her designer sadness.

'Good morning,' she said finally, with the microphone skills of a TV veteran. She glanced at each of the cameras in turn with an eyelash fluttering expression of poised grief.

'I'm here today to beg the public to come forward with any information they have about the tragic death of my husband, Cameron Crewe.'

'It's Petula Parrish,' Tabitha moaned.

'I know, right?' Jason breathed.

From the collective orgasm being experienced by the press corps as they absorbed the late Cameron Crewe had been married to the very beautiful, very pregnant Petula Parrish, I was the only person in the universe who had no idea who this person was.

I frowned. 'What am I missing?'

Jason and Tabitha both looked at me like I was from another planet.

'Do you honestly not know?' he demanded.

'Would I have this blank expression on my face if I knew?'

'She's the Saucy Chef,' said Tabitha with a soppy look on her face.

'She has to be one of the most famous TV chefs of all time, do you live under a rock?' Jason demanded.

I glared at them both. 'I live in the real world where TV chefs aren't that important.'

'That's not the real world,' said Jason in outrage.

'They're married,' Tabitha breathed. 'This is massive. I thought they were rivals.'

'This story just became the biggest food celebrity news of the year.' I had never seen Jason this excited about anything.

'Bigger than Cameron Crewe's murder?' I said skeptically.

'MUCH bigger,' Jason and Tabitha said in unison.

Petula was talking again, and so I hushed them both—they could fansquee at me later, when there wasn't evidence to be gathered.

'Custody battle?' Tabitha reminded me with a quick whisper in my ear before falling silent.

Given that there weren't any other rumours about Cameron Crewe's children, we had to assume he and Petula were estranged or on the verge of splitting up. You wouldn't know it from today's stage performance.

Assuming he had been telling the truth when he mentioned a custody battle to Daisy and Dot, instead of just bullshitting to make them throw a little sympathy his way.

'My family has suffered a great loss,' said Petula. 'I ask that you respect my children and myself during this time of mourning.' She waved forward two slender, bored-looking teenagers, a boy and a girl with identical pixie cuts. 'Otto and Cherish have lost their beloved stepfather, while I have lost the father of my unborn child.'

Jason swung around Tabitha, pushing her out of the way so that he could tug on my arm. 'That kid! Otto!'

I pushed him off me. 'What about him?'

'I've seen him before. Week Two, Soup Kitchen.'

'He was here in Hobart?' I had assumed Petula and the children flew in today or last night, which was why the police had put off the press conference to this morning.

'He was working at Teasperience. He's the first Lief!'

Well now. That was a whole bunch of suspicious circumstances, right there.

'Do you think I should wait until I'm definitely cleared of murder before I ask Petula for her autograph?' asked Tabitha.

———————

Once the press conference was over, we headed for the door. Stewart met us outside, his enormous camera still slung around his neck and an expression of wide-eyed innocence all over his face.

'Where have you been, young man?' said Tabitha sternly, which clued me in that she knew exactly what he had been up to. Whenever there is scheming and shenanigans, those two are slap bang in the middle of it, holding hands and acting out vintage detective novels with innocent expressions.

'Collecting head shots,' said Stewart. 'Facial responses to big news are so interesting, aye?'

'Stop being mysterious,' I said irritably. 'It doesn't suit you. Back to yours for a debrief, Tabitha?'

'The house, not the café,' she agreed. 'I have dough rising.'

'When do you not have dough rising?'

We went back to the house. Tabitha knocked the air out

of her bread dough, and Stewart pinched Ceege's computer in order to show us his shots from today's press conference.

While they occupied themselves, I used my phone to Google Petula Parrish, the Saucy Chef. Her show, *Bring the Sauce*, was on its third season on SBS, so I guess I was officially behind the times. I did vaguely recall my mother and Nonna watching the show, though I'd never paid much attention.

The things that woman could do with hollandaise had to be classified as pornography. In a five minute clip of her show I watched her lick, smooth, slink and squirt her way across a kitchen like food prep was her own personal phone sex channel.

'What do you think?' Tabitha called from the kitchen, where she was still working away.

'No wonder she's pregnant. This whole show is some kind of sacrifice to the fertility gods.'

'Check out *No Choux, No Shirt*,' said Jason from where he was leaning over Stewart's shoulder. 'That's the series where she cooks something pastry-related for a hot male celebrity each week, and he has to eat it shirtless.'

'And now I see why she's your favourite,' I said dryly. Then I did a search for *No Choux, No Shirt*, because why not?

'So, people's faces,' said Stewart, beckoning me over to the computer. 'Windows to the souls and all that.'

'If you say so.'

'Ever spent time on a stage?'

'Can't say I have.' Backstage, yes.

'People never guard their expressions in an audience,' Stewart went on. 'They're watching, so it never occurs to them they still can be seen.'

That I knew. 'What do you have for me?'

'This is our own Kari Nagarra at the moment when everyone else was losing their shit about the Petula Parrish secret wife reveal,' he said, calling up a still image. Kari's expression was perfectly calm, with Tom beside her, his face mostly hidden by his own camera.

'Note lack o' surprise,' Stewart said.

'Duly noted.'

Tabitha put her head in from the kitchen, drying her wet hands on a tea towel. 'That's not all *that* suspicious. Kari was Crewe's producer, of course she knew shit that the tabloids didn't.'

'There's nothing suspicious about any single thing that's happened lately, unless ye count the dead body,' said Stewart. 'No' until ye start adding them up.' He pulled up images of Crewe's three kitchen assistants: Earl, Grey and Lief, standing separately in the crowd behind the most ardent journalists. All three of them were almost unrecognisable without their uniforms, but each wore a touch of grey or green about their clothing. Clones indeed.

'That was when the murder weapon was described,' he added.

'Why were you focusing on them at that particular moment?' I asked.

Stewart gave me a skeptical look. 'Have ye not watched all the vids yet?'

'I've been busy,' I said defensively. 'And also, food porn is not my drug of choice.'

'The knife skills that Chef Crewe demands in his kitchen are quite specific. I was hoping the press conference would address whether he was stabbed or—'

'Or what?' I said blankly. 'How many different ways are there to kill a person with a knife?'

'Projectile,' said Tabitha. She exchanged a look with Stewart, one of those 'I am looking directly into your brain' looks that was their personal brand. It's one of their more irritating features. 'Chef Crewe's kitchen staff members are trained in knife throwing tricks as well as chopping carrots.'

'He's still doing that?' I knew this about Cameron, of course I did. The first time I met him, I was hired as part of the security team at a demonstration Expo where he had his assistants juggling fruit and tossing knives around like the world's deadliest cocktail waiters.

'Oh aye,' said Stewart. 'That's why he likes a site where the customers can see into the kitchen.'

'Nothing like trying to caramelise onions with knives flying through the air,' said Jason sourly. 'Doesn't work so well in this store as in his Sydney one—there, he has a paper blind up with back-lighting so the customers can see the silhouettes of the kitchen staff chucking knives around from the best tables. Here he just had his boys come out to the tea bar and do the occasional knife trick. But Stew's right. They've all got the training.'

'And if Chef Crewe received tha' knife to his chest from a distance, it puts shade away from Tabitha,' Stewart finished. 'But we don't know.'

I nodded grimly. 'We need to find out.' The police always kept key details out of press announcements, to prevent false confessions. Which, fair enough, really. But it made my job harder. 'Could be nothing.'

'Couldnae hurt,' said Stewart. 'Unless another suspect has circus skills they've been keeping quiet?'

'That depends,' said Tabitha. She sank down on to the couch near him, and put her feet up on the coffee table with a sigh that suggested maybe, just maybe, she was capable of relaxing for a minute or two. 'Does whisking count?'

A phone rang from the kitchen.

'Ugh, that's mine,' said Tabitha, starting to lever herself up again. 'Hope I didn't drop it in the dough again.'

'I'll get it,' I said, since I was on my feet already, and she looked done in. I snagged her phone from the kitchen counter, and walked it back into the living room. 'It's Leo.'

'Ugh,' said Tabitha, more fervently than before. Don't answer it.'

'Too late.' I pressed the button. 'Hello, this isn't Tabitha.'

A huff of a sigh on the other end, matching Tabitha's 'ugh' for fed-upness. 'Can you put her on, Xanthippe?'

I looked over at Tabitha whose eyes were wide and frantic. She mimed something and it took me almost no time at all to realise that she was acting out the phrase 'plausible deniability'.

I spend way too much time around these people. I need other friends.

'She can't come to the phone right now, because bread dough.' I hoped that the dough she was kneading in that kitchen was for bread, because Tabitha's bread is amazing. 'Is there any way we can find out if the knife that killed Cameron Crewe was thrown at him from a distance, or used up close?'

Tabitha, Jason and Stewart were all miming something bizarre at me, like they were at a nightclub. I tipped my head on one side at them, which only encouraged them to mime it even harder.

'You're not funny,' my brother grouched.

'That's a lie, all the people in this house think I'm hilarious.'

All three of them stopped miming and looked deeply

disappointed in me.

'Tell Tabitha we need to talk, soon. I'll drop around tonight.'

'I'm pretty sure she's going out, but I'll pass the message on,' I told him, and hung up. 'What the hell was that?'

'Gay bar,' said Tabitha. The boys nodded in agreement.

'And why did you feel the need to mime it at me while I was trying to interrogate Leo?'

They all rolled their eyes at me, simultaneously.

'We need to talk to our morgue source,' said Tabitha.

'Easy enough, as it's glitter and gimlet night at the Grind,' Stewart added.

Now it was my turn to roll my eyes at him. 'You are way too straight to have that information immediately to hand.'

He spread his hands wide, grinning. 'And yet.'

'Right,' said Jason. 'If I have to be seen with you lot in public, I'm calling for reinforcements.'

———————

I refused to let Tabitha dress me. Sure, a little black dress is boring, but it works much better as camouflage than dressing like a disco ball exploded on you, which pretty much covers what Tabitha did to Stewart.

'You don't even question it any more, do you?' I asked, straightening his bright silver tie and flicking a finger at the purple hair chalk he hadn't been wearing an hour ago.

'I never did,' he admitted with a lazy grin.

Ceege, who made it home in time to join the party, looked fabulous in a zebra print frock, but he was already side-eyeing the band and grouching about how he was going to pay for it tomorrow, clubbing on a work night.

Jason dressed up by changing into a different band t-shirt, putting on a little hair product, and adding a couple of piercings, 'because my generation has some fucking subtlety, OMG Tabitha, I can't even look at you right now.'

Tabitha was dressed like the Green Fairy, with tulle skirt, glossy retro pumps, and LED light-up wings. She performed a piece of hairdressing magic to give herself sparkly green glitter roots along her hair parting. (I refused to let Tabitha touch my hair. I regret nothing.)

'I've changed my mind,' Jason had said the minute he set eyes on her. 'I think we should let her go to prison.'

'On a Tuesday night?' I questioned her, and thus her life choices.

'It was the most convenient outfit to pull together at short notice,' Tabitha protested. The worst part was, she was probably not even lying about that. 'Shut up, all of you. We have a mortician to mob.'

———————

'A coffee-themed bar,' Stewart sighed in admiration, as we moved across the dance floor, the entire surface of which was covered in a pattern of glossy coffee bean photography. 'This is why I can never leave this city.'

Quinn saw us coming. A long-time friend and enabler of Tabitha's most indulgent habits, his training and subsequent employment in police pathology had proved useful in the past.

'I knew you were going to do this to me,' he moaned, slumping back on the latte-coloured leather couch in the corner of the bar where he was chatting comfortably with mates before our posse arrived. 'As soon I heard you'd been taken in for questioning, Tabs. I'll get fired. You will totally get me fired.'

His friends peeled away to the dance floor, knowing an uncomfortable conversation when they saw one. Ceege sat on one side of Quinn, and Tabitha on the other. Stewart perched on the couch arm next to Tabitha. Jason and I both took a discreet step back, shielding the three of them from view from the rest of the club. If we also took the opportunity to pretend that we weren't with the Disco Pals, that was up to our individual consciences, and no one should judge us for it.

'We're your friends, and we love you,' said Tabitha warmly. 'We're not going to make you tell us anything you don't want to.'

'No in words, that is.' Stewart looked meaningfully at Tabitha.

Tabitha was so delighted she clapped her hands. 'Charades!'

Quinn looked like he was far too sober for this conversation.

Give me strength. 'I'll buy the first round of gimlets,' I volunteered.

Everything's better with gin and lime juice, right?

WEEK FIVE

Spinning Teacups
vs
Angry Feminist Defence
Force Alpha

[Cut to: Teasperience Hobart]

KARI NAGARRA: Chef Crewe famously says that Teasperience is about more than food and drink. It's a carnival ride—an artwork long before you open your mouth. His kitchen assistants are required to be patisserie chefs, baristas and high class waiters, all rolled into one … but that's not all.

EARL [flatly]: Taristas.

KARI: Sorry, Taristas. That's … a tea barista, yes?

EARL: We also brew coffee, but tea is central to the Teasperience experience, so Chef Crewe requires that we reach a standard of artisan excellence far beyond most service professionals. Apparently there wasn't a word for 'tea barista' before. There is now.

KARI: Can you do the knife thing?

[Earl turns and hurls a knife which bursts through two of the paper lanterns hanging from the ceiling, and hits the teacup target pinned to the back wall of the café]

[Kari fans herself]

KARI: That's pretty hot. Can you all do that?

EARL [as if he has lost the will to live]: It's one of many skills we're required to perfect before we're allowed to work front of house at any Teasperience salon.

KARI: And that explains your names, right?

[Earl looks distinctly uncomfortable.]

EARL: I don't know what you mean.

KARI: Well, Earl and Grey and Lief. You can't tell me those

names are for real. It's part of the Teasperience theme, yes?

EARL: Contractually I am obliged to tell you that those are our actual names.

[Awkward pause]

EARL: Also I can juggle friands.

═ 15 ═

Tabitha and her Plots
(before the murder)

'I'm pretty sure ye didnae have to come in disguise,' says Stewart, tugging me along the pavement.

I'm wearing one of Ceege's faded INXS t-shirts with a black cardigan, plain jeans and very large sunglasses, my hair tucked under a slouch beanie. The Wonder Woman Converse sneakers are brand-new. It's not a disguise, as such, but anyone who knows me wouldn't recognise me.

'It's not like I want people to know I'm consorting with the enemy,' I hiss back.

'It's no' the enemy, Tabitha, it's a coffee shop. And a party. To which you were invited.' Stewart leads the way through The Chocolate Teapot kitchen, to the private backyard with the yummy herb garden.

Their yard has lawn and pretty roses and climbing ivy, not to mention an enormous covered verandah that goes on forever, and actual produce they can use to add that special something to their recipes. The courtyard behind my urban café is mostly gravel. I'm not bitter.

'Lovely to see you,' says Daisy, enveloping us both in a hug. 'Help yourself to drinks.'

Maaka and Bruce from #Sconebros, already ensconced on floral banana lounges at the far end of the verandah, wave their microbrews at us in greeting.

'See, no worries about consorting with the enemy,' Stewart says in a low voice.

'You're kidding yourself,' I reply. 'This is a competition. It doesn't matter how friendly everyone is, there will always be someone who takes the rivalry too far.'

'Aye,' says Stewart, with a skeptical look at my beanie of disguise. 'I wonder who.'

Daisy commandeers Stewart to bring out more snacks, so I sit on the edge of the verandah with Kari and Tom. 'Almost didn't recognise you without a camera,' I tease him.

Tom waggles his hands at me. 'Look, I can hold a cup and a plate at the same time!'

'This was a nice idea,' says Kari, more relaxed than I've ever seen her.

Daisy and Dot, being the nicest people in the known universe, decided we should all hang out and socialise after the Week Five challenge. We've spent far too long immersed in the Teasperience Method, which is all about taking the simple pleasures in life—a cup of tea, cinnamon toast, a slice of shortbread—and overthinking the concept,

KEEP CALM AND *Kill* THE *Chef*

rendering it into a format that entirely misses the point.

I never want to discuss reconstituted tea flakes, buttered steam or crumb infusions ever again.

Well, okay, one or two of the crumb infusions were divine, but I don't want Chef Crewe to have the satisfaction of knowing I recognise his occasional moments of genuine kitchen genius. His head is big enough.

Speaking of which... 'No guest of honour?' I guess.

'I'm sure he'll make an appearance,' Kari says dryly.

It's an amiable group. Lara and Yui are over there, wheedling the sous-clones to teach them how to throw knives.

'I'm not having any of that in my kitchen!' I yell at them, but my baristas have perfected the art of ignoring me.

'I don't know how you do it,' says Tom, his eyes on the cheerful youngsters like he'd rather be filming the action with a lens at his eye. 'Working in a professional kitchen. I did a year of it when I first left school, and it drove me up the wall. Couldn't hack it.'

'Not every assistant chef has Cameron Crewe as a boss,' I say brightly. 'I, for instance, am a delight to work for.'

Jase, in the middle of a friendly argument with Bruce about the flexibility of scones as a throwing weapon, pauses to point and laugh at me. I stick my tongue out at him.

Stewart, walking past with a tray of sandwiches and chocolate snail pastries, gives me a sideways smile. 'Confidence is important in the workplace.'

187

'I feel so attacked right now.'

'I wouldn't do a cooking show again,' Kari confesses. 'This has been more fraught than I was expecting.'

'Eh,' says Tom. 'Most reality TV show crews get shouted at. Goes with the territory. Doesn't matter whether it's a car show or a building show or whatever, you're gonna get something chucked at the camera sooner or later.'

'Not usually a knife,' Kari points out. 'The trolling and the cyberbullying were bad when I was starting out as an online activist, but there were no actual projectiles whizzing past my head.'

'Cooking shows are the best,' Tom says firmly. 'Real ones on network television. The residuals are great, and once there's an overseas deal or two going, you're living the dream. A literal gravy train.' He pauses, and makes a note on his phone. 'Gravy Train. Anyone used that for a cooking show yet?'

I make a face. 'I'm imagining Australian Ninja Warrior, but with gravy.' He's right, actually, that could be commercial dynamite.

Dot emerges from the kitchen in a velvet smoking jacket and trim striped trousers, carrying a tray of delicious savouries. She takes one look at the knife-throwing mob over by her iceberg roses, and marches over to give them what-for.

'There's something to be said for cranky ladies of a

certain age, scolding people who aren't me,' I say happily.

Dot confiscates the throwing knives from Earl and Lara, then pivots on the spot and throws three of them in a perfect triangle formation at the trellis on her side fence.

Kari, Tom and I watch with our mouths open as Dot collects the knives, and makes Earl pack them away in his carry case.

Tom gives Kari an accusing look, and she throws her arms up in the air. 'Yes, you're right, there's bound to be irreplaceable footage at a party like this, how dare I suggest you take a couple of hours separated from your camera so you can relax!'

———————

Winter in Hobart means it gets dark early. By the time Zandra kicks out the few remaining customers from The Chocolate Teapot so she can join the party out back at 5PM, the sun is already fading from the sky. Daisy and Stewart rig up fairy lights around the verandah, and Dot charms the #Sconebros into building a bonfire with her. Someone digs up sparklers, and Zandra rolls out a deep pot of pumpkin soup to keep us warm.

So much for rivalry between the cafés. This lot are goddamned jolly, and I have to admit I'm enjoying their company. When Zandra pulls out a guitar, though, and her aunts kick off the dancing, I feel a wave of melancholy about my lack of ~~boyfriend~~ fiancé.

Café Wars was a great distraction from The Bishop Thing, but it's starting to hit home that we are over, and I didn't fight all that hard to keep him. (I could blame *Café Wars*, but let's face it, this was coming even without that added complication.)

'A gentleman would lend me his jacket,' I note to Stewart as he sits near me, passing over a mug of soup.

'Chivalry is dead,' he says heartlessly. 'That's fourth wave feminism for you.'

'Did fourth wave feminism fetch me this soup?' I blow on it, inhaling the warm scent.

'No, that was first generation Scottishism.'

'Oh.' I smile at him over the mug. 'It's good soup.'

Stewart looks as if he's going to say something. I breathe in pumpkin fumes as I wait in anticipation.

It's the worst possible time for Cameron fucking Crewe to make his entrance.

'Here you all are!' he roars, in good form. Good form, for the record, is way less fun than bad form. Cranky, swearing, aggressive Chef Crewe is hell to manage, but smarmy happy Chef Crewe (who has obviously downed more than a few beers before coming out tonight) is a particular grade of arsehole that I have no patience for at all.

If this evening doesn't end with someone throwing a mug of soup at his head, my name's not Tabitha Darling.

Crewe pours effusive compliments on his hostesses, as a blatant excuse to make a beeline for Zandra (whose impressive resting bitch face instantly takes on whole new levels of 'leave me the hell alone'). Kari catches my eye and withdraws from the verandah, into The Chocolate Teapot kitchen.

So. Subtle.

I set down my mug, avoiding Stewart's curious face, and follow Kari.

'How are things really?' I ask as she leans over the sink, running the tap cold to pour a glass of water.

'I'm at the end of my rope, Tabitha. I know we got into this for—reasons—but what if it's all for nothing?'

'Hey, it's still a solid line on your resume,' I joke.

Kari turns around, leaning against the cupboards. She looks rough. 'I just—having to smile and put up with all his bullshit, *still*. I don't think I can manage another three weeks.'

'Do you want to finish up early?' I ask, genuinely concerned for her. 'I mean—I know we said to give him enough rope to hang himself, but...'

'How much is enough?' she finishes for me. 'Don't mind me. I feel guilty complaining after what happened with—you know. Your bloke.'

Ugh. 'That wasn't because of this,' I insist. Well. It was. 'Well, it was, but—if not this, it would have been

191

something else. Something very similar. I can't not get involved, not with people like Ani in the firing line.' Ani and all the other women, going back years. Even Xanthippe, though I was sure she'd never admit it. Ugh.

'I can stick with it for another three weeks,' Kari decides, resolute. 'We're nearly there.'

'Nearly there,' I echo.

We hear a commotion outside—shouting and rustling and oh, a fight.

'I so should have let Tom bring his camera,' Kari groans. 'He'll never let me hear the end of this.'

We hurry out, to find Cameron Crewe lying dazed on the grass, Zandra looking seriously pissed off, and Jase pulling Stewart back from some kind of skirmish.

Stewart. The least violent person I have ever met in my life.

'I leave you alone for two minutes!' I holler at my boys.

Stewart looks wild-eyed and furious. It's a rare look for him. *Must not swoon.* 'He had it coming,' he growls. 'She told him to keep his hands to himself.'

Zandra has her arms crossed defensively over her punk outfit. She's the most likely victim of Chef Crewe's wandering hands.

'I thought chivalry was dead?' I say.

'Hey, everyone else at this party is armed with knives, I thought me punching him was the diplomatic option,'

Stewart shoots back, flexing his hand.

Stewart punched the celebrity chef. And I missed it.

Cameron groans at my feet.

'I didnae even hit him that hard,' Stewart says, worried now.

'He's drunk,' sighs Kari. 'A lot more drunk than he looked. I've seen him like this before—he may not even remember what happened.'

For a moment, everyone at the party attempts not to meet each other's eyes.

'Right,' says Daisy, taking the lead with a voice of brisk efficiency. 'Well, when Chef Crewe wakes up, I suggest we all make it very clear to him that he slipped on the damp grass and accidentally hit himself in the head with a mug of soup. Any objections?'

She gives Earl, Grey and Lief a particularly hard gaze. All three of them mumble and shake their heads. That makes sense. Even if their loyalties are to their boss (which has to be questionable at the best of times), no one wants to be anywhere near him when (if) he finds out the truth.

'All right then,' Daisy says, her voice melting into sweetness. 'Carry on, dears. Let's not end the party yet.' She discreetly pours some soup over Cameron Crewe's collar, discards her mug nearby, and begins the process of waking him up, carefully and with motherly attention.

'I want to be her when I grow up,' I whisper under my

breath, awed by her poise. 'She is my favourite and my best.'

Stewart gives me a hopeful smile. 'Cuppa?'

'Cuppa,' I agree.

16

Xanthippe Should Never Drink Gimlets (after the murder) (also after a long night at the bar)

I woke up in my old room at Tabitha's house, under an unfamiliar doona, and stared at the ceiling for a few minutes before piecing together the circumstances that led me here.

This. This is why I shouldn't drink gimlets, no matter how stylish and retro they are. Mojitos at least come with vegetation, a sprig of mint to help the body prepare for the morning after. Gimlets are pure pale green doom.

Too late, I realised Tabitha chose last night's outfit to match the drinks theme.

A body shifted next to me, and I flipped back the doona to see the dark curls and glitter-streaked face of TV presenter, Kari Nagarra. Huh. That was unexpected. I vaguely remembered her arriving at the Grind, but I wasn't sure if it was before or after we all decided the fourth gimlet was a bitching idea.

'Ugh, coffee,' she muttered, and dragged the doona back

over her head, protecting us both from an awkward conversation.

Wearing last night's camisole and a pair of clean boxers stolen from Jason's drawers, I wandered out into the rest of the house, stepping over a snoring, still-zebra-frocked Ceege in the corridor on my way.

Tabitha and Stewart were fast asleep on the couch, both fully dressed, in a position that the council for the prosecution could only describe as 'canoodling'. His arm was slung around her, anyway, and her face was squashed into his shoulder.

Quinn was curled up in one of the armchairs, also fast asleep, his fake eyelashes making spider shapes on his cheeks.

I found Jason fresh-faced and clean clothed in the kitchen, cooking what appeared to be an egg white omelette with Italian parsley. 'Morning, sunshine,' he said cheerfully.

'Sorry I stole your bed.'

'S'okay, I wasn't here. Went home with the coat check boy.'

I gave him a meaningful look, because apparently I'm still part of this makeshift family that Tabitha has gathered around her. 'You're being safe, right?'

'Yes, Mum,' he said sarcastically. 'You know my generation are more carefree with our online information than we are with our dicks, right?'

I fumbled at the coffee machine until Jason moved me

gently out of the way and started making me a macchiato. 'That's not reassuring,' I told him darkly. 'Also, I'm only eight years older than you.'

'What's that in dinosaur years?' he teased, but followed up with a cup of coffee, so I forgave him instantly. 'Don't fret, I exchanged Facebook info with him, we made out twice and then we spent like six hours playing Skyrim.'

Kids today. 'Be cyber smart, don't share passwords.'

Jase patted me on the head. 'I just upgraded your status to Grandma. Don't freak out, you're still a cool Grandma.'

'Did we get the info we needed last night?' My brain was such a gimlet-induced wreck of gin and glitter that it wasn't ready to boot up anything work-related. Like, waking up properly.

Jason shrugged at me. So helpful. 'According to Quinn, Chef Crewe was stabbed at close quarters, not from a distance. Which means our suspect list doesn't get narrowed down to his knife-throwing employees, except for the part where...'

'Yeah, yeah, everyone who works for him wanted to kill him. But surely it—'

'It doesn't narrow it down to people big and strong enough to take him in a fight, either. His system had coffee in it, laced with sleeping pills and aspirin. So he was sluggish and likely to bleed out faster. Premeditated. If someone wanted to stab a big, belligerent bloke like Cameron

Crewe, that'd be the way to do it.'

Damn. That didn't let Tabitha off the hook at all.

'So,' I said, trying to bring this part casually into the conversation. 'Do you happen to recall at what point in the evening Kari Nagarra joined the party?'

Jason stared at me. 'Grandma, did you bang a girl in my bed?'

'Definitely not!' I insisted. 'I'm—like ninety-five percent certain that I didn't. I would have remembered that.'

There might have been some kissing. I'd definitely kissed someone last night. The memory would come back eventually.

There was a knock at the kitchen door and I headed for it because anything was better than looking at Jason smirking at me.

'But were you safe with your passwords?' he teased, just as I opened the door and came face to face with the pained expression of my brother, Detective Sergeant Leo Bishop of Tasmania Police.

'Excuse me,' I said politely, turning my back on him. 'I just have to strangle today's youth.'

Still laughing at me, Jason backed up against the doorway and lobbed an orange into the living room. A loud squeak told us that he had made his target. Subtle. That boy is subtle. But yeah, good call.

I tamped down my murderous instincts and contributed

to the 'being a good friend' plot by delaying Leo with a cup of coffee. By the time we made it to the living room, Tabitha and Stewart were awake, perfectly respectable, on either side of the couch, with a mostly-still-asleep Ceege propped between them.

Quinn was now mysteriously absent from the room.

Impressed with everyone's tact and diplomacy, I nipped back into the kitchen to steal Jason's omelette, with only slight resistance on his part.

'Coward,' he accused, with his mouth full.

'You don't want to deal with me when I'm hungover and hungry,' I replied.

He conceded the point.

I could already hear raised voices from the living room. Bloody hell. 'Keep that warm for me,' I told him, and stalked after my short-tempered brother.

———

Tabitha and Leo stood in the centre of the room, bristling like cats at each other, while Stewart tried to pretend he was furniture. Ceege opened his eyes at one point, saw what was going on, and slumped on to Stewart's shoulder, preferring unconsciousness. I couldn't blame him for that.

'I can't believe we're still having this conversation two years later,' Tabitha flung at Leo, her arms crossed defiantly. 'I am an adult, and not a child, and I don't think you can judge me for wanting to investigate a murder in which *I am a suspect*.'

Her speech would have come across as slightly more dignified if she was not still dressed as the Green Fairy. At least her wings had stopped randomly lighting up. That might have taken the wind out of her argument.

Leo leaned back on his heels, glaring down at her. 'Why do you always think the worst of me? I'm not here to lecture you, Tabitha. I'm here to make sure you share all the relevant information with your little—Baker Street Irregulars.'

Tabitha made a face. 'The proper pop culture reference is Scooby Gang.'

'What can I say, I've read a lot of Sherlock Holmes,' he shot back.

Leaning against the door frame, I cleared my throat. 'So, you're not here to stop our private investigation?'

Leo gave me an incredulous look. 'Are you kidding me? Someone is blatantly trying to set Tabitha up, and using police resources to do it. Of course you should be investigating!'

Tabitha's mouth opened and shut like she was a goldfish. Well, a glittery greenfish.

Jason pushed his way into the doorway beside me, and handed me my half of the omelette, on a plate. 'I feel you're going to need to keep your strength up,' he informed me.

I accepted the breakfast offering. 'This is why you're my favourite, kid.'

Stewart finally decided to stop acting like he wasn't in the room, which may or may not have had something to do with the fact that Tabitha was staring at my brother with little hearts in her eyes. 'Coffee,' he announced, levering himself off the couch. 'We all need more coffee for this.'

Well, he wasn't wrong.

———————

Ten minutes later, we all had coffee and there was a second drip filter working on the next round that would be required shortly. Quinn had been reclaimed from where he was trying to hide under Tabitha's collection of 1950s cocktail dresses.

My brother was officially in on the extracurricular mystery-solving shenanigans. Clearly, this was the end times.

'So, you're not here to shut down our investigation,' Tabitha repeated, as if she was waiting for Leo to spring a trap.

Leo sighed. 'No. I'm here to make sure you tell Xanthippe everything you've been up to over the last six weeks. They're looking for a fast arrest on this one, Tabitha, so it's time to stop bullshitting and let people help you.'

Something I've always been good at is reading a room— getting the measure of a situation fast, and reacting to it.

And what I saw right now, surveying this particular room, was awkwardness. Not surprise. No one was looking directly at me—not Stewart, or Ceege or Jase, let alone Leo and Tabitha—but they were all waiting to see how I would react.

Apparently I had just spent the last two days interrogating the wrong people. I should have been paying a lot more attention to Tabitha.

Summoning as much dignity as was possible while wearing Minecraft boxers and a glitter-streaked camisole, I sat down in the nearest armchair. 'All right, then. Let's have it.'

Leo stepped back, leaning against a wall, because god forbid he actually relax for five minutes.

Tabitha radiated guilt, from her glitter roots to her fairy wings. 'So when I told you that I was signing up to *Café Wars*, I may have left a few details out about my motive. And I may also have—failed to elaborate even after Cameron Crewe was found dead.'

I waved a hand impatiently at her. 'If it saves time, we can shelve the part where you explain *why* you didn't tell me everything.' No point in fighting about that now, when I could save it up and have a more convenient blow up later. My curiosity was beating out my anger.

No, that's a lie, I was livid, but I'm nothing if not pragmatic.

'So,' said Tabitha, bobbing up and down on her

stockinged feet as she gathered what she was going to say. 'Let's be methodical.'

'Wouldn't hurt,' I said evenly.

She counted off the facts on her fingers, one after the other. 'One, Kari Nagarra and I knew each other before she approached me for *Café Wars*. Two, we had a shared ulterior motive for doing the show. Three,' and she hesitated on that one. 'We were basically out to destroy Cameron Crewe. Four...'

'No, wait, I think we have enough to be going on with,' I interrupted. 'Tabitha. *What the hell.*'

'Not murder him destroy him,' she insisted.

'Thanks for the clarification,' Leo said sourly.

'Shush,' I told him. 'As the last person in the room to find out about all this, I get to ask the questions and make the snarky commentary. The rest of you may silently witness my rage and provide refreshments.'

When no one complained, I turned back to Tabitha and made a 'go on' gesture. She took a deep breath.

'Kari wants a career as an investigative reporter, not a bullshit feel-good cake presenter. Which, each to their own, personally I've made a good living at feel-good cake, but I could see her point of view. And the first story she wanted to break was Cameron Crewe.'

Everyone in the room winced.

'Murder was not in the plan,' Tabitha said quickly.

'I don't know who killed him, and I don't know why. But I'm not surprised he had enemies. Every one of his Teasperience bars in Melbourne and Sydney was built on the shattered remains of a beloved independent business. If they wouldn't sell to him directly, they found themselves under siege—failed health inspections, leases pulled out from under them, dramatic rental hikes, staff leaving in droves. No one could pin it on Crewe directly, no one could prove it, but everyone knew he was behind it.'

'Kari had a lot to go on, plenty of anecdotal evidence, but nothing solid enough to build a story on,' added Stewart, and of course he was involved with this. It had his paws all over it.

'Plus there was his treatment of women and former employees,' Tabitha added, scooting quickly over the topic of whom she had told, and when. 'His lawyer has covered up so many harassment claims—anyway, Kari had plenty of people willing to go on the record about what a shit he was, including some of his former employees and the businesses he screwed over, but *Café Wars* gave her the opportunity to collect new footage that could do double duty in her planned expose, and to...' she hesitated at that one.

'Oh, say it,' Leo growled. 'Why stop there.'

'She wanted him to implicate himself on camera,' Tabitha sighed. 'One way or another. He destroyed businesses, it was *his turn*. And I was right,' she added furiously.

'The night he was killed, I just found out the arsehole tried to buy our building. Luckily Darrow wouldn't have a bar of it, but I hate to think what Crewe might have done to put the pressure on...'

Tabitha trailed off, as a room full of people who loved her tried not to think too loudly about what an excellent motive that gave her for murder.

'So,' I said, to get this straight. 'You went undercover on a reality TV show to expose a powerful, amoral and possibly dangerous celebrity chef to perform some kind of cake-themed vigilante justice?'

'Cake-themed vigilante justice is the best kind of vigilante justice,' Tabitha said earnestly.

'And you knew about this?' I accused, turning to my brother.

'I found out,' he said flatly. 'Once it was already underway.'

That made no sense. The rest of the gang supporting Tabitha's shenanigans, sure, that was no shock to me. Of course she would have confided in Ceege and Jason—and Stewart's always been in her corner, even when she's furious at him. Hell, if I hadn't been wrapped up in getting my detective agency off the ground, I would have joined in cheerfully enough.

But Leo, how could Leo have even tacitly endorsed ... oh. *Oh.*

'You found out in Week Two,' I realised. Week Two, Soup Kitchen, that was when he came back from that police conference, and within a week he and Tabitha were both iserable and she wasn't wearing the engagement ring any more. 'This is why you split up.'

Ceege, Jason and Stewart all looked like they would rather be anywhere than here, but to hell with them, if I had to witness this, they could suck it up.

'Yes,' said Tabitha, chin high.

'No,' Leo corrected, causing her to whirl around and stare at him. 'I mean—it wasn't just that...'

'Can we please move past this bit,' Tabitha begged.

'Please,' Leo added.

'Fine,' I said, because really, none of my business, except for the part where Tabitha dragged this whole tangled web of insanity directly into the room and placed it at my feet like a dead mouse. 'Moving on, this whole fake reality TV show...'

'It's a real show, it's only my motivations that were fake,' Tabitha protested.

'And is it a wild coincidence that Stewart took a job with The Chocolate Teapot the same week you signed up for the show?' I looked past Tabitha's fairy wings to give Stewart a meaningful look.

'Yes,' Tabitha said quickly. 'Of course it was a coincidence, I wouldn't ask him to...'

'No,' Stewart said quietly. 'Not a coincidence. Tabitha didnae bring me in on the plan until Week Four. But I heard about it from Jase back when it all started, when Kari was still searching for cafés to sign up. I wanted to help, so I took Daisy and Dot up on their job offer, and talked them into registering.'

Tabitha was going to get whiplash if she kept spinning around to stare at people when they said surprising things. Her face was unreadable as she stared at Stewart. 'I was so mean to you for taking that job.'

Stewart shrugged and gave her half a smile. 'Were ye? I hardly noticed.'

═ **17** ═

Xanthippe is Restrained and Mysterious
(after the murder)

There were so many heated meaningful looks zig-zagging between the group, it was astounding the couch didn't combust.

An alarm went off on Jason's phone, and we all jolted. He checked it. 'Xanthippe? We have an appointment in thirty.'

Leo twitched at that. 'Relevant to the case?'

'We'll let you know,' I said, which showed how much I have matured because I didn't go with the more obvious response of 'bite me'. Leo gave me a sarcastic look that showed he didn't believe in the new diplomatic Xanthippe one bit. 'Do I have time to swing by the office and get showered and changed first?'

Jason eyed my makeshift pajamas, and glitter-streaked hair. 'I'm going to say yes, because you look terrible. Move fast, though.'

'Got it.' I went back to his room to reclaim my dress,

since I wouldn't fit into a borrowed pair of his skinny jeans, and I've learned the hard way that borrowing clothes from Tabitha is a rabbit hole no one needs to fall down.

Kari Nagarra lifted her head out of the doona again as I wriggled the little black dress back over my head. 'Is there coffee yet?'

I had totally forgotten she was there. 'So much coffee you wouldn't believe.' I found my shoes under the bed. 'There was, uh, kissing last night, yes?' Smooth, Xanthippe.

Kari nodded thoughtfully. 'I definitely kissed someone.'

Ah, a woman after my own heart. 'I hate to smooch and ditch, but I'm late for a thing. Tabitha will caffeinate you, and/or feed you, depending on what damage the gimlets did last night.' Under other circumstances I might feel guilty about leaving her with Tabitha, but apparently they were much closer friends than I'd ever realised, so…

Kari gave a wide, warm smile that lit up her whole face. 'I wasn't drinking the gimlets last night.'

Huh. 'Do you need a lift anywhere?'

She shrugged, and half the doona fell off her. 'I'll call Tom to pick me up. We have a meeting with Petula about the future of the show.'

I blinked at that. 'The wife?'

'Oh, yeah.' Her smile wasn't going away any time soon, which was fine with me, because it was one hell of a smile. 'We had to sign a confidentiality agreement about anything to do with Crewe's personal life—i.e. his secret marriage, famous wife, sulky stepkids, and the impending divorce. It's void now because of his death, of course.'

Why do chatty and pleasantly bed-dishevelled sources only start revealing interesting info once I have a time constraint? 'I would really like to hang out later. Would you—'

'Sounds good. I put my number in your phone.'

I fled before my mouth started flirting. Then I darted back, picked up my phone from the bedside table with a smile, and headed off again.

'This had better be a very useful meeting,' I informed Jason as we made for my Spider.

'Wow, you look even more trashed than when you first woke up,' he said helpfully.

Goddamn it.

'I take it we're interviewing suspects?' I asked as I peeled the Spider out of its parking spot and headed for the city centre.

'The sous-clones,' Jason confirmed. 'Earl, Grey and Lief, not their real names. They said they'd come to the office at ten.'

It was nearly that now. Hopefully I'd have a few minutes for a quick change. 'Has Ceege called in sick for work yet? I don't think his eyes were even open when we left.'

'Huh,' said Jason, and sent a text to Tabitha. 'Sorted.'

'I haven't had many clients actually come to the office,'

I told him as I parked the Spider on the only available meter, and hurried for the stairwell behind the café. 'Not a single Bogart and Bacall meet-cute since I got started. Maybe I'll ask Darrow to arrange that for my next birthday.'

'Should I have told the sous-clones to dress up like the 1940s came knocking?'

'I'd hate anyone to strain themselves.'

I took the stairs faster than Jason, who didn't need to make an effort beyond a saunter. In the office, I headed for my back room (not a bedroom yet, it didn't count as a bedroom until I unpacked) and considered the possibility of a shower, longingly. Later.

It was unlikely I'd be able to pull off 'professional and intimidating' without devoting half an hour to hair, make-up and wardrobe, so I went for 'restrained and mysterious' instead: white shirt, black trousers, my hair scraped back and my sleeves rolled up enough that you could see my tattoo, even if you couldn't read what it said.

My ugg boots were calling to me, because whatever the hell had happened after the third gimlet, dancing had definitely been involved. I went for boots and hoped for the best.

When I emerged from my costume change, I found Jason sitting at my desk, wearing my fedora, and three weirdly similar young men sitting opposite him.

I knew for a fact I did not have that many chairs. Where

had Jason stolen them from, and could I get away with keeping them?

'Gentlemen,' I drawled politely. I had not missed that there was no chair for me, but that was fine. I perched on the desk, deliberately blocking Jason's view of our witnesses. 'Thank you for coming.'

I had followed enough of the vids by now that I could tell the difference between them while they were together, though I was likely to embarrass myself if I happened across one on his own. They really did look distressingly similar.

'We were already interviewed by the police,' said Earl, crossing his arms aggressively. 'Dunno what else there is to say, or why we should be saying it to you.'

'The police are looking for a fast arrest, and that means they'll home in on the easiest suspects they can find,' I said, breezily casting aspersions on the entire profession. 'A little bird told me that anyone with knife throwing skills is going to be at the top of their list. Are you sure you don't want to help me with my investigation?'

All three of them exchanged nervous glances.

'So that is how he was killed?' whispered Lief. 'No one would tell us. I mean, we knew about the toffee knife...'

Grey snorted. 'Everyone knows about the toffee knife.'

That was interesting. Who was everybody, and why was that particular detail (so pointedly left out of the press conference) doing the rounds?

'Did Inspector Fitzgerald tell you about the toffee knife when he was questioning you?' I asked.

'He asked enough,' said Grey. 'Was obvious it was important—and there was only one toffee knife in those displays, the one that Chef Darling made.'

'You can't actually stab someone with toffee,' added Lief. 'Especially not throwing it. I don't reckon they've found the real murder weapon yet.'

That made sense. If they had it, they'd have an excuse to haul Tabitha back. That reminded me, I had to find her an actual lawyer for next time—and there would be a next time, if we didn't sew this up fast.

'They're looking for a knife,' grunted Grey. 'Went over the kitchen with everything they had—took every knife out of the place, including ours.' He sounded outraged, like this was unreasonable evidence gathering on the part of the police forensics team. 'How are we supposed to apply for new jobs without our own knives?'

'Might not have to now,' Lief said hopefully. 'Not with the new—' He broke off suddenly, looking unhappy.

'You idiots talk too much,' Earl growled. 'She's not the police. What the fuck do you think she's going to do to you if you don't co-operate?'

WEEK SIX

Coffee to Die For

═ **18** ═

Tabitha Thinks Murderous Thoughts
[hours before the murder]

It's possible I've gone overboard. Give a woman like me a theme like 'coffee to die for' and what do you think is going to happen?

The Teasperience pop up bar is closed for the day so we can arrange our displays, and film the bits for this week's episode.

Kari and Tom set up partitions around the bar, so we can keep our work secret until the reveal. My table is already sticky with fake syrup blood, running in scarlet strings between the props—a black toffee apple axe, a golden toffee shard dagger, and a scattering of homemade licorice bullets dipped in silver fondant instead of chocolate.

I'm about to start arranging the coffee-themed pastries in my own hot murderous mess when my phone rings. I peel off the toffee-flecked gloves and step outside for a few minutes, breathing in the chill winter air instead of the stifling tea bar. 'Hello?'

'Darling,' says the warm, chocolate voice of my landlord, former business partner and longtime patisserie patron, Darrow.

'Where have you been?' I ask. 'Why make a grand gesture like presenting Xanthippe with a retro detective office, if you're not going to swing by to find out how grateful she is?' I choose not to investigate how that relationship works.

'Is she grateful?' he asks, sounding more amused than hopeful.

'Not especially, but she's enjoying herself.' Café La Femme runs so much more smoothly since Zee took herself up to the second floor, but I do miss having her around.

'Listen, Darling, I can't talk long, I'm on a cruise ship and the reception is terrible...'

'You're on a what now?'

'I want to check in with you. What's the name of that chef you're running around making YouTube vids with?'

'Cameron Crewe.'

'Thought so. Might interest you to know that he's looking to settle that pop up of his more permanently in Hobart.'

'Okay?' That's vaguely interesting, I suppose, but not exactly...

'He put in an offer on my building.'

I blink. 'Which building?' Darrow owns a lot of real estate around Hobart, but it's mostly residential. Still, he couldn't mean...

'Your building, Darling. Café La Femme's building.'

'The first floor office isn't big enough for a Teasperience bar...'

'I'm sure it's big enough for his boot cupboard or chef hats or whatever storage he needs. Don't be dense, Darling. He's after the whole building. He wants to replace Café La Femme with Teasperience.'

Darrow is on a cruise somewhere, so if he betrays us, I won't be able to kill him. Is that a deliberate move on his part? 'Are you going to sell?' I demand.

A long pause, and then a low chuckle. 'Are you kidding? I *just* got Xanthippe to forgive me for past crimes. I'm not going to sell off a building that has her birthday present as its top floor. Thought you should know this bloke tried it on, though.'

Oh. That's a relief. Creepy stalkerish gift-giving habits for the win. 'Thanks for the head's up.'

'Start making that tiramisu ice cream again and I'll consider us even.'

'Not in the middle of winter, Darrow.'

'You're a hard woman.' He rings off, leaving me fuming. Failed attempt or not, Crewe is trying to do exactly what he's done to so many others. Only now he's trying to do it to me.

———

I storm into the Teasperience bar, heading for the kitchen.

Stewart, assisting Dot as she constructs her own coffee pastry triumph, sees the murderous light in my eyes and leaps forward to intercept me. One of these days, that instinct of his is going to get him into trouble.

'Everything all right here, Tabitha?'

'I'm going to stab him in the face,' I rage.

Stewart wraps an arm around my waist. 'How about we *not* get into a slapfight with an all-powerful celebrity chef?'

Out of the corner of my eye, I can see Tom the camera-man reacting with interest, tilting his camera in my direction. I meet Stewart's gaze with my anger blazing out of my eyes. 'Out. Of. My Way.'

To his credit, he lets me go the second I ask. I barge into the kitchen with Tom powering after me like I'm fulfilling all his gonzo documentary wet dreams.

'Chef Tabitha, what are you doing back here?' Cameron says smoothly, tossing his bowl of proving dough to Earl, his nearest assistant, who has to drop a bag of rice to catch it. 'I'll fine you two cookies if you insist on breaking the rules of the challenge...'

I don't just see red, I see 220 degrees Celsius, the perfect baking temperature for puff pastry. 'I know what you're trying to do!' I shriek at him. 'Trying to buy my building? Is that the true *Café Wars* grand prize? You figure out which of us has the best business and you steal it? I might have known this was your MO, you've never had an original cooking thought in your life!'

Cameron Crewe turns an interesting shade of burnt orange. 'Leave my kitchen, little girl,' he says in a fierce, angry hiss. 'Leave my kitchen. Leave this entire space for one hour, and I will forget what you just said to me, because I am a fucking professional. But if you speak one word of disrespect to me again, I will not only kick you out of my show, I will make sure you never sell so much as a muffin top in this city ever again!'

I open my mouth to retaliate, because what the hell power does he think he has in Hobart? This is my town. My customers love me. He's some big city blow-in who thinks he is the Big Banana.

Before I can say any of that, Stewart is there again, tugging me gently away, back through the bar—he scoops my handbag up on the way, what a gentleman—and out the front door into the mall.

Behind me, I can hear Crewe screaming at Tom to delete that footage, or he'll spend the rest of his career shooting cheap-arse wedding videos.

'Self preservation, Tabitha,' Stewart says once we are outside, with the metal door clanged firmly behind us. 'Take some deep breaths, sweetheart.'

I burst into tears, which is embarrassing for both of us. At least I get a Stewart hug out of it. He gives me a good squeeze, letting me soak the shirt he's wearing beneath the official The Chocolate Teapot apron.

'I can't take much more of this,' I mope into his shoulder.

'All in a good cause, aye?' he murmurs.

'It doesn't feel like that.' I pull away from him, because his arms are way too comforting for his own good. 'Do you know what that bastard has gone and done now?'

'I got the gist,' he says, frowning. 'Do ye want me to ask around, find out if he's angling for Daisy and Dot's place too?'

'Thanks,' I say, mopping the last wetness from my face with my own apron, the one Lara and Yui designed for me with the Café La Femme logo and images from Stewart's mural all over it. 'That man is fucking poison.'

'So we'll bring him down,' he says with that crooked smile of his, the one that warms me all the way down to my feet. 'Together.'

I lean in, because those are kissing words, but Stewart moves back quickly, putting a pointed amount of space between us. 'Take an hour, Tabitha. Get your head together before we film the next segment. Right?'

'Right,' I say softly, trying not to show the hurt at how quickly he dodged my kiss. *Don't go there, Tabitha. Bad timing. Bad everything. Badness.* 'Later, then.'

Stewart gives me an awkward sort of wave and lopes inside, leaving me on my own in the busy mall.

Imagining all the ways that Cameron Crewe might meet his death.

19

Xanthippe Gets Saucy
(after the murder)

'What next?' asked Jason.

I eyed him suspiciously. 'Are you short of something to do? Don't you have classes?'

He leaned back on my desk chair, as if he was contemplating putting his feet on the desk. Just try it, kid.

'Mid year break,' he informed me.

'Exams to study for?'

'It's not that kind of college. I need to practise my pavlova whisking skills for a thing, but I can do that later.' He paused and reconsidered. 'Actually my shift in the café starts in an hour. But until then, I'm completely at your disposal.'

'Good to know.'

'You're not pissed off at Tabitha, are you? About the whole—' He gave a vague wave to encompass everything I'd learned this morning.

'Of course I am. I don't like it when clients keep

important information from me, and it's much worse when they're friends.' I gave him a pointed look.

'You mean me?' Jason looked flattered. 'Are we friends? I thought you found me irritating.'

'I find everyone irritating, don't take it personally.' I stood up, stretching. 'Take the day off the case. You have a life, and I have to shower.'

'Don't you want to track down that Otto Parrish kid, the one who was the previous Lief? And we still need to find out what happened to Ani from #Sconebros, and...'

'Jason,' I said pointedly. 'You have shit to do. I have shit to do—Tabitha is not my only client. And I need a shower. So get out of here.'

He looked hesitant. 'You're not giving up on her, are you?'

Loyalty. What is it about that woman, that she inspires so damned much of it?

I leaned over and picked a bit of glitter out of Jason's hair. 'I signed on for keeping Tabitha Darling out of trouble long before you came along, sunshine. Everything's going to be okay. We can take a break.'

Back in the day I was getting her into as many scrapes as I was bailing her out of, but the point stands.

Jason took off my fedora, and made himself scarce. Good kid. Good instincts.

_____

The water pressure was nothing to write home about, but at least I didn't have to share a hot water heater with Tabitha and the boys any more. I let my thoughts wander under the spray, and when they kept darting back to the case, it wasn't Cameron Crewe or the sous-clones or Petula Parrish's tea-brewing son that came to mind.

It was Kari Nagarra. She was at the heart of all this—she was the reason Tabitha had gotten involved in the first place. Kari said from the start that she was likely to be questioned by the police, but I wasn't sure if they even looked in her direction.

As I washed away a good part of the gimlet haze from the night before, I recalled that she was a really good kisser. With my romantic luck, that added an extra point to the 'suspicious' column.

After drying my hair, I assembled a sharper outfit. The nice thing about being a private detective rather than say, an office administrator, is that you can factor in a black leather coat as 'business casual'.

If I added a little more raspberry lipgloss than I would usually wear mid-week, well. There was no one to see me do it. Fruit flavours are useful. They make people under-estimate how serious you are, or how dangerous you are, and that comes in handy in my line of work. Also, smelling delicious makes me happy.

I strode back out into the main office, ready to call a

certain hot YouTube presenter and ask her a bunch of pointed questions while looking effortlessly amazing.

There were two men standing to attention near my desk—black suits, buzz-cuts, sunglasses and Bluetooth headsets. Not cops. Professional heavies.

'I definitely locked that door,' I noted. Speaking of the door, they were between me and it, and there were no other exits from this apartment. I should remember to call my landlord and request a rope ladder for situations like this. 'Are you here to pass on a message?'

They gave me 'lady, please' expressions and the taller of the two spoke briefly into his phone.

My smoky-glass front door opened, and a curvy brunette sauntered in. She had fashion labels on her fashion labels, and dynamite legs under tailor-cut linen trousers. This wasn't a woman who fretted about finding decent maternity wear—she snapped her fingers, and the perfect clothes fell into her lap.

Petula Parrish, the Saucy Chef. That meant these two goons were bodyguards, and probably not about to use violent methods to frighten me off the case. That was a relief. I hate to use a taser on men in nice suits.

There was a gleam in Petula Parrish's eyes that told me, she wasn't here to be my friend.

Whenever I'm not sure how to react to a situation, or I think it's a good idea to appear unthreatening, I smile my brightest smile and ask myself, *What Would Tabitha Darling Do?*

'You look so familiar,' I declared, shaking my hair out to make it look extra pretty. 'Are you on TV or something?'

Petula smiled, a broadcast quality smile that told me nothing of what she was thinking or feeling. 'Xanthippe Carides. I think you know exactly who I am.'

'Someone who thinks she doesn't need to make an appointment,' I chided lightly, but why waste the power dressing? I could only keep up the Tabitha smile for so long before it started to ache. I dropped into my seat behind the desk. 'How can I help you, Ms Parrish?'

'I understand you have been conducting a private investigation into my husband's death.'

I gave her my most inscrutable face. 'Who told you that?'

'It's hardly relevant.'

'To you, maybe. But I don't like people spreading untrue stories about me. I'm afraid you've been misinformed.'

Petula blinked at that, a twitch of annoyance crossing her face. 'Excuse me?'

'We're talking about a recent suspicious death which has an active police investigation running. It would be deeply inappropriate for a private investigator to take on a case like that. My work tends to be more about the cases without active police interest. Missing persons, divorce and civil claims, minor thefts. That sort of thing.'

Petula did not frown—she had a good line in resting bitch face without actually looking bitchy. It was an impressive skill. 'But you have been asking intrusive questions about my husband's death, of many of his co-workers and other witnesses.'

I shrugged a shoulder. 'Many of those co-workers and witnesses are my friends. I do have an investigation running that has overlapped with Chef Crewe's death, but I have been doing my best not to overstep my bounds, or get underfoot with the police.'

That last part was quite an understatement. I was exceedingly proud that I'd got through several days of this without a single awkward lecture moment with a serving officer, other than my brother. But getting through a week without an awkward lecture from him is a basic impossibility.

I might have known that Saucy Petula was not the kind of woman to leave a room without tossing some final line over her shoulder like she was flipping a perfume-drenched silk scarf. 'I hope your Ms Darling wasn't put out by my husband's interest in this building. Business is not the same as personal.'

Oh, it was like that, was it? I smiled with my sharpest teeth. 'Luckily, our landlord has sentimental reasons to hold on to this building. He was never going to sell.'

'My husband could be very persuasive,' Petula shot back. 'And ruthless, when it came to getting what he wanted.'

She flounced, the door banging behind her and her two suited bodyguards.

Okay, that was weird, right? Was she threatening me with the ghost of her husband? Or was something else going on?

= 20 =

Xanthippe Has a Motive For Murder
(after the murder)

The café was bustling when I came downstairs—it didn't surprise me at all as I rounded the corner to see Tabitha at the counter serving customers. Getting her to take even one regular day off was next to impossible.

I looked at her through the glass for a minute. She chatted away with one of her favourite bohemian old lady customers, serving up a slice of what I could tell from a glance was her famous pear crumble tart. Tabitha only made it in the dead of winter, when fresh seasonal fruit offers its most limited selection.

Yui flashed in and out of the kitchen, but disappeared for a while, leaving Tabitha alone in the main café. When a crowd of hipsters made their way in, I snuck in with them and took my old place behind the counter, near the coffee machine.

Tabitha gave me an arch look somewhere between gratitude and skepticism. Just like old times. She called me the coffee orders as they came in, and I tried not to screw them up too badly while she flirted with the customers, served them their snacks, and kept the engine running smoothly.

When Yui returned, cradling a freshly chilled New York cheesecake for the glass display, I made myself a macchiato and sat down at the last spare table.

A while later, Tabitha joined me with a couple of veggie paninis. 'Have you had lunch?'

'Not yet.'

'I suppose I'll let you have one of these, then.' We ate in silence. She still had her glitter roots in, though they weren't as intense as the night before, and she'd matched them with a sixties mod dress in lime cotton.

Tabitha thinks winter is for other people.

'I think we've talked more in the last week than we have all year,' she noted, picking artichoke out of her sandwich.

'And yet you're still leaving out details.'

Her phone beeped, and she ignored it. 'I can't help that there's so much to catch up on.'

'You need to get better at triaging vital information.'

'Being a responsible witness in a murder investigation isn't something I feel the need to get good at,' she huffed, and her phone beeped again.

I raised my eyebrows. 'Avoiding a boy?'

'In a manner of speaking.'

'You can tell me, or I can take that phone off you and

massively invade your privacy.'

Tabitha quirked an eyebrow at me. 'Don't both those options involve a massive invasion of privacy?'

'Well, sure. I was giving you an opportunity to pretend you had control over the situation. You're welcome.'

With a sigh, she unlocked her screen and handed the phone over. 'I was going to tell you.'

'Sure you were.'

It wasn't a boy. At least, not one of the boys we liked.

Instead, it was a long thread of abusive, threatening text messages, going back weeks.

Finally, I set the phone down and looked at Tabitha. She avoided my gaze, as if those muffins under her display counter were really worthy of more than ten seconds of intense scrutiny.

'Tish,' I said heavily.

'I know, right?' She managed a smile.

'This is the kind of thing you tell people about straight away. You report it to the police, and to your friends, especially those who are capable of physically protecting you.'

'I know. Awkward timing.'

'You broke up with Leo, not the entire local police! You should have reported it.'

'I did report it!' Tabitha said impatiently. 'I'm not completely irresponsible, Zee. I did it three weeks ago— Inspector Fitzgerald used the report to support his theory that I stabbed Cameron Crewe, hid the weapon, and then re-stabbed him with an ironic piece of confectionary.'

'Oh.'

'Uh-huh.'

'Well, that sucks.'

Tabitha took her phone back. 'I didn't figure out the connection until that afternoon, when we were setting up the Death By Coffee display. But of course Crewe was behind the threats. He wanted Café La Femme. He must have been working to scare me before he even approached Darrow for the purchase. I guess because he would have had to buy out my lease, once he had control of the building, or wait another eighteen months to put me out of business.'

'Did the police track the source of the messages?'

'Burner phone, no way to ID who was behind it. And it's not like Crewe would have done it himself anyway. He was one of life's true delegators. Besides, he's dead, and the messages keep coming.'

'You're sure he was behind it?'

Tabitha gave me her most sarcastic expression. I hadn't realised her face was capable of so many sharp angles. 'He's done it before. That's why Kari and I were going after him in the first place. We're lucky he was killed when he was, or he would have escalated his plan. As soon as Crewe gave up on buying the building legitimately, it would have been bricks through the window, suspicious fires, bomb threats, the works. Anything to drive the businesses away from the building and make it easier for Darrow to sign on that dotted line.'

I thought of my beautiful detective office, and felt a growl build in the back of my throat. 'I would have liked to see him try.'

'See,' said Tabitha with a gentle smile. 'You had a motive for murder too. You just didn't know it.'

WEEK SEVEN

Bringing the Sauce

KARI NAGARRA: Café Wars was hit by tragedy last week with the violent death of our patron, legendary Chef Cameron Crewe. But the shocks didn't stop there—at a press conference about the alleged murder, the world discovered that Chef Crewe was secretly married to another culinary superstar, Petula Parrish: the Saucy Chef. Petula, thank you for joining us.

PETULA PARRISH: Thank you for inviting me, Kari.

KARI: We thought that Café Wars died with Chef Crewe...

PETULA: Which is absolutely not what he would have wanted. This project meant so much to him.

KARI: You have come forward to save the show—so we can realise your husband's vision.

PETULA: He loved nothing better than celebrating the art of the local café, and sharing his love of food with the nation. [Wipes a discreet tear] We have to finish the show, for Cameron.

KARI: You heard it here first, Café Wars isn't going anywhere. Stay tuned for Week Seven, which is going to be our best week yet as all three of our cafés dedicate their culinary talents to create a brand new Teasperience signature dish in honour of Chef Crewe, taken from us too soon.

PETULA: The challenge for this week is to Bring the Sauce. I want a sexy, delicious, beautifully arranged dish featuring a special sauce of some kind—sweet, savoury, as long as it kisses the tastebuds and leaves the customer longing for more.

KARI: You heard the lady. Sauce up, contestants!

≡ **21** ≡

Tabitha's Alibi
(Tabitha Doesn't Have An Alibi)

It's been the same dream all week. I'm back there, sitting in my car, so angry with Cameron Crewe and his schemes that I could hit him with a frying pan.

I've been angry all day. Walking around didn't calm me down. When I returned to the Teasperience kitchen to film the Coffee To Die For segment, Crewe pretended nothing happened between us. I even won the challenge, for my masterful use of gothic black toffee.

I'm not calm.

I have way more toffee blisters on my hands than a good chef should.

I should be home right now, eating pizza with Stewart and Ceege and Jason and spending a blissful several hours thinking about anything but *Café Wars*. I turned down that invite because I'm still stinging from that whole near kiss situation. Stewart and I and kissing doesn't work out (not the kissing part, we're great at the kissing part, it's the consequences that suck).

It's me. I suck. Stewart has always been pretty fucking gracious about the terrible timing that continues to hover around him and me and kissing.

Part of me wants to wail, *why doesn't he want to kiss me now*, but I know the answer to that too. Neither of us is stupid.

Bishop and I have been breaking up in a hundred different ways for a long time now, but as far as everyone else is concerned, it only happened a month ago.

My head is full of ugh boys and grr chef, and when a text comes up on my phone from an unknown number saying,

HEY CHEF DARLING, NO WORRIES BUT YOU LEFT YOUR TOFFEE AND FONDANT CUTTING TOOLS IN THE TEASPERIENCE KITCHEN, DID YOU WANT TO COME BACK TO PICK THEM UP?

there's so much going on that I don't stop to think about the weeks of other anonymous calls from other unknown numbers.

I assume it's Tom or one of the sous-clones, or that assistant of Kari's who turns up every other shooting session and spends most of it texting her friends. I'm already here, sitting in my car. It doesn't take a lot of effort to walk down a couple of flights of stairs out of the Argyle Street carpark, and pop back to Teasperience.

No one's locked the kitchen door yet, so I push it open, take four steps inside the room, and stop short at the puddle of blood slowly cooling on the milky tea-coloured floor tiles.

Cameron Crewe is lying there, with my golden toffee knife wedged triumphantly into the hole in his chest. For a startled moment even I wonder if I did it.

I make the call.

Soon there are flashing blue lights against the walls of the kitchen, and I'm probably in shock, because it doesn't occur to me to call anyone to meet me at the station. I allow Constable Steve and Constable Tara help me into the back of their car. It's Tasmania Police, they're practically family, all of them, of course I have to answer a few questions, that makes sense...

The dream never ends there—I don't wake up straight away, but I skip past hours of questions and other hours of being deliberately left alone before more questions. This is where the dream gets creative. Sometimes I get Bishop interrogating me about the baking times of cheesecake, sometimes it's Nin demanding I do better with my time-keeping, or Stewart drilling me on the history of Alfred Hitchcock movies. The only thing all my interrogators have in common, across the different versions of the dream, is how flat they sound, how unemotional, completely unlike themselves.

They sound exactly like Inspector Fitzgerald did that night—the skeptical expression, that undertone of aggression, the overwhelming sense that this person is *not on my side*. It aches to have my friends and loved ones acting that way, but I mostly know it's not real. This isn't how it happened.

The dream always ends the same way, with Xanthippe's voice on the other end of the line, sounding tired and pissed off at me, and an overwhelming sense that...

Everything's going to be okay, right? If Xanthippe sounds like herself, if she's legit cranky, then real life must be right around the corner.

Then I wake up, and get mad at myself. What does it say about me, that I'm more traumatised by a senior policeman not thinking I'm adorable than by the sight of Cameron Crewe, dead on his own kitchen floor?

It's 5AM and I'm awake, even though I'm not opening Café La Femme today. It's Week Seven, Cameron Crewe is still dead, and I have to be upbeat about tarragon sauce for the internet.

It's not our usual schedule for filming, but Petula Parrish wanted to do it on Saturday. Kari and Tom are jumping to her tune—why would they not? They need this show to be done more than anyone.

Taking Saturday off when you work in a café is a big deal, but according to Nin I haven't taken a Saturday to myself in months, so no one is going to give me shit about it.

It's hard to find positive energy to smile and cook in front of cameras when I'm still fretting about the Cameron Crewe case, but every day that doesn't end with me being brought back in for questioning makes me relax a little more.

The police are investigating. Xanthippe's nosing around after any spare crumbs they may have missed. Reality can return anytime it likes.

I'm going to be okay.

———————

By 6AM I'm downstairs with bouncing hair, and a winter ensemble with a tropical theme: an orange-and-yellow plaid skirt, and a wool coat lined with a bright print of mangoes and pineapples.

Ceege isn't anywhere in sight—he's been working all hours to make up for pulling an accidental sickie the day after Glitter and Gimlets. I'm startled to see Jase and Stewart on my couch, dressed for the day. Stewart is wearing his best jeans without holes.

'Have you two not gone to bed yet?' I ask suspiciously.

'That's libel,' says Jase.

'Slander,' Stewart corrects.

It's way too early for any comedy double act not involving

me. 'So ... to what do I owe this early morning honour?'

'We're escorting ye to the filming,' says Stewart, as if it isn't in question.

'You—why?' He literally works for the opposition, and he's planning to hold my hand?

'Xanthippe's finally having a real bed delivered to the new office, and we promised her we'd keep an eye on you,' says Jason.

I narrow my eyes at them both. 'Does she think it's her physical presence that has stopped the police arresting me all week?'

Both boys shrug. 'No one asks questions when Xanthippe gives orders,' says Stewart. 'Unless it involves coffee, which she knows nothing about.'

That's fair.

———————

Petula Parrish is putting in so much flair and effort that it only makes it more obvious how Cameron Crewe was phoning it in with *Café Wars*. Instead of a few grudging scenery shots of Hobart to remind viewers where the series is set, this week's challenge takes place on the lawn in front of Parliament House, a hop, skip and jump across the road from the buzzing Salamanca Market. Tourism central, even in the middle of winter.

There's a crowd gathered, and at least three camera operators, as part of a crew of eight instead of our usual bodgy 'Kari and Tom and nameless assistant' situation.

Anyone would think this was going straight to Channel Ten, and not YouTube.

'Don't you mind?' I ask Tom when we stop for a ten minute break because Petula has to get hollandaise sauce cleaned out of her long, billowing brunette curls. 'All these people horning in on your territory.'

'Nope,' he says, looking more relaxed than he had the entire time he was working for Crewe. 'Petula's put me forward for a job on her next SBS show, *Sauce Around The World*. We're presold to eight countries already, filming in August. The only way is up, baby.'

I high-five him. It's good to see the positives coming out of the colossal mess that is my winter so far.

Kari admits that Petula offered her a job too, but all the publicity coming in from the secret wedding revelation and the final weeks of *Café Wars* means she can pick from a long list of offers.

Good for them. Kari and I failed to expose Cameron Crewe for the horrible human being he was, but at least Kari and Tom came out ahead.

———

The actual challenge is pretty fun. Each of us—me, Dot and Maaka—has a table in front of us, covered in ingredients, with access to ice and a single burner. There's a station up the front where Earl and Grey grill steaks and fish, toss salads, poach eggs, and whip up the occasional surprising dessert. Petula yells out a type of classic sauce, and a number of minutes, anywhere from four to fifteen. We then race into gear, constructing the best sauce we can, and rush forward to dress the plate we are given.

My sauce allemande rocks, my bechamel is a gift from the gods, and I totally get away with my parsley aioli. I produce teriyaki dipping sauce, salted caramel pouring fudge, smoky chipotle mayonnaise, and a miso-mustard butter chutney that tastes so good I take the time to write down the recipe.

There are disasters too, but I choose not to dwell on them.

By the time we reach the final round, in which we have twelve minutes to make our own ketchup from scratch (let us never speak of it again), our aprons are spattered, we are singed and exhausted and half-hysterical and it's honestly the best time I've had in ages.

Every time I catch Dot's or Maaka's eyes, we burst out laughing. It feels like we're veterans of intense vinegar-themed trench warfare, which is probably the opposite of what a TV cooking contest is supposed to bring out in people.

My boys are there, laughing and cheering with the rest

of the audience. Cooking for a crowd is way more enjoyable than doing it front of a single camera.

Petula Parrish is actually pretty cool. Who would ever have guessed?

We're done by lunchtime, and when I say 'done' I mean halfway roasted, despite the chill in the air. All I want is a shower because I have tomato chunks in my hair, but I parked my car near Café La Femme that morning, which means a leisurely walk with Stewart and Jase, back up the hill.

I hear the sirens first, but don't think anything of them, not until I actually see the fire truck blocking the intersection up ahead of us.

My intersection. My café.

Thank goodness I went for boots today and not cute heels, because I can run the last half block until I'm close enough to see the crowd gathered around the intersection, blocking off half of Macquarie Street.

When I sway on my feet, Stewart catches me around the waist, as if he expects me to dash full on into traffic. 'It's the first floor,' he says urgently. 'No' the café, it's...'

Black smoke, belching out of the windows of Darrow's beautiful, heritage-listed sandstone building. Stewart is right, it's the middle floor, the one that had a tourism blog business, and now has some kind of ... who even uses that space these days?

As long as everyone gets out, we can spare the first floor, right? These are the kinds of crazy thoughts that go through your head when you realise the business you have devoted years of your life to is literally on fire.

Among the crowd of onlookers, I see my people: Nin and Lara and Yui, talking earnestly to fire officials in the grounds of St David's Cathedral. Evacuated. That's all right, then.

How much does smoke damage cost to repair? As long as the fire didn't spread to the rest of the building, maybe this isn't as bad as it looks...

My eyes drift up to the top floor. No smoke coming out of those windows yet. 'Someone call Xanthippe,' I say in a steady voice, well aware that Stewart hasn't let go of me yet. 'Someone call her phone right now.'

≡ **22** ≡

Xanthippe and the Dead Body Room
(we're all caught up now)

I told the truth about the bed; I want to make that very clear. Life is too short to spend any amount of time on a futon.

But if I chose to multitask the crucial 'waiting for delivery' window by inviting my brother over, at a time when the three most interrupty people that I know happened to be busy down at Salamanca Market in front of a film crew, I don't think anyone would blame me.

'So, this is your place now,' said Leo, eyeing the blatantly film noir office that took the place of the flat's former living room. 'It's very you.'

'I know you don't approve,' I said dryly.

'You're an adult,' he sighed. 'And apparently licensed in this state as a private investigator. I don't have the grounds to complain. Certainly not about your retro taste in decor.'

And yet.

'Admit that you're jealous of my hat stand,' I teased him.

Leo didn't quite manage a smile, but I've long since given up on earning more than a bemused twist of his face. 'Why am I here, Xanthippe?'

'I want to know how you're doing,' I said. 'You know, post-breakup, checking in, it's what people do! Especially people who are siblings.' It sounded more reasonable in my head before he was here, standing in front of me, reminding me how few proper brother-sister interactions we've managed over the years.

We have a mess of cousins who are always in each other's faces, teasing and scrapping and mocking each other's significant others with the same tones of voices they used to reserve for arguing about which Planeteer they wanted Captain Planet to drop into a volcano (trick question: the answer is all of them). Leo and I were never like that—the age difference was too wide, and he lived with his dad mostly, so there was a kind of stiff formality between us right up to the point that he joined the police, and I fell into the kind of teenage scrapes that the police highly disapprove of.

Right now, he was looking at me with suspicion. Not 'arrested for streaking on university grounds' suspicion, but not too far off it, either. 'What are you up to, Zee?'

'I'm trying to be a good sister, shut up, I'm new at this,' I grumbled. 'Let me practise.'

His face softened for a minute. Sap.

'Also I'm pretty sure this bed I'm having delivered is coming in like eight parts and I don't know how to put it together,' I added, because emotions are squishy, and manly emotions are the squishiest. The best way to deal with men+feelings is to provide some kind of practical task to distract them with.

'Make me a coffee and I'll think about helping you with the bed,' Leo said, which wasn't quite pouring his heart out to me about all the Tabitha!feels, but it was a start.

I might have known that the whole brother-sister business would backfire on me, because once my Heatherington Deluxe (the people who name beds have watched too much *Downton Abbey*) was set up in the bedroom where Tabitha didn't once find a dead body (I was totally using the dead body room for my personal Pilates studio), Leo drank the last cold dregs of his cup of coffee and asked me about my love life.

For real.

Well, he didn't say those exact words, because this wasn't a 1970s swingers movie, but he did cough before saying 'So the Lotuscrasher is the one who set this place up for you, right?'

'His name is Darrow,' I said, but I was amused by the nickname and totally going to steal it. 'And yes. It's weird and inappropriate of him, but he gave it to me for my birthday and it's my favourite weird and inappropriate thing he's ever done.'

Leo gives me flowers every birthday, which never fails to be awkward.

Speaking of awkward...

'Are you two getting back together?' he asked now, sort of maybe frowning, then deliberately flattening his face in order to look completely neutral.

'He's angling for it,' I sighed.

'And what about you?'

Huh. I would never admit this out loud, but turns out it didn't suck to have Leo taking an interest in my life. Even if it was all a lead up to let me know how much he disapproved of my taste in men. I hadn't got around to letting him know yet that my taste in men also included women. 'I'm not a fish,' I said for now. 'I think he's currently avoiding me so I can't let him down gently. I haven't called him on it, because him avoiding me supports my own plan of avoiding him. It's a self-sustaining system.'

Leo arched an eyebrow at me. 'Are you paying rent?'

Oh, hell. I hadn't thought of that. 'I should, shouldn't I?'

'Hey, I'm not the one who took first year Women's Studies...'

'Bite me.'

He checked his watch. 'I have to run.'

'Don't think I didn't notice how little we talked about your feeeeeelings,' I said, because I felt there had been a shortage of brat in this conversation.

He shook his head and grinned at me. 'We can work up to that. Baby steps.'

———————

I had one more piece of DIY to install after Leo left. Petula Parrish strolling in with her entourage the other day while I was in the shower had raised a few security concerns. My smoky glass doors were pretty, but the lock was too basic for my liking.

I'd moved over my toolbox with the rest of my stuff from Tabitha's, which meant I had everything I needed to install a reassuringly solid bolt on the front door.

There were more chores to tick off my list before I returned to the case of Who The Hell Stabbed Cameron Crewe And Can I Give Them a Freaking Medal? The bitch about freelancing is, weekends come out of your pay packet. The job taking up most of my billable hours all week was as pro bono as it gets. So. Other work.

I checked my emails on the tablet I kept in the bottom drawer, next to the half-full whiskey bottle, and did some internet research on one of my other outstanding cases, to prove to myself that I wasn't one hundred percent Tabitha Darling's unpaid saviour.

Fifteen minutes later, a text chimed on my phone, from an unknown number. I wasn't going to check it because hello, busy here, but that lasted about two minutes before I broke, and reached for my phone, swiping it open...

To stare into the face of a dead girl.

I swear I stopped breathing for at least a minute. The picture was partly blurred, but it captured the image it was going for—the limp, unnaturally twisted limbs, the half-lidded eyes, the greyness of the skin. A mess of blood crusted around her throat, spilling on to her t-shirt. Hours old blood, at least. Maybe days.

I knew her, that was the worst of it. I recognised her. If only I could remember where...

A thought flitted across my brain, and I moved without thinking about it, calling up YouTube on my tablet, hitting the channel for *Café Wars* and scrolling back until I got to the video I needed.

Week Two, Soup Kitchen.

I fast-forwarded until there was a shot of Ani from #Sconebros, the girl who watched the celebrity chef smash her soup pot, because she wouldn't let him grope her behind the scenes. The girl that supposedly went home to New Zealand. Her contact information never made its way to me, and I never followed it up.

Alive, she had light brown hair, a slightly wonky front tooth, a sarcastic smile and a sad look about her eyes.

Dead ... she looked flat and entirely lacking in quirk. But it was her.

Before I could think about calling someone to report this, another picture beeped through. This was a wider shot, from a more gruesome angle, in better focus. It wasn't the clearer image of the dead girl that made me sit up and take notice, though.

It was the view of the mountain in the background, half cut off by a sandstone wall. I knew that view, and that window. It was the same as mine, only one floor down.

This photo had been taken in the office below me. What the actual hell? I thought it was an accounting firm.

I'm not proud of what I did next, but I had spent the last several months convincing myself that I was a private detective.

————

Xanthippe Carides' Rules For What To Do When Someone Texts You The Images Of A Dead Body

1) Contact the police, because come the hell on. There are times for private detectives to shine and this is not one of them. Take your phone directly to the police station so they can try to trace the call, do not pass GO, do not collect $200.

2) Call your brother, which has the added bonus of being compatible with 1) because your brother is a fucking police officer.

3) Do Not Under Any Circumstances Go To Investigate the Location Of The Background Of The Picture Even If It's Only A Flight of Stairs Away

4) If You Do 3) Then At Least Don't Be Stupid Enough Not To Tell Someone Where You Are Going.

5) If You Want A Suggestion for 4) I Recommend You Revisit 2) But Honestly Anyone Would Do At This Point. The Teenage Sidekick. Tabitha. Stewart. Your Mother. Yes, Even Your Mother.

———————

I wasn't making the best choices that day. Even as I headed down there, I had a rough draft of the Seems Obvious In Retrospect Rules running around in my head. But it felt like a no-brainer to check whether the body was still in residence before I headed out to share my new and disturbing plot twist with Tasmania Police, or Leo, or Tabitha.

The door was locked. Of course the door was locked. Guess who has two thumbs and taught herself to pick locks when she was fifteen? This person.

Two minutes later, I was inside, and that was where things got strange. This was, quite obviously, an accounting firm. Or, I don't know, some kind of dull open plan office, much like it was back when Stewart worked here with the blogosphere.

There was no dead body on the floor. I could see where

it had been, and could even see where the photographer had to stand, to get those exact angles. They must have been trying for some extra arty flair, to go to all the trouble to take that particular shot that captured the view out the window as well as the sprawled dead body...

Oh. Well yes, there was that. Taking the trouble. They had to move the desks, and even then, there was no reason to take that particularly arty shot, unless they were deliberately planting a clue about where the body was being photographed.

As that thought slotted into place, I backed up to the door, about to high tail it out of there before the person who sent me those images decided this was the perfect opportunity to kill me too...

Pain exploded in my eyes and skull, and I hit the floor.

= 23 =

Xanthippe Carides is Not
A Black Belt in Karate

Here's the thing: Tabitha has a vastly overinflated idea of how good I am at martial arts.

Sure, I spent my teen years obsessing about Karate, Taekwondo, Muay Tai, kickboxing and everything in between, but my short attention span and recurring issues with authority meant that I gave up and moved on before coming close to mastering any given discipline.

I love my judo throws, and I am damned handy in a bar fight, but my overall self defence style is what could politely be called eclectic, and more accurately called a freaking mess.

Even so, being a black belt in karate or anything else would not have saved me from being knocked unconscious from behind by a dickhead wielding a plank of two by four.

That's my excuse, and I'm sticking to it.

Somewhere, my phone was ringing.

The smoke was bitter against my mouth, harsh enough that I didn't want to open my eyes. My nose hurt. Ugh, now that I was properly waking up, a whole bunch of things hurt, the back of my head most of all.

I'd never suffered a concussion before, but I'd done enough first aid courses that the symptoms came readily to mind. Loss of memory, loss of consciousness, grogginess, possible nausea or vomiting, dizziness, drowsiness...

I was ticking all of the boxes, though I don't remember anything in the list of concussion symptoms about imagining smoke.

My body was too wrecked to even cough, but I did manage to open my eyes, long enough to find out that yes, blurry vision, there we go. I caught hold of the metal waste-paper bin under my desk in time to throw up in it, so at least I still had my lightning reflexes.

Lightning reflexes, and a concussion.

My phone was ringing, but I had no idea where it was, and the smoke—the smoke and the head trauma, lovely combination—was making it hard to put all the pieces together. Still, I was in my office. I wasn't in my office before, was I?

It was a different office. Someone had moved me.

Not just me, I realised, as there was a zip-up bag on the floor nearby, a sports bag long enough to carry skis or fencing swords or a whole lot of soccer balls or—and this was the thought that whirled most rapidly into my head—a dead body.

There was smoke and I had been moved while unconscious and chances were very high that the sports bag contained Ani from #Sconebros. Someone wanted to make very sure that we both disappeared.

The building was on fire. This looked bad. This looked very bad.

I crawled to the window and dragged it open. This helped slightly with the breathing situation. I could hear sirens, which was good, and my phone again, which was way past helpful and all the way through to irritating.

Ugh, thinking was hard. But the pictures of Ani's body were on my phone. If she and I both burned to a crisp here, there would be no evidence of her death.

I was going to have to find my phone, wrap it in a sock, and chuck it out the window.

Turned out, it was on my desk. Which I couldn't see well, what with the smoke making my eyes water, and the extreme dizziness, but once I got there, it was sitting right out in the open. A bunch of missed messages, and I couldn't focus enough to read them.

Huh. Why would my attacker have left my phone with all the evidence right there on it … unless they deleted the photos. That made sense. Sometime soon I would have to remember how to click through and check. Other things to worry about right now. Like how to preserve a corpse in a sports bag from a fiery death.

Also, was it too late to save my new bed?

I got myself to the door, and was grateful for glass instead of wood, but the stairwell was so thick with black smoke, it didn't seem a viable option.

Window. It was always going to come down to me climbing out a window.

I dragged the sports bag to the window first, levered it up over the ledge, and kept shoving until it fell down, down, to the courtyard below with a sickening sound that made me rethink whether there was anything left in my stomach to throw up.

So much for burning the evidence. Take that, arseholes!

Two floors doesn't sound high, not until you think about it, not until you're leaning out of a window and the concussion is making your ears ring and your eyes blur, or maybe it's not the concussion, maybe it's everything else, maybe it's smoke inhalation, maybe it's previously-undiagnosed acrophobia.

Possibly in this exact moment, it didn't matter why my head was spinning.

Here's something else you might not know about me: while my martial arts prowess is sketchy and imperfect (as opposed to my martial arts bluffing and posing prowess which is second to none), my drainpipe climbing skills are excellent.

I'm not going to admit that Catwoman was a major influence on me growing up, or that David Niven in the *Pink Panther* was the other major influence, but let's face it, a girl doesn't start practising roof climbing at ten years old for no reason.

Yes, I'm a parkour hipster, I was leaping across rooftops before it was cool. I was totally capable of shinning down a drainpipe to safety. As Tabitha would say, I'm just that awesome.

I turned and threw up again, on the floor of my office. Damn it. Hands shaking. Not awesome. Not awesome at all.

I clambered up on to the window sill and sat there for a moment, waiting for my eyesight to settle. One drainpipe. It was in focus and everything. We were going to be fine. I leaned out, securing one hand firmly on the joist where the pipe connected to the side of the building. Right. Any minute now.

Just as I was able to hurl myself at the wall and do my woozy drunk Spider-Man impersonation, something bright and red filled my vision. A massive fire truck backed into Tabitha's courtyard, knocking over one of her favourite tables.

Tabitha was there, too, ahead of the truck, yelling something.

I'm almost certain she wasn't screaming at me to jump. Which is a good thing, because I had forgotten how.

———————

Yes, I was rescued, ladder and everything. I'm not proud. Hell, I was barely conscious by the time the hot fireman in the bright yellow suit got me to ground level, though I was awake enough to dry heave on his shoes.

Luckily for us both, my stomach was empty by then. Yay.

I think Tabitha is a lot less intimidated by me than she used to be. But hey, I didn't burn to death or break a limb trying to climb down a drainpipe with a concussion. I'll take the win.

≡ **23** ≡

Tabitha Comes Across as an Unreliable Witness

'They're keeping Zee in overnight,' I say shortly. Judging by the facial expressions of the mob that has taken over my living room—Nin, Lara, Yui, Stewart and Jase—that isn't nearly enough information. I shrug limply and head for my kitchen. 'That's all I've got.'

Ceege brought me home from the hospital. I was all for hanging around Xanthippe's room like a creeper, but Leo was there, and Zee's mother and a bunch of other relatives, which made things awkward.

Leo understood me wanting to be there, but there was only so much I could take of their Mama's deathglare. I don't know if she blames me for Zee's near death experience, or is still sore about the break up, but either way I am not her favourite person right now.

That's okay. I'm not my own favourite person either. Zee almost died, while I was fretting about my café.

Darrow hasn't replied to any of my messages. You'd

think 'Someone set fire to your building and came close to killing your ex' is the kind of text message you REPLY TO.

I don't have any answers yet for the questions my staff has about their jobs, or my friends have about my current state of mind. What I do have is a buttery short-crust pastry recipe that shouldn't go to waste, even if there isn't a café to stock tomorrow.

Stewart is the first one to leap to his feet and try to talk to me. 'Tabitha...'

'I'm making mango cream pie,' I interrupt him. 'You can help.'

He looks like he had a lot more to say, but goes easy on me when he sees the frantic expression on my face. 'As ye wish.'

———————

This is a good chance for us to talk. Surely we have issues to air, serious business to discuss? Matters to get off our collective chests.

Instead, I silently assemble butter and flour and ice water. Stewart fetches everything I ask for, and together we make enough dough for at least four pie crusts.

His presence is comforting. His lack of talking, even more so.

Somewhere the doorbell rings, but I ignore it. Surely the benefit of having my house full of people is that I don't have to worry about that sort of thing.

Some hope. Ceege raps gently on the kitchen door. 'Oi, Tabitha? Cops.'

I wash my hands quickly, wiping off the last of the flour with some paper towel, and head into my living room.

Inspector Fitzgerald stands there, with Detective Senior Constable Heather at his side. She at least looks apologetic. He looks like, in his ideal world, he would be allowed to arrest everyone in the house for making him stand next to a TV screening *Footloose*.

'Tabitha Darling,' says Fitzgerald in a self-important voice. 'We'd like to ask you some questions down at the station, concerning the suspicious fire at your place of business.'

Suspicious fire. Yes. That's one way to phrase it. 'I'll be right with you,' I say, and turn to Stewart. 'How confident are you with blind baking? If you can't hack it, I'd rather you cling-wrap the crusts and leave them in the fridge for me to bake later.'

'Tabitha,' he replies in a low voice. 'Shall I call your lawyer to meet ye there?'

I frown at him. 'I don't have a lawyer.'

Stewart had a pained look on his face. 'Tabitha,' he says in his low burr. 'You hired Xanthippe all week, but no lawyer?'

'We've established that I'm terrible at being a suspect,' I whisper frantically. 'It doesn't suit me at all.'

Inspector Fitzgerald clears his throat.

'Coming!' I announce cheerfully.

'I'm calling a lawyer,' Stewart mutters.

'I'm finishing off the pies,' Jase volunteers.

'Apple,' says Nin.

I give her a dirty look. 'Mango cream.'

Nin employs her eyebrows of judgement at me. 'Trying too hard.'

'They're Xanthippe's favourite.'

'Mango isn't even in season.'

'We'll discuss this later,' I say loudly.

Nin continues to be unimpressed with me, as I'm escorted out of my house in police custody. I'm glad someone around here has their priorities straight.

———————

It is a strange thing that I know at least three quarters of the local police by name, but hardly any lawyers. Most of my knowledge comes from feeding police officers, not being arrested by them.

Still, there's a very nice young woman called Matilda in a smart suit waiting for us at the police station. Further proof, if I needed it, that Stewart is magic.

'I don't mind answering their questions,' I tell her, straight out.

'Good. I'm here to make sure you only answer the

questions that you want to,' Matilda replies, shaking my hand.

That sounds okay. I can get behind that.

Fitzgerald is deeply unhappy about Matilda's presence. How churlish of him. He sits back and folds his arms while Constable Heather takes the lead in interviewing me.

'The fire service haven't given us their report on the scene yet,' she says conversationally. 'But we're treating it as a suspicious fire until they tell us otherwise.'

'Good,' I say indignantly. 'It *is* suspicious. Someone set fire to my café! That sort of thing doesn't just happen.' Near my café. On top of my café. Same difference.

'Why do you think arson was involved, Tabitha?' asks Heather gently.

'You don't have to answer that,' interrupts Matilda, in case I had missed the memo.

'Because this is what Cameron Crewe does,' I say impatiently.

Both police officers exchange glances. Even my lawyer looks baffled.

Fitzgerald speaks at last. 'Are you saying that Cameron Crewe, the celebrity chef who died six days ago, set fire to your building?'

No, obviously I'm not … huh.

'I'm not ruling out the possibility,' I say, and fold my arms to mimic his.

'There's no reason to be hostile,' says Heather gently.

'This is an appropriate amount of hostile,' I snap back. 'Someone set fire to my building. Xanthippe nearly died. And—someone did die.' I still remember the awful noise of that sports bag hitting the ground, as I was unlocking the gate to let the fire engine through to the courtyard. A sickening squelch of bone and flesh.

'Are you referring to the contents of the sports bag?' Heather asks.

I stare at her. 'That's kinda cold.'

'Silverside.'

'I'm—what now?'

'Several hundred dollars worth of silverside. Corned beef, you know?'

'I know what silverside is.' I'm jarred back to my memory of the courtyard, staring at a smoky, woozy Xanthippe as they checked her vitals before loading her into the ambulance.

Xanthippe shoved her phone into my hand and said something along the lines of 'I found her Ani, I didn't let her burn.' I assumed ... hell, *Xanthippe* assumed...

'I need to discuss something with my lawyer,' I say suddenly.

'Ms Darling, you are not currently under arrest,' Inspector Fitzgerald growls. 'But that does not mean we have endless time and patience.'

I know what he's doing—trying to make me feel

intimidated. But he hasn't arrested me yet, so I still have some power here.

'I have some information to share,' I say calmly. 'I want to check it out with Matilda first.'

Fitzgerald throws another deathglare in my direction, but he and Detective Constable Heather give us the room.

'This sounds promising,' says Matilda. 'What have we got?'

I'm getting rather attached to her. I wonder what her favourite kind of pie is.

———————

Fifteen minutes later, when the Inspector and Heather return, Xanthippe's slightly cracked phone is sitting face up on the table between us. 'So here's the thing,' I say in my serious voice, or as serious as I've ever been able to make my voice. 'Remember how during that very long night of you asking me aggressive questions about Cameron Crewe, I told you that I had been receiving threatening text messages for weeks? You didn't seem terribly interested, but you did try to use the police report I filed about it to scare me into admitting all kinds of things that weren't true.'

'Go on,' says Inspector Fitzgerald, giving nothing away.

'Well, I may not have chosen to emphasise it at the time...'

'Due to stress, lack of sleep and general shock,' Matilda puts in.

'Yes, that. But I think those messages were sent to me by one of Cameron Crewe's employees. I found out on the day of his death that he made an offer on my café's building. His business model for opening new bars has always involved pushing established, successful and independent operators out of prime positions.'

'What makes you think it was someone working for him, and not Crewe himself?' Detective Constable Heather asks me.

'Um, because I've met him? That man hasn't chopped an onion for himself in the last five years. Also, whoever sent me those messages is still out there.' I push Zee's poor battered phone towards them. 'Check out the images Xanthippe Carides was sent earlier today, before the fire started. They're from an anonymous number—not the same one that contacted me, but the texting style is similar. All caps shouting, and all that.'

I have to hope that sharing this is what she meant me to do when she took the password lock off her phone.

Heather blanches at the images of the dead girl saved to Zee's photo app. Fitzgerald is unmoved.

'Think about it,' I say. 'There wasn't a body in that bag, okay,' hooray for that, 'but someone *wanted* us to think that there was one. Like someone wanted to lure Xanthippe down to the first floor, with these pictures.'

'But if Xanthippe died in the fire, and her phone was

destroyed, no one would have known about those pictures,' Heather objects.

I shrug. 'Maybe they didn't think she would check it out without forwarding the pics to someone she trusted. Maybe they were trying to get her to find the fire and put it out before it spread too far—it might have been intended as a warning. I don't know. You're the police.'

'Indeed we are,' says Fitzgerald. 'And while this conspiracy of corned beef and faked photographs is a charming diversion, I think I would prefer to continue asking the questions, if that's all right with you?' His voice was like acid on the skin.

'So, you're not interested in the information that whoever was sending messages on behalf of Crewe is likely to be the same person who killed him?' I suggest.

'Right now, I'm interested in who started the fire,' says Fitzgerald smoothly. 'What exactly is the nature of your relationship with Xanthippe Carides?'

Matilda leaned forward, on alert. 'You don't have to answer that.'

'She's my friend. Who almost died today, because she was hit on the head and left in a burning building!'

'That's one interpretation of events.'

I stare at him, mouth open. 'How else do you interpret it?'

'It's not the first time that Ms Carides has faked a crime…'

'How do you even know about—no comment.' Shut up, Tabitha. Engage shutting up mode.

Fitzgerald lifts his eyebrows at me. Seriously, his eyebrows are vicious. They could give Nin a run for her money. 'I am not the media, Ms Darling. I know you like your headlines, but...'

'What exactly are you accusing me of?' I hear my voice rising in panic.

'And we're done here,' Matilda says crisply. 'I'm not sure why you feel it is necessary to question my client with such hostility, Inspector, but she is a victim of today's fire, and she came here of her own volition to help you with your inquiries.'

'We'll need a witness statement about Ms Darling's movements today, her insurance details, and that phone,' says Inspector Fitzgerald.

'I'll supervise the witness statement,' says Constable Heather in a low voice.

Fitzgerald nods once, and then storms out.

'Are you going to arrest me if I state for the record that your boss is an arsehole?' I ask Constable Heather.

Matilda clicks her tongue at me. 'Oh, you're going to be a handful.'

= **25** =

Xanthippe Takes Drastic Measures

'You're sure about this,' said my brother as we approached Tabitha's house.

I rolled my eyes at him. He'd been acting like a broody hen ever since I woke up in hospital with him hovering over me. 'I'm fine, Leo.'

'You don't even have a room here any more...'

'Well, since my office is too smoke-damaged to set foot in right now—' No one was allowed in the building until it was deemed safe given the extreme fire damage on the first floor. 'This is the next best option.'

'You don't think it would be better to go home for a few days...'

'Mama's place is not home,' I said pointedly. 'And I think living under the same roof would be a terrible idea, thanks for asking.'

'You could stay at mine?'

I tried to hold it in but couldn't help laughing at that

suggestion. 'Yeah, no, same answer. I love you, Leo, but let's keep things at a sensible distance, shall we? I can curl up on a couch at Tabitha's until everything else is sorted.'

What I didn't say was that Tabitha, Ceege and Jason were squishy and vulnerable, and someone had to keep an eye on them. Whoever was behind this took me down, and I'm tougher than the three of them put together. At least, I thought I was before someone hit me on the back of the head and left me in a burning building with a (apparently fake) corpse in a sports bag.

What was with that, anyway? Why send me a picture of Ani's dead body, and then try to burn down the building with a bag full of meat? What was the intended endgame of that scenario? Why not burn the actual body?

I still had my key from when I lived here, so I let myself in by the kitchen door at the back. The kitchen, it turned out, was full of pies.

Not just pies. Mango cream pies. The madam president of pies. They are my favourite thing that Tabitha makes for the café, though she hardly ever puts them on the specials board. I have a suspicion that every time I hint that she should make them more often, she adds four weeks to their next appearance, so I've learned not to ask.

'Huh,' I said aloud.

The internal door opened, and Tabitha's cat Kinky Boots slinked out, eyeing the table full of pies. I tensed, prepared to defend them at any cost if necessary. Before I had to make a decision, Ceege followed Kinky Books into the kitchen and picked her up.

'Mangoes aren't even in season,' I said.

Ceege laughed at me. 'She missed you, babes. And she felt super guilty.' Somehow, I didn't think he was talking about the cat.

'Is she around?'

He shrugged. 'Tabs? She had to go meet with Darrow's insurance people or something. Cuppa?'

'Hell yes.' I dropped my bag in the corner. It held the smoke-ruined clothes I'd been wearing during the fire, and not much else. I had hopes of saving the leather jacket, but the rest would have to be trashed. 'Is it okay if I stay here?'

'Duh.' He put the kettle on.

I don't think I properly appreciated the benefit of living here when I actually did. 'You're the best, Ceege.'

'I know.' He went on to prove it, by making me a cup of tea. 'How you feeling?'

I coughed. 'Lungs sore, throat sore. Smoke is the worst.'

'And here I thought you were just doing cabaret sexy voice.'

'I wish. Feel the lump on my head, though.' I leaned in, to show him.

Ceege kept his hands to himself. 'That's super gross, Zeecakes.'

'Sorry, I'll try for an elegant cheek scar next time, or something that can be covered by an eye-patch.'

He passed me the Convict City Roller Derby mug. 'What's your next plan?'

My plan. What was my plan? My office was inaccessible and/or charred to a crisp. My hair smelled more like hospital than I smelled like fire, but that wasn't a major improvement. Someone had tried to kill me.

'I'm going to take a bubble bath,' I announced.

Ceege snorted. 'Who do you think you are, Tabitha?'

The idea was growing on me. 'I could do worse than act like Tabitha. She's the mystery-solver around here.'

'Mostly by accident.'

I ignored him. 'I've had zero luck as myself, lately. Tabitha has a better hit rate than I do with untangling stupid, messy mysteries on this scale.'

There was a gleam in Ceege's eye. 'A bubble bath isn't going to cut it. To think like Tabitha, you have to do everything she would do.'

I nodded seriously. 'Ballgowns?'

'Ballgowns.'

We dressed up in girl clothes. I washed my hair in Tabitha's bathroom, and stole one of her Oscar frocks. She and Ceege had a pet dressmaker with a talent for making comfortable replicas of famous designer wear, who was happy to work for baked goods and home IT support.

'I hate how good you look in fake Valentino,' Ceege complained, as I arranged myself comfortably on the couch in red strapless satin.

'It's a curse.'

He was in black sequined tulle, Marilyn Monroe style. I'd missed seeing him in frocks since he went all serious dayjob on us.

'Right,' I said. 'Thinking like Tabitha.'

'You need to talk to more people,' Ceege suggested.

I groaned behind a cushion. People were the worst. 'I've done nothing but talk to people all week, it's horrible. I was promised a lifestyle of hard drinking, taking dodgy pictures in the middle of the night, and organised crime payoffs.'

Ceege frowned at me. 'Possibly you shouldn't have based your career plan around detectives in old movies?'

'If old movies don't speak the truth about our lives, what's the point of anything?'

He grinned approvingly at me. '*Now* you sound like Tabitha.'

By the time Jason rolled in with a case of beer on his hip, we progressed to making an elaborate mind map of the case so far, using marshmallows and licorice strips.

'What the hell are you doing?' the teenager proclaimed in

his 'I am the only grown up in this household' voice.

'Oh, I know this one,' volunteered Stewart as he trailed into the house behind Jason. 'They're pretending to be Tabitha. Works every time.'

'Do you actually live here?' I grumbled at him.

'Gotta have a Scotsman to kiss, to make the Tabitha experiment more authentic,' Jason said solemnly, giving Stewart a shove on his way to make coffee.

Truly, his coffee skills were the only reason that kid had lived this long.

'I was promised pie, not kisses,' Stewart shot back, following him.

'Stay away from those pies, those are my survival pies, no one eats them but me!' I yelled after them into the kitchen.

'Sorry, I cannae hear ye, there's all this mango cream muffling your words...'

'Back to the case,' I said, giving Ceege a stern look.

'I can't remember, are the pink marshmallows the suspects, or the victims?' He had a suspicious ring of white powder around his mouth, as if he had been eating suspects when I wasn't looking.

I gave up on the lolly map and pulled out a notebook to make a proper list of priorities. 'Throwing knives was a red herring, but the three sous-clones are still damned suspicious.'

'Four!' Jason called from the kitchen.

'Aye don't forget the mysterious Otto Parrish AKA Previous Lief,' Stewart agreed, wandering back into the room with a plate of pie and only one fork.

I nodded, making a note of it. 'Our man Otto was in Hobart until he was fired by Crewe in Week Two, though we don't know his movements between then and Week Six. Did he go back to Sydney?'

'Petula Parrish definitely didn't fly in until the morning of the press conference,' said Ceege, his tulle rustling as he leaned in for more marshmallows.

I stared at him. 'And you're sure of this because…'

'Because I read gossip magazines? Duh. The paps have been on High Baby Bump Patrol for months. They took pictures of the Saucy Chef in Sydney airport even before they knew where she was headed—and those pics went viral once they revealed the whole secret marriage, dead chef thing.'

I was starting to realise why Tabitha never bothered much about social media—she had Ceege to cover her blind spots.

'Pretty sure Petula wouldn't be the murderer,' said Ceege. 'She dresses way too nice to do her own stabbings.'

'That reminds me of something Tabitha said,' I mused. 'That Cameron Crewe wouldn't do his own dirty work—driving tenants out of their businesses. He'd hire someone to do it. That brings us back to Earl and Lief and the other Lief and Grey.'

'Or some other person working for him we don't know,' added Jason, as he brought in a coffee pot and tray of cups. This hospitality training of his was working out great. Stewart swayed towards the coffee pot like a vampire scenting a tasty neck. 'He must have a long line of pissed off former employees back in Sydney. It doesn't have to be a local who killed him, or set the fire. Assuming they're the same person?'

Stewart downed a third of a cup of coffee before pouring for the rest of us. It smelled amazing. Real coffee with a hint of hazelnut and not a whiff of hospital canteen. 'We should check in on the other cafés, aye? I never heard whether The Chocolate Teapot had anyone offering to buy their building, but they might no' have told me if they had. Family business, ye know.'

'I need to talk to the #Sconebros crew, see if anyone knows what the deal is with them telling us Ani went back to New Zealand,' I said. 'This sounds like a plan.'

'I'm not wearing a frock,' Stewart informed me.

I sighed, looking down at my own red satin. Fake Valentino would look so good in my matching sports car. 'I'll change.'

Stewart came with me to #Sconebros. Tabitha still wasn't back from her insurance appointment, Jase had a culinary college exam to prep for, and Ceege was refusing to remove his Marilyn Monroe for the rest of the day.

I borrowed black jeans, a hoodie and even underwear from Tabitha's room without asking. I was pretty sure the jeans were originally mine. I'd have to buy new clothes soon, damn it. Every time I thought about my flat and my stuff and the fire, my brain shut down, not prepared to deal with all that shit yet.

Speaking of denial, the #Sconebros tent was nowhere in sight. 'Did they move on? Pop up somewhere else?'

'The couch is still there,' Stewart noted, hurrying along the beach.

The bright acid-green couch was indeed still sitting on the sandy grass of Marieville Esplanade, along with the vinyl coffee table. The rest of their set up—everything from the tables and tent, to the blackboard—was gone as if it was never there.

'If I still had a flat, I would totally steal this couch,' I mused. 'Where the hell did they go?'

As we stood there, a van pulled up, taking over two parking spaces. I saw Maaka at the wheel and he hesitated, as if he was about to back right out again rather than talk to me.

'Wave and look unthreatening,' I said to Stewart,

pasting a friendly smile on my face.

'I always look unthreatening, it's my best talent,' Stewart commented. He lifted a hand in Maaka's direction.

Maaka made his decision, and loped over to us. 'Hey, bros, help a fella out moving a couch?'

'I hope you're talking to me, because I'm the one with the muscles,' I said.

Stewart stepped on my foot. 'Low blow, bro.'

I wrinkled my nose at him. 'Stewart, you're not allowed to say bro unless you do something about your accent. Why aren't you Australian yet?'

'Working on it, lassie.'

I kicked his shin, but only a bit.

Stewart and I took one end of the couch, and Maaka the other. 'I didn't realise you were a pop-up,' I said, keeping my voice light and casual. 'Where to next? There's a lot of good beaches to choose from.'

Maaka made a fair attempt at a shrug considering he was taking more than his share of the couch's weight. 'Yeah, nah. We're done. Bruce and the rest of my staff got offers to work on Petula Parrish's new show in Sydney—she's launching some restaurant chain to go with it.'

'You didn't fancy fame and fortune on minimum wage?' I asked.

'Not for me, bro. I hated working the Sydney restaurant scene. Too cut-throat, too many wankers. And after what happened to Ani...' He shook his head slowly. 'Nah, I'm going home to Wellington. Got my ticket booked and everything, flying out straight after the last filming session for *Café Wars*.' He laughed hollowly. 'Be funny if I won considering I don't have a café any more.'

'Does anyone know what happened to her?' I blurted. We got as far as the van, and lifted the beautifully horrible piece of furniture into the back. I could see the awning and other #Sconebros furnishings stacked in there. 'I mean— other than the picture I gave the police. Have they found Ani?'

'Nah, bro, still searching. They reckon she's somewhere in the building that nearly burnt down.' His usually cheerful face had closed over. 'I don't know what to think. Thought I knew her. But I found these hidden when we took down the kitchen.' He fished around in the van and pulled out a sealed plastic bag containing several cheap phones. 'You should have them, I reckon. Still on the case, aren't you, glam detective?'

'Aye, she is,' said Stewart, before I could answer. Was there even a case worth solving any more? As long as Tabitha stayed in the clear, my job was done. Right?

The two of them went back to grab the vinyl table and finished loading up. I leaned against the van and turned on one of the phones, using the plastic bag to keep my prints off it. It came to life with an easy buzz of pale green light, and I scrolled through recent messages.

They were all made to a familiar number—Tabitha's number—and full of aggressive, empty threats. Well, maybe not so empty. Another phone proved to be the one that had sent images of Ani's body to me, the day of the fire. I left that alone and opened a third, only to stare at the contents.

'I'm off, bro,' said Maaka, giving Stewart a complicated handslap thing. 'See you at the Bikky Battle, Week Eight.'

'Righto,' Stewart agreed. We both stepped back as Maaka pulled out of the parking space, driving off with the last pieces of #Sconebros packed into the back of his van. Stewart blew out a long breath. 'So, that's two o' the three *Café Wars* contestants, out of business.'

I gave him a dirty look. 'Tabitha will stage a comeback. You know she will.'

'I meant for now.'

'Whatever.' I tossed the bag of phones into the back of my Spider. 'We need to check on Daisy and Dot.'

'I'm worried about how they're coping wi' all this,' he agreed.

'I was thinking more, asking them about the secret death threats that our mystery phone-bandit has been sending them but okay, that too.'

≡ 26 ≡

Xanthippe Gets a Clue

I felt severely underdressed as Daisy served tea to Stewart and me on her back verandah, away from the main part of the café. Maybe I should have kept the frock on.

'Yes, there were some nasty phone messages,' Daisy said in a low voice, sounding distressed. 'I'm sure you can imagine the sort of thing.'

I didn't have to imagine it, because I made Stewart read the messages aloud to me while I drove over. Then we had to sit in the car quietly for fifteen minutes while he got over being unspeakably furiously Scottish about what kind of arsehole would send messages like that to nice old ladies who run tea shops.

'Why did ye not tell me about this?' Stewart asked now. The edge to his voice suggested I should have made it twenty minutes, not fifteen.

'Nothing to bother you young ones about,' Daisy said, fiddling with a crocheted doily. 'There isn't much they could threaten us with—Dot and I own the property out-right. I don't know if you've dealt in real estate in recent years, but the threats had not escalated to a point that we'd even consider trying to sell. We didn't tell Zandra either. She would have jumped to all kinds of conclusions, or possibly gone around hitting and spray-painting any suspects. It was best ignored.'

'I heard that!' complained their punk niece, joining us from the kitchen. 'The cheek of it. I hardly ever spray-paint people out of revenge.'

'So reassuring,' Daisy sighed.

'Did messages stop after Cameron Crewe died?' I knew the answer to this one, as we had the phones that had sent the messages. I knew that the most recent was sent yester-day, which had to mean that Ani wasn't the one sending them, despite the presence of the phones at #Sconebros.

Maaka thought Ani was behind it all, but she was already dead when the last message was sent. Wasn't she?

Mind you, sending someone photos of yourself looking like a corpse shortly before burning down the building—that was a hell of an effective way to fake your own death.

My life. Most people get through entire careers without ever having to think about methods of faking your own death.

Daisy and Dot looked at me expectantly, which made me realise I had let some of the polite conversation drift along without actually listening.

'They were wondering if there was any news about Ani,' Stewart said in his low burr.

'That poor girl,' said Daisy. 'She was Zandra's age.'

'Well,' said Dot, and pressed her mouth together. 'Not saying she deserved anything that happened to her. But I don't think she minded the attention from Chef Crewe at all.'

'Aunt Dot!' said Zandra, livid. 'You do remember what he was like at the party here, don't you?'

'Oh I know he had no business putting his hands all over you, dear,' Dot said firmly. 'And I have no objection to how our knight in shining armor handled the matter.'

Stewart looked startled and—was he blushing?

'I missed something,' I said, leaning into him. 'What haven't you been telling me, McTavish?'

Zandra mimed a punch above her aunts' heads, and blew Stewart a kiss.

'Have there been hijinks I don't know about?' I demanded.

'Chef Crewe had an accident involving a mug of soup,' said Stewart with a completely blank face.

Zandra mimed another punch, to the eye this time, and made a 'pow' sound effect to go with it.

'Stop that right now, young lady,' said Daisy, but she was laughing.

My phone buzzed with an unknown number. I looked at

it, hesitating. Stewart leaned over my shoulder. 'D'ye want me...'

'Oh please, save your protective streak for literally everyone else we know.' I answered the phone. 'Who is this?'

'Uh, Xanthippe?' The voice was vaguely familiar. 'This is Quinn. Assistant forensic assistant at the morgue. You know, Tabitha's friend from the Glitter and Gimlets night...'

'I remember you.' I shook my head to let Stewart know it was nothing to worry about, and walked a little distance from the table, across The Chocolate Teapot back yard. 'How can I help?'

'I called Tabs, but she wanted me to talk directly to you. You're investigating the fire at Café La Femme now?'

'In a manner of speaking.' Which was to say, if I found out who was responsible, I planned on punching them in the face a bunch of times.

'I spent some time with the arson crew, sifting through the building yesterday,' said Quinn. Oh, I didn't like the sound of 'sifting'. Especially if they felt the need to have one of the mortuary technicians involved.

'How's the second floor looking?' I couldn't help asking. My precious detective office.

'We didn't go up that high, but the first floor is holding together structurally—just about. It's not bad enough to condemn the building, from what the building inspectors were saying.'

I felt the urge to grab a paper bag and start huffing into it. 'Never mind the building, what were you doing in there? Don't you spend your work day in that little cold room poking at dead bodies?'

'They were looking for a body,' Quinn said dryly. 'Something about photos of a corpse on that floor before or during the fire?' Yes, made sense. 'As it's an ongoing investigation, I'm obviously *not* supposed to tell anyone that we found exactly zero dead bodies, especially not the body of a certain missing person called Ani Wilson, who is a person of interest in the Cameron Crewe case.'

'Got you,' I said, keeping it cool. No Ani in the building, despite the photos. Did that mean my outlandish 'faking her own death' theory was correct, and she was actually alive somewhere? Huh.

'And I'm definitely not supposed to tell you that the body of Ani Wilson was pulled out of the Derwent in the early hours of this morning.'

I did not feel faint. Faint was for heroines in those old-fashioned musicals Tabitha watches instead of paying for psychotherapy or sleeping pills. 'Can you tell me how long ago she died?'

'Course I can't tell you that, what do you take me for?' said Quinn. 'Four hours. Definitely no more than four hours, she was pretty fucking fresh if you know what I mean.'

Private investigator or no private investigator, I didn't ever want to know exactly what he meant.

'Four hours, you're sure?' Faked her own death … and then died anyway. Creepy.

'Yep. Those photos of her corpse that someone delivered to the police? Definitely fakes. Unless there's some sort of time travel subplot going on here…'

'Let's assume not. Um, thanks, Quinn. I appreciate this.'

'I didn't do anything,' he said quickly. 'Less than nothing. And if coincidentally Tabitha has promised to join my team for Hollywood trivia night for the next six months, then you can consider us square. Let us never speak of this again!'

'Works for me.' I hung up, and turned back to Stewart and the others. 'When does Week Eight start?'

'That lovely Petula Parrish sent one of her assistants around to inform us the last filming block would be on Wednesday,' said Daisy. 'I'll be glad to be done with it all, I can tell you.'

'Excellent. That gives me a couple of days to figure out what Tabitha is scheming, and get in on it.'

Stewart blinked. 'What do ye—'

'Oh come on, give me some credit. Am I really supposed to believe that Tabitha Darling spent all of today dealing with insurance forms?'

He looked guilty. It wasn't a long way from his usual

facial expression, but I could tell the difference. 'How much do ye know?'

'I spent several hours wearing a ballgown and thinking like Tabitha today, so let's assume I've guessed everything.'

His suspicious look was much easier to read than his guilty look. 'Let's ... not?'

Well, it was worth a try.

'I know that Tabitha's got far too much style and curiosity to give up on sleuthing when a big fat murder mystery falls into her lap. She hates giving up on things she's good at. That's how she got talked into running a café in the first place.' I pointed a finger at him. 'Has she solved this already? Am I a red herring?'

Stewart looked shifty. 'Surely she would have told someone if she solved it?'

I loomed over him, still holding on to my vintage teacup. 'Yes, yes, she would have told someone. And I think we all know who she would have told—that is, everyone that isn't me. Is this why Jason volunteered himself as sidekick, to follow me around? Have you and Tabitha been playing detective all along?'

Stewart hesitated, then shrugged hopelessly. 'Where she goes, I follow. Ye know that.'

'Yes, it's all very romantic,' I grated. 'But right now, I'm distracted by planning a murder all of my own, and you just volunteered to be the first corpse!' I got into his face with my most intimidating gaze. 'Where. Is. Tabitha?'

'She went to visit Petula Parrish at her hotel,' he admitted reluctantly, with a guilty look at Daisy and Dot. They didn't look surprised either. Was everyone in on this apart from me?

I blinked. 'You let her go alone, to search for a murderer?'

'The Saucy Chef isn't a suspect,' Stewart protested. 'She wasn't even in the state when Cameron Crewe was killed.'

'No, but her son was. And we've already established that celebrity chefs don't do their own dirty work.' I grabbed Stewart's arm. 'Come on. Let's get out of here and rescue Tabitha *before* she actually needs rescuing, for once.'

Tabitha Brings the Sauce
(and the Mango Cream)

Cherish Parrish, daughter of the Saucy Chef, is a droopy sort of girl when there isn't a camera on her. She wears a whole lot of product in her hair, but her smile doesn't meet her eyes.

'You'll want to talk to my mother,' she mutters, like there is no other reason a visitor might be at the door of their hotel suite.

'Tabitha Darling. I have an appointment,' I say brightly. Making friends with the downtrodden is an excellent way to gather info. Cherish doesn't seem to care.

'I'm not her secretary,' she sighs, and walks out of the suite with a towel over one shoulder, either looking for the pool or, well, there might be other reasons. It's not polite to inquire that closely.

The hotel suite is larger than most flats I've ever been in—not only featuring bedrooms, balcony, and by the looks of it, multiple bathrooms, but also a sunken lounge area in the centre of the main room, and a massive display kitchen.

Who pays this much for a hotel room and cooks their own meals? No, wait, that's me, I would totally do that.

Petula Parrish has either been expecting me, or she spends most of her life in a constant state of pose. She sprawls on the white couch in a Cruella De Ville jacket over a fine linen suit, with cucumber slices resting on her eyelids. Her belly is perfectly round, like she was sculpted out of bread dough. The suit has to be custom-made—I've never seen maternity clothes quite so well-fitting before.

'Tabitha Darling,' she says in a breathy, made-for-audiobooks voice. 'Trying to get ahead of the competition, are you?'

Must not hyperventilate in the presence of your culinary hero, must not. This isn't the first time I've talked to her given her new role in charge of *Café Wars*, and the chaotic filming session at Salamanca. Still, it doesn't get any easier to face off against the Saucy Chef like she's a real person.

'Not sure if you heard,' I say, playing it cool. 'But my café burned down. So the prize stopped being worthwhile and cruised all the way to tragic irony some days ago.' Every time I say 'my café burned down' it hurts a little less. No, that's not true. It's never going to hurt less.

She removes the cucumber slices and bats her raw eyelashes at me. Has any human ever seen Petula Parrish's eyes devoid of makeup, mascara and extra lashes?

Such an honour, I can barely stand it.

'You've all had such bad luck since you signed up with Cameron's show,' she agrees coolly. 'If you have any questions about the Week Eight Bikky Battle, I suggest you contact Ms Nagarra.'

'No, I'm good for that, thanks. All themed up and ready to bake. I was hoping to talk to your son Otto.'

Petula arches her neck in order to more effectively stare down her nose at me. 'Why on earth would you want to do that?'

'He was working in Chef Crewe's kitchen, for the first two weeks of *Café Wars*.'

Petula's face hardens. It's a barely imperceptible shift, but it makes her look more angular and threatening than her usual squishy, seductive TV personality. 'No he wasn't.'

'Um, yes he was. We all saw him. He was calling himself Lief, but he was definitely … I mean, you can check the videos.'

I watched them myself and noticed how often the first Lief tugged his hat down or turned at the last moment, to avoid being properly framed by the lens. He clearly didn't want to be there. Was that why Chef Crewe (AKA his secret step-dad) replaced him so quickly?

Petula stands up, arching her back like a goddess emerging from the foam. 'OTTO!' she howls into the bowels of her palatial hotel suite.

There is a pause and a brief scurrying sound, before her son emerges. He doesn't look capable of handling the hard grind of working in a professional kitchen, least of all for a demanding boss like Cameron Crewe.

Otto is about Jase's age, barely twenty if that, a scrawny kid in torn jeans and a designer hoodie. Total sad sack. His sneakers are so trendy that they practically hover two centimetres off the ground, but he hasn't bothered to tie the laces. Kids today.

'Were you working for that bastard when he started his little show?' Petula roars. 'I thought you were on a road trip of discovery with your stoner friends.'

Otto's eyes widen, and he takes a step back. 'Chef … uh, Cameron offered to teach me the business, and the pay was good.'

'You got a JOB?' Petula is ropable. 'We weren't *talking* to him then, you little shit. He must have been trying to pump you for information about my lawyers…'

'What does it even matter?' Otto yells back at her. 'He fired me after two weeks because he said I cracked eggs like a pussy. Can't wait to see what kind of dickhead you hook up with next time around!'

I back slowly towards the door. There are times when observing other families going into meltdown is a way to glean useful information, and then there's the fine art of knowing when to make yourself scarce. I don't want to be in that room when Petula realises she let her showbiz façade slip in front of a civilian, and a stranger. That manicure of hers could do damage.

In the last instant, before I leave, I notice a scattered handful of hotel keycards on the glass table, and I pocket one. No one sees me do it.

Mother and son are still screaming at each other when I let myself out of the suite. Xanthippe and Stewart lean against the apricot walls of the corridor, facing the door. Waiting for me. Busted.

Stewart gives an apologetic wave.

'Given up the amateur detective lark, have we?' says Xanthippe, quirking her eyebrow. 'You know it's bad manners to hire someone for a job and then do the work yourself.'

'They burned my café, Zee,' I say with a hint of tremble in my lip.

She catches hold of my elbow and drags me to the lift. 'That lip wobble of yours would be much more sympathetic if I wasn't on to your game. Time to pool our resources, Tish.'

'I made you mango cream pie,' I remind her hopefully.

'Believe me, sweetheart, that's the only reason I haven't pushed you out a window.'

———

The secret to a good cream pie is that the crust has to embody the perfect balance of smooth and firm textures. The filling should taste somewhere between amazing and ambrosia. I'm a fan of pairing sour flavours with the sweet—lemon meringue is a classic for a reason, and it's my personal mission to make rhubarb the new blueberry.

I prefer to source my fruit locally, but nowhere on this island is good for growing a decent mango until climate change pushes us closer to the apocalypse. We import our mangos, bananas and avocados from the hot and steamy end of the country.

Xanthippe loves mangoes. She doesn't care about food the way I do. She prefers scent to taste, and is capable of living on the same noodle recipe for two weeks in a row, with occasional peanut butter sandwiches to liven things up. She eats steamed vegetables all the time with *nothing on them*, not to keep her figure trim, but because she doesn't get excited about what she consumes.

It used to drive me around the bend, her disinterest in food adventures, until I figured out about the mangoes.

I went to a therapist a couple of times, after the whole kidnapping incident the year before last. He told me I have a pattern of using food to manipulate people. I responded by sending a batch of the best brownies he was ever going to taste to his office. I then severed all contact.

In retrospect, he may have had a point.

Finding a food that Xanthippe genuinely cares about is a gift that keeps on giving—I feel so much better having a recipe stash for when she's having a crappy week, or nearly died in a fire or whatever. Something I can withhold when she is pissing me off. It's reassuring.

When we return to the house from Petula Parrish's hotel suite, I realise that I've been waiting a long time to throw a mango cream pie directly in Xanthippe Carides' perfect face.

I would never act on that impulse. What a terrible waste of pie. And yet...

I'm not entirely ruling it out.

'What are we doing, Tish?' she explodes as soon as we are back inside my kitchen. 'Are you so nostalgic for my brother's lectures on irresponsibility that you want to turn me into your new bad guy?'

'No! Maybe. What?'

'I'm gonna...' says Stewart, edging towards the living room door.

'Stay there, traitor,' I snap at him, at the same time that Xanthippe says:

'You're part of this too, McTavish, don't you move an inch!'

'I'm a little scared of ye both right now,' he informs us. 'And I cannae deal with this without coffee.'

I wave him towards the plunger. 'Knock yourself out.'

Xanthippe sits down at my kitchen table, with a spread

of mango cream pies between us. I check they've cooled properly and begin popping them away in the fridge. You don't let good food spoil because of drama.

I leave one pie out, deliberately. I fetch plates, a whacking great knife, cake forks, then arrange all of them between us on the table. 'So we need to talk.'

Xanthippe leans in, cuts herself a piece of pie and puts it on a plate for herself. 'You start. Who killed Cameron Crewe?'

'The same person he was paying to scare me out of my business,' I say automatically.

'Suspects?'

'The creepy kitchen assistants, including Petula Parrish's creepier son Otto.'

Xanthippe raises an eyebrow. One of these days I'll train myself to do that. It's unfair to be surrounded by people who can do eyebrow gymnastics while I'm stuck with ordinary facial expressions. 'And?'

I cut myself a piece of pie. 'And everyone who works at The Chocolate Teapot,' I mutter.

'Hey!' Stewart protests.

'Except Stewart.'

'Aye, well. Since when are Daisy and Dot suspects?'

I cut him a piece of pie, to soothe his outrage. 'Daisy and Dot and Zandra. Since they are the only *Café Wars* contestants whose business hasn't tanked in the last week,

Stewart, get with the program.'

'You're missing Ani,' Xanthippe says, taking a bite of mango cream. She might be pissed off at me, but that doesn't stop her exhaling softly as the flavour hits her mouth—and it doesn't stop me glowing with professional pride.

'I liked Ani,' I admit reluctantly.

'I like Daisy and Dot,' Stewart huffs, but we both ignore him.

'I appreciate you telling Quinn to share the intel about Ani's body with me,' Xanthippe adds grudgingly.

'It sucks that she's dead. I wanted to help her—Kari and I both did. She was one of a long line of Crewe's victims. But unless she threw herself into the river out of guilt...'

'Quinn would have told us if suicide was a likely ruling. Wouldn't he?'

'Then she can't have killed Crewe.'

'That's not logical, Tish.'

I take a big bite of mango cream pie. 'I don't like the idea that there are two murderers running around. Seems like overkill.'

'Oh by all means, let's just agree that the idea of murder is generally distasteful and have a tea party instead!' Xanthippe is at the end of her rope. Still, I choose to believe she's less stressed than she would be without the influence of pie.

'Tell Tabitha about the phones,' Stewart urges her.

Xanthippe nodded. 'Maaka found a bag of phones when he dismantled #Sconebros. If one of his employees sent all the threats, they could also have faked Ani's death before the fire. She must have been involved. It's not easy to put corpse makeup on someone without their consent.'

'Threats were made to The Chocolate Teapot too,' Stewart says pointedly, continuing his agenda of pretending his adorable bosses are above suspicion.

'Someone silenced Ani,' I say slowly.

'Seems like,' said Xanthippe.

I thought about that for a few moments. 'You know you don't have to do this any more.'

Xanthippe stares at me like I've cut my head off with a butter knife. 'I don't what?'

'I panicked when the police kept treating me like a suspect. But they haven't actually arrested me, and I have a decent lawyer in case they do. So you could let the case drop. You don't have to help.'

Xanthippe drops her cake fork. 'Tabitha, someone didn't put that toffee knife in Crewe's chest because it would look super cute on Instagram. They were trying to frame you! They burned down our building! Giving up is your way of dealing with this shit, not mine.'

Her words sting. 'That's not fair.'

'Isn't it? You're the one who keeps playing detective like

it's a party game, and dropping it the second that the pota-
to gets hot. This isn't something you flirt with when you
feel like it, Tabitha. You're horribly good at solving crimes,
but you know that's mostly been down to luck.'

'I'm also good at pie,' I mutter.

'Yes,' Xanthippe says resentfully. 'You are excellent at
pie.' She eats more mango cream, to spite me. Or to prove
a point. Who can say why she does anything?

'So,' says Stewart after a long pause. 'How do we feel
about the theory that Ani knew who killed Cameron
Crewe, and someone killed her to keep her quiet?'

'Conflicted,' I say. 'I still think we need to be looking
more closely at Petula Parrish.'

'But she wasnae even in the state.'

'I know, but she was secretly married to Cameron Crewe,
and they were splitting up. Now he's dead, she gets his TV
show, his restaurants, she's handing out jobs like they're
candy, and as the cherry on the cake she gets the publicity
boost of being a grieving widow … she's made out like a
bandit from his death.'

The perfect alibi feels too good to be true. Has to be
suspicious, right?

'It's not enough,' Xanthippe says flatly. 'None of this is
enough—why do you think the police are having such
trouble? Why do you think no one has arrested you? We
need *evidence* to move forward.'

'Or we need to get everyone so rattled that the guilty person blurts out all their secrets over tea and scones,' I counter.

She gives me a tired look. 'That method is going to stop working for you sooner or later. Can we leave it as a last resort?'

'Fine.'

We eat our pie in silence.

'You're right,' I admit eventually.

Xanthippe stares at me, scraping up the last of the crumbs from her plate. 'I'm what now?'

'You're right. I'm not a professional detective, and I'm never going to be. My methods are slapdash, I already have a real job to care about, and if my life gets threatened, I'm likely to freak out and give up on the whole deal for six to twelve months. Based on past experience.'

Xanthippe gives me a highly cynical look. 'I am really regretting the ballgown thing.'

'The ballgown what now?' There was a ballgown thing and I missed it?

'Never mind, go on with the part about me being right.'

I sigh heavily. 'I have a natural talent for digging out secrets. That doesn't make me a detective. However, my whole chat-loudly-and-cause-distractions methods have their uses. For instance.' I slip the small white card out of my pocket and hand it over. 'I totally stole a keycard to

310

Petula Parrish's hotel suite. And I am not the person to do anything useful with it.'

Xanthippe gazes at me like I'm a stranger. 'Can I borrow Jason?'

'No, Jase is still technically on probation, he can't afford to get arrested. You can have Stewart.'

'Hey!' Stewart protests, then shrugs. 'Aye, fair enough. Let's go.'

= **28** =

Xanthippe Breaks and Enters

Stewart wore his chef whites from the show, which turned out to be a perfect infiltration-of-a-hotel outfit. I borrowed a plain black dress and white apron from Tabitha, and we all agreed not to discuss the fact that she had everything required to cosplay a maid easily to hand.

'So ye agree with Tabitha that Petula Parrish looks guilty?' Stewart asked as we went up in the lift.

'You mean apart from her airtight alibi? No, I think Tabitha is offering up her hero on a platter as some kin of personal sacrifice because she'd rather it turn out to be a hard-nosed celebrity than someone we like and trust.' I nudged him. 'Like your Daisy and Dot.'

'That does sound like Tabitha,' he said, looking mournful.

I eyed him sharply. 'I'm not going to ask.'

'Fine.'

'She was dating my brother. I have conflict of interest.'

'Aye,' said Stewart, giving me a piercing look. 'But ye

hated those two being together.'

'What? No I didn't. Shut up.' Now was not the time for soul searching about the innate awkwardness of your high school best friend dating your distant and disapproving big brother. 'Chef face on.'

Stewart went obediently blank-faced. 'Are we going with room service emergency, if we get caught?'

'I could have got you one of those trays with a giant silver dome over it to make you look less break and enter-y, but it was too much work.'

I checked my new phone. We had called upon the assistance of Team McTabitha, a group of teenage girls with home-printed t-shirts who leaped out randomly at Stewart whenever he ventured out in public.

They communicated with each other mostly via Snapchat, and had been doing a great job of stalking our three targets ever since Petula Parrish and her two children shared breakfast at the hotel buffet. 'Currently, Petula is at Teasperience setting up for tomorrow's Bikky Battle, Cherish is shopping aimlessly, and Otto appears to be kicking a tin can at some puppies in St David's Park,' I reported. 'Let's go!'

We let ourselves into the suite as if we belonged there.

'What are we looking for?' Stewart asked.

'Rubbish bin, electronic devices, appointment diary. A scrap of paper telling us who she's been talking to, and who might be enough in her thrall they'd be willing to take on a little job like stabbing her husband.'

'Apart from her legions of fans, do ye mean?'

'I'll take Otto's room,' I said firmly. 'That kid's got to be guilty of something.'

———————

Sadly Otto was mainly guilty of putting complex password protection on all of his electronic devices, which meant that a search of his hotel room taught me nothing about him except that he never picks up his damn socks.

I was about to rejoin Stewart when he hurried into Otto's room after me. 'Someone's here,' he whispered frantically.

I checked my phone. Team McTabitha informed me that the Parrishes were all still out and about at their various activities. 'Not one of the family.'

'They had a keycard,' he hissed.

'So did we, that doesn't mean anything.'

It was possible one of Petula's army of employees had access to the suite, not to mention hotel staff. I leaned into the door and peered through the crack. Definitely someone moving around in the main living area.

I caught a flash of bright pink hair, and realised who it was. Not an employee after all. An intruder like us, currently rifling through a bunch of papers left out on the bar.

'It's Zandra,' I mouthed to Stewart.

'What?' he said out loud and pushed open the door. 'Zandra, what the hell are ye doing here?'

'You are so not subtle,' I grumbled as I followed him. 'I'm returning you to Tabitha first chance I get. You are a terrible sidekick.'

'Stewart!' Zandra exclaimed. 'Why are you here?'

'I asked ye first,' he demanded.

She put her hands on her hips. She was wearing a bright orange shirt with blue suspenders, over a mini skirt and ripped fishnets. Quite apart from the pink hair, hers was the worst infiltration-of-a-hotel outfit I'd ever seen. 'Did you think I was going to ignore what you and the aunts have been keeping from me? Death threats much? It's so obvious Petula had something to do with it.'

Obvious to me, yes, but why was it obvious to Zandra? 'Do you know something we don't?'

'That Kiwi barista girl was still sending the threats to my aunts more than a week after Cameron Crewe died!' Zandra snarked back at me. 'So someone else must have paid her to do it. Either Parrish, or your cute little pigtail side salad girl.'

I blinked.

'I think she means Tabitha,' said Stewart, as awestruck as I was by that splendid piece of descriptive phrasing.

'Obviously I mean Tabitha,' groaned Zandra. 'She's the only other person who had the motive to drive my aunts out of business.'

'Tabitha wouldnae do that,' Stewart said in alarm. 'She loves your aunties.'

Love was an overstatement given the way Tabitha was known to hold grudges, but even I didn't think she would stoop to death threats.

My phone buzzed. 'Damn it, Cherish is on her way back. We missed our window!'

What a waste of a good keycard theft.

———————

I left Stewart to escort Zandra back to The Chocolate Teapot and her aunties.

Given my melancholy mood, it's hardly surprising that my feet took me across town to check on a certain fire-damaged building.

Café La Femme looked awful. The building was intact—knock wood, it was going to stay that way—but the sandstone bricks were blackened in patches, the windows were streaked with soot and the glass on the first floor had shattered under the heat.

The café itself hadn't suffered much in the way of smoke or scorching, though when I leaned into the windows I could see that the first floor ceilings were blackened and blistered.

It was going to take money to repair damage like this.

There was police tape everywhere, and a notice on the side stairs that the building was closed for renovations. No one should enter without permission.

Fuck that. My key still worked.

I made it all the way up to the second floor, deliberately looking away from the blackened mess that was the first floor office. Kept going up, until I saw my door.

Xanthippe Carides, Private Detective.

The flames had made it up this far. Standing right in front of the glass panel in the door, I could imagine the heat licking up around me—could see the traces of it in the black, bubbled surface of the varnished wood.

There was a layer of ash coating my door. When I wiped it with a tissue, the glass came away clean. I stared at it for a minute. I'd half thought I might take the opportunity to throw a few things in a bag—reclaim the important items that weren't too badly smoke damaged. Right then, in that moment, I couldn't think of anything that I could be bothered saving.

The air tasted vile, like exhaust fumes and plastic. I turned around, and went outside again.

Tabitha's courtyard—it's shared by the whole building and I'd been in residence for months, but I always thought of it as Tabitha's courtyard—wasn't looking as pristine and welcoming as usual. There were grooves in the gravel from the fire truck, and the chairs and tables were still scattered around. There was litter here and there, whipped in by the chill Antarctic winds that rush up from the docks at this time of year. I picked up a few chip packets and Coke cans, not wanting Tabitha to see the place looking this bad. Presumably she'd come back to check on it at some point.

'Hello, Carides.'

I paused, very slowly, and turned around with my hands full of garbage. 'Darrow. About time you turned up to sort out this mess.'

My ex is a beautiful man. Wide shoulders in an expensive suit, long chestnut hair, and a voice that sounds like sex on the radio.

He has style, imagination, a sense of humour, and a stupid amount of money. He's the kind of man that's very hard to dump.

It hadn't occurred to me until this instant that there were a lot of similarities between Darrow and Cameron Crewe. A similar physical type, they both throw their ego around like it's worth its own wardrobe and townhouse. They both take—took, in Cameron's case—command of situations, presiding over every room and conversation they step into.

The main difference now was that only one of them was still alive.

'Naturally,' Darrow said. 'Can't have my favourite source of sticky hazelnut puddings out of business for long. How do you think Tabitha would feel about running a food truck? Just until the building's back up to code.'

I blinked at him. 'I can totally see that. Better make her think that it's her idea, though.'

'I'm not new.'

No matter what went wrong between us, we'd always have our long-standing tradition of bitching about Tabitha behind her back.

Darrow looked up at the windows, his face troubled. 'Glad you got out in one piece, Carides.'

'I don't know who did it yet.' It was an itch I couldn't scratch. The best thing about detective work was the impersonal nature of it. People brought their most embarrassing problems to me, and I replied with facts and figures, tangible results like film or photographs, delivered as unemotionally as possible.

I wasn't their therapist. Most of my clients appreciated my cool attitude to their messy personal bullshit.

This case, though, this case had been personal to me from the beginning, even before my building went up in flames.

'I liked it,' I confessed. 'The office. The private detective thing. Sure, I like the work and I'm weirdly good at it. But the office. I loved that stupid office. You did good.'

Darrow looked at me, very serious, and then his face broke into a beautiful grin. 'I can get you a truck too, babe.'

I huffed at him in frustration. 'Are you kidding me right now?'

'I know a bloke.'

'You always know a bloke. I'm not setting up as Xanthippe Carides, Private Detective on Wheels. No trucks. I want my damn office back exactly as it was.'

This time, his smile was like a golden sunrise. 'Really? Even the hat rack? I thought the hat rack was a bit much…'

'Even the hat rack,' I grumbled. 'Shut up. Buy me a beer.'

WEEK EIGHT

Bikky Battle

vs

Xanthippe's Dynamite
Detective Skills

vs

Tabitha's Jammy Luck

KARI NAGARRA: It's the final showdown between our three Café Wars *contestants: The Chocolate Teapot, Café La Femme and #Sconebros. Petula, what can we expect today?*

PETULA PARRISH: Think Battle of the Bands, but with biscuits. Australian cuisine has a lot to offer the world, but one of our unsung heroes is the good old bikky. Each of our contestants has been asked to pick a theme and present a display of five different kinds of biscuit. Our judges will consider many factors including visual appearance, crunch and texture, dunkability, and that special wow factor.

KARI: We'd better roll in a lot of cups of tea to help those cookies crumble!

PETULA: What better way to pay respect to my beloved husband Chef Crewe and his life's work in Teasperience, than with a Bikky Battle finale in Café Wars*!*

≡ **29** ≡

Tabitha Has Her Suspicions

One of the odd quirks of reality TV is that time on the show doesn't equal time in real life. Contestants spend 'a year' (three months) in a historical haunted house, or spend eight weeks (twenty-eight weeks) pretending they don't know how to cook, for a mainstream TV audience.

Café Wars wasn't like that. We ran our businesses same as usual, and filmed the challenge vids—plus Kari and Tom would drop by at random times to pick up background footage, interview us while we were prepping, or spring a surprise Chef Crewe visit. A week of the show meant a week of real life, pretty much, and the episodes were uploaded within a couple of days of filming. I don't know if they managed it that way because Kari's assistant is brilliant at scheduling, or because they understood that the format required people who could only accept so much disruption to their day jobs, given how little we were being paid...

Or maybe Cameron Crewe had no idea what he was doing. That's always a possibility.

Petula Parrish (or more likely, her producer, a short-statured hipster named Fredde) did things differently. She needed to wrap this up and get back to her shiny Sydney life. If it wasn't for the fire, we would probably be done and dusted by now, but she gave us a few days to collect ourselves.

In Maaka's case, that was literal—he collected his café in a van and drove off with it. Only one of the three *Café Wars* businesses is still trading. What exactly did those lovely ladies of The Chocolate Teapot do to stay safe?

I hate feeling suspicious about people I genuinely like. But I learned the hard way that the people you least want to be guilty are often the ones who have the worst secrets to hide.

My kitchen—and it is my actual kitchen at home, since the café is off limits to me for weeks, maybe months, depending on how quickly Darrow gets the renovations underway—smells like Christmas. There's a heavy wet rain blatting against the windows, and it was hailing only a few minutes ago. The perfect weather for cookie baking.

Every year, I tell myself I'm going to bake Christmas cookies, until I remember that I live in the Southern Hemisphere. Rolling shortbread on a thirty degree day is a special kind of culinary hell. The best time for spiced cookies and

328

themed shortbread is winter, but I usually haven't recovered from normal Christmas by the time the cold winds of Hobart come around. Still, this is my year. The episode is going to air at the very beginning of July, and I can't resist 'Christmas in July' as my Bikky Battle theme.

Bikky Battle. Huh. These people have no idea what they are dealing with. Murder and arson be damned, my priority for the next twenty-four hours is to win this contest.

Kari and Tom are here to film my acreage of biscuits rolling out of the oven. Tom promises he can edit around Stewart, so it isn't obvious I've ~~stolen~~ borrowed him on his day off from The Chocolate Teapot.

When we pause for a break in filming, Jase commandeers Tom to join them in the living room for something X-box related. I'm teaching Stewart to pipe lemon icing beards on to gingerbread Santas while Kari sits on my counter, swinging her legs and testing the merchandise.

I think she might be stalling in the hopes that Xanthippe will show up, but I'm managing not to tease ... yet.

'Do you mind about Petula?' I ask, covering the worst of Stewart's beards with bright red jaffa noses. 'Honestly, McTavish, I don't know why you're so terrible at this. You're magic with a paintbrush in your hand.'

'Paint isnae usually this sticky,' says Stewart. He has icing on one eyebrow. I'm not going to tell him about it for at least an hour, because *adorable*.

'What is there to mind?' asks Kari.

'*Café Wars* was your baby. You were producing and presenting the show. You could have taken over from Crewe, but suddenly there's this whole other chef calling the shots, and she's brought in this Fredde bloke to take over your producer credit.' I shrug. 'I'd mind. I'd mind so hard they'd hear me screaming from the street.'

'So true,' Stewart confirms.

Kari really doesn't seem bothered. 'I'll get the credit on my CV either way. Realistically, for the next ten years, I'm better off trying to pitch myself as a presenter, not a producer.'

'That's depressing.'

'It's the reality of being a twenty-something female in the entertainment industry.' She quirks a smile. 'Petula's promised us all work on her new show.'

'Yes, she's good at that,' I mutter. Petula Parrish's Magical Jobs Emporium is one of many things I don't trust about that obnoxiously beautiful, talented cooking goddess.

If she tries to take Jase, I'll set fire to her hair.

'Are ye gonnae take her up on the offer?' Stewart asks Kari.

Oh, I missed this. We always made a good team at investigations and shenanigans, before I decided I was never, ever again going to try to solve a case best left to the police.

That was why I wanted him to work for Café La Femme so badly. We make a good team.

'I don't think so,' says Kari in a wondering sort of voice, like a lightbulb just clicked off over her head—like she's making the decision now, in the moment. 'If I learned one lesson from Cameron Crewe, it's that television is a horrible business. Everyone I've met in this industry has deeply skewed priorities—the promise of the next contract turns reasonable people into monsters.'

'I reckon Crewe was a monster either way,' mutters Stewart.

'I won't argue with you there,' Kari says dryly. 'I think people get so wrapped up in being seen on two million screens, they forget about what real life is supposed to look like. I thought with YouTube, I'd miss out on most of the industry bullshit, but all I found was more bullshit.'

I'm rather fond of Kari Nagarra. Not only as a partner in scheming, but as a person. She's totally good enough for Xanthippe. I'll have to do some matchmaking before Kari takes off back to the mainland.

'Tabitha, what have you done to your kitchen? You made the excellent mango smell go away,' Xanthippe complains as she strides through the door, making her usual dramatic entrance. She catches sight of Kari and smiles with more warmth than her face usually provides. 'Hi.'

'Hi,' says Kari, swinging her legs a little more elegantly.

'Want to watch some boys being stupid at an X-box?'

'Sure.'

They head to the living room together, exchanging secret smiles. No matchmaking required.

Stewart meets my eyes briefly as he clears the iced Santas off the trays to make room for the next batch. I feel a sudden wave of melancholy. Of course he picks up on it. He wouldn't be Stewart if he didn't. 'The café will be back good as new soon enough,' he says in a comforting voice. No one does comforting voice like Stewart and that Scottish accent.

'I know,' I say awkwardly. Which is stupid, because we are rubbish at awkward. We're great at relaxed and cozy and hanging out and cuddling after a night out even after failure-to-launch kissing incidents. We're fine. 'Why don't you want to kiss me anymore?' I blurt out.

Oh wow. That's a thing I did. I guess we're doing the awkward thing all the way.

Stewart doesn't blush or fumble. He licks some icing off his thumb, and gives me a perfectly ordinary smile, like he's not freaking out at where this conversation is going. Who even is he right now? 'I always want to kiss ye,' he says. It sounds like an obvious truth, something he doesn't even have to think about.

'So that wasn't you ducking your head away in the alley the other week?' I press.

The calmer he is, the more I want to throw things and make a fuss. But a horrible sentence from the previous month has ingrained itself deeply in my psyche—Bishop saying 'I can't take any more of the crazy drama, Tish,' because apparently setting a trap to blackmail a major celebrity into outing himself as a terrible person is one step too far in a ~~girlfriend~~ fiancée.

I stay calm, waiting for whatever infuriating brush off Stewart is going to give me. Waiting for him to tell me he's sick of my crazy drama too. Waiting for him to tell me I'm ridiculous.

Stewart meets my gaze straight on, and there is such warmth there I want to wrap myself up in it. 'I'd like to kiss ye,' he says after a thoughtful moment. 'But our timing's always terrible, and ye broke up with Bishop five minutes ago, and I know better than to push. We're friends, and I'm fine with that. Do ye want the shortbreads frosted?'

'Only knaves and poltroons put frosting on shortbread,' I murmur, my eyes still fixed on his. 'How long do I have to be single before you trust me enough to try again?'

'I have no idea.' He's so damned casual, like this is an ordinary conversation.

Two can play at that game. 'Okay. I'll wait.'

For the first time in this conversation, Stewart looks impatient with me. That feels like a win. 'I'm not asking … *Tabitha*. Patience is not what I'm asking for, here.'

'Tough. You can't stop me waiting. Patiently.' I lean in to dust icing sugar over the shortbreads, and accidentally on purpose dust him all up the front of his shirt. 'Oops.'

Stewart holds up a cinnamon shaker and smirks.

Oh, it's on.

Ten minutes later, we emerge from the kitchen, coughing up clouds of spicy and sweet Christmas cheer. Both of us will taste powdered cloves for days.

Ceege rolls his eyes at us. He's been wearing his Marilyn Monroe black tulle all day and won't tell me why. I think it has something to do with Xanthippe. I'm tempted to put on my Grace Kelly seafoam gown since we're being fancy, but my pores are clogged with cinnamon, ginger and icing sugar.

'Enough kitchen related foreplay,' Ceege declares. Stewart's ears go red—good to know someone can still embarrass him, since I've lost the knack. 'Let's do shots!'

The living room descends into approval and delight, despite my attempts to convince them all that *Café Wars* is important enough to warrant an early night.

I'm not even convincing myself.

It's not enough that we're a gang of twenty-somethings doing tequila shots on a week night. It has to be Truth or Dare.

'Are you actually fifteen years old?' Jase accuses us in mock outrage, but he joins in readily enough.

'We can't do dares!' I remind them all, jumping on the nearest couch to make my point.

Ceege was already nodding solemnly. 'Dares are forbidden in this household since the Great Bedazzling Incident.'

'If we're going to do this, we have to play Stand Up Truth,' I explain. 'The rules are simple. You stand up to make a statement, and if it's true about anyone in the room, they stand up to drink a shot with you. If your truth is unique, you don't have to drink.'

'It has the added bonus that if you can't stand up straight, you know it's time to stop drinking,' Xanthippe adds dryly.

'Safeguards are vital,' I agree.

Ceege goes first with 'I look awesome in high heels,' which is not only an undeniable truth, but encourages Kari and me to get the party started.

I tease Xanthippe for refusing to rise for that one. 'Come on, shut up, you look good in everything and you know it.'

'High heels make me cranky,' she insists.

'Cranky looks good on you too.'

'Get on with the game, Tish!'

Jase declares 'I can make Baked Alaska,' which has me on my feet again. Some kind of conspiracy, perhaps?

Xanthippe manages a universal truth with 'I once hitch-hiked through Poland,' and is far too smug about it.

Stewart pretends to consider a cop out option like speaking Gaelic or something (is that even a thing he could do?) but then he grins and says: 'I've saved Tabitha's life.'

'I'll drink to that,' says Xanthippe, on her feet again.

I meet Ceege's eyes and he bats his eyelashes at me, then hefts himself to his feet too. 'We never speak of it,' he says, saluting me with his shot.

I glanced at Jason. 'You could make a case...'

'Shut up, you saved my life more,' he mutters. I lean over the circle to give him a soppy kiss on his forehead. Apparently we're at that stage of the evening.

The game speeds up after that, getting more and more ridiculous. Most embarrassing moment? Probably when Kari admits she has a McTabitha t-shirt on under her jumper, and Jase tries to buy it from her.

Tom stands up at one point and confesses: 'I really, really hate cooking shows. And reality TV in general. But cooking—I don't even know how to poach a fucking egg. Why does anyone want to poach eggs anyway?'

Ceege leaps to his feet and salutes Tom. 'I do know how to poach a fucking egg but I am *with* you on cooking shows.'

I gasp. 'Traitor. How am I only now hearing about this?'

'Tabby, babes, I love you, but if I never have to watch another minute of the Food Channel, I will be a happy man.'

Kari gets to her feet.

'Not you too!' The world is topsy-turvy.

'I didn't hate them until I tried to make one, obviously.' Oh, I can see that.

The boys sit after downing their shots and exchanging some kind of bro-bump, but Kari stays up. 'Cameron Crewe was a vile, horrible excuse for a human being, and part of me is really glad he's dead,' she says in a shaky voice.

Xanthippe pours herself another shot, gets to her feet, and gives Kari a hug.

Jase gets to his feet too, and then Tom. Stewart looks troubled, and undecided.

I've never felt so much like a coward for not drinking a shot. 'We should stop now.'

'You know,' says Tom with a twisted smile. 'I once saw that bastard throw an omelette in a waiter's face? Because the customer made him bring it back to the kitchen and Crewe reckoned there was nothing wrong with it.'

'Was that here?' Xanthippe asks in surprise. She lets go of Kari.

'Nah, in Sydney. Years ago.'

'It wasn't the big stuff,' Kari mutters, sitting back down next to me. 'It was the—what's the word? Micro-bullshit.'

'Micro-aggressions,' says Stewart.

Kari snaps her fingers. 'That. He'd taunt people, but

337

keep it just the right side of civil, sometimes for hours. So you'd look like a crazy person if you reacted to it.'

'He wasn't,' I say, and then close my mouth when everyone looks at me. 'Never mind. Doesn't—mind.'

'What were you going to say?' Xanthippe asks.

Words cannot describe how defensive I feel about this. 'It was one time, okay? Bishop had just broken up with me, and I felt really terrible, and I was fighting with my friends, and nothing was going right. Crewe noticed I was having a terrible day and I thought he was going to mock me or whatever, but instead he let me play with the dry ice. We pretended we were Heston Blumenthal for like an hour, and it cheered me up.'

Yep, they're all looking at me. I pour myself a shot. We're running low on tequila. 'I know he was a dickhead, but only like ninety-nine percent of one,' I add, feeling like an idiot.

'I suppose there are worse eulogies,' says Xanthippe grimly.

'How's this for a unique truth?' I force myself to stand and raise my glass. 'I killed Cameron Crewe.'

They're all staring at me with only slightly more concern than when I said he wasn't always completely horrible. Laughter bubbles up in my throat. 'Just me, then? No one else has anything to add?'

Xanthippe hooks an arm around my waist, drawing

me away from the party. 'Okay, game's over. Divvy up couches, call cabs, or fight over Jase's bed—'

'Hey,' protests Jase, but only vaguely.

'McTavish, a little help here,' Xanthippe says. I feel the comforting presence of Stewart pressing in at my other side. Well, all right then.

'I'm not that drunk,' I protest as they drag me up the stairs to my room.

'Sure you're not,' says Xanthippe, taking off my shoes. 'Stewart, water.'

He disappears into my bathroom. While he's gone, Xanthippe expertly changes me into my pyjamas.

'You're way too good at that,' I grumble.

'One of my many superpowers.'

'You drank more shots than me.'

'I'm tougher than you, Tabitha. You're made of cake and nail art.'

'That is slander, sometimes I make pie.'

Under her supervision, all three of us drink enormous glasses of water. Before I quite realise what's happening, I'm tucked into bed with Stewart on one side of me (minus his shoes and jeans), and Xanthippe on the other (in a borrowed pair of silk pyjamas that I bet I'll never get back).

'I'm fine, you know,' I mutter. 'I don't need to be watched like a—person.' I intended a more appropriate simile, but tequila.

'Don't throw up on me and we'll all be fine,' Stewart requests.

'Not even upset,' I grouch into the pillow. 'Only a chef. Plenty of chefs in the world. Plenty of cafés in the world. Plenty of beautiful sandstone buildings in the world.'

'If you start crying right now, I'm going to throw half a dozen of your favourite shoes out the window,' Xanthippe complained. 'Selected at random, not in pairs. Shut up and go to sleep.'

'Worst best friend ever,' I tell my pillow.

It's nice, not being alone.

––––––––––

I wake up to find myself pressed up against the long line of Stewart's back, with Xanthippe nowhere in sight. Subtle, Carides, really subtle.

'This is awkward,' I mumble into the back of his neck.

'Can it be awkward later?' he retorts. 'I'm still asleep.'

'Did we mean to get everyone hungover the day of the last *Café Wars* shoot?'

'Let's blame Chef Crewe, seems like his sort of crime.'

'So true.' I roll away from him, and stare at my ceiling. 'Game face on?'

'D'ye still think you killed him?' Stewart lifts himself off on an elbow.

'I never thought I killed him. I was trying to—you know.

Gathering of the suspects. Get a reaction.'

He frowns at me. 'Most of the suspects were no' in the room.'

'That was a miscalculation, yes. But I can improve on it.' I climb out of bed. 'What would be a good outfit for crime solving? Can I get away with tweed again? Or should I be super ironic and go with prison stripes?'

'Aye, it's too early for this.' Stewart disappears back under the covers.

'Boo.' I look at my phone, which miraculously ended up on the charger despite the state I was in last night. 'Did you two let me drunk text?'

'Possibly?'

'I think I came up with a *plan* last night.'

'Ye mean, tequila came up with a plan.'

I take a flying leap on to the bed, ruffling his hair despite his groans and half-hearted attempts to kill me with a pillow. 'Stewart! *Tequila* came up with a *plan*. Today's the day we fix everything.'

All I have to do now is pick the right outfit, and this murder has basically solved itself.

Too easy.

KARI NAGARRA: What's been your takeaway experience from Café Wars?

[Close up of Daisy and Dot of The Chocolate Teapot]

DAISY: It's been lovely to spend time with these enthusiastic, creative young people, sharing delicious food. That's what running a café is all about.

DOT: I enjoyed the food throwing challenges!

[Close up of Maaka of #Sconebros]

MAAKA: I've been thinking a lot about what's important. A café's not just a business. It's a place where people come together to share stuff. Also, a café that refuses to serve coffee is a pretty [bleeped out] stupid idea.

[Close up of Tabitha of Café La Femme]

TABITHA: I learned you should never leave confectionary weapons lying around, or someone might use them to frame you for murder.

[Camera shifts slightly]

KARI (off mike): Tabitha, you can't say that.

TABITHA: It's what we're all thinking!

TOM (off mike): I was definitely thinking that.

[Kari clears her throat]

[Cut to:]

[Mid-shot of Kari with her arm around Tabitha in a friendly way]

KARI: So how has Café Wars changed your life?

TABITHA: I'm not engaged any more. My non-existent love life is a hashtag. I did this show in the first place to expose the criminal activities of its star, who is now dead, and to promote my business, which is closed because some arsehole burned the building down!

KARI: Can you answer the question as if all those things didn't happen? Also, the building did not completely burn down.

TABITHA: Tell that to my customers who have nowhere to eat.

KARI: Can you just—say something upbeat and non-sarcastic for this vid? Literally anything. Please?

TABITHA: I can't rein in my sarcasm when your cameraman is wearing a McTabitha t-shirt.

KARI: Okay Tom, she has a point, that shirt is deeply inappropriate.

TOM (off mike): It was the only clean one left.

[Close up of Tabitha of Café La Femme]

TABITHA: Café Wars totally changed my life! Thanks for watching.

≡ 30 ≡

Xanthippe is Gathered,
Along with the Suspects

Here's a tip for drinking tequila: don't do it on the night before you're going to be observing a loud, raucous recording of a TV cooking show. Petula Parrish's 'Bikky Battle' came in three stages. The first was some sort of bizarre cookie Olympics, staged up on the Domain, in the piercing winter sunlight and freezing cold.

I was wrapped in a wool coat, two scarves and a beanie. I never wear beanies unless someone forces me to climb above sea level during winter in Tasmania. 'Is there snow on the mountain? I think there's snow on the mountain.'

'Barely even a frost,' said my brother, standing beside me in a coat large enough for two police officers, and maybe a dog. 'All those years on the mainland turned you soft.'

'I wasn't expecting you,' I said, giving him the side-eye. 'This isn't your sort of thing.'

Leo showed me his phone. 'I got a couple of texts from Tabitha in the early hours. She sent me today's filming

345

program and this message.' He handed his phone over so I could read:

Bwa ha ha, I HAVE A PLAN, gathering of the suspects, police presence would be awessscakes.

'Ah,' I said, giving him back his phone. 'Full disclosure, we were totally shit-faced last night.'

'I figured,' Leo said steadily.

'But you came anyway?'

He looked at me like I was crazy. 'I may not be Tabitha's anything any more, but as a police officer and a fellow human being, 'gathering of the suspects' is a flag I can't afford to ignore.'

'Can't argue with that.'

Tabitha, Dot and Maaka were in the middle of an egg and spoon race, with cookies instead of eggs. I had to assume it would look great on YouTube, because all three of them looked miserable from where we were standing.

We weren't the only non-combatant observers. Several members of the McTabitha fan army and a couple of glamorous ladies from Daisy and Dot's bowling league were also in attendance.

'For what it's worth, she didn't mention any kind of suspects showdown to me,' I added.

'Huh,' said Leo. 'So Tabitha's running on some wild tangent without calling in proper back up or explaining anything to anyone? You surprise me.'

'I'm sorry things didn't work out between you two,' I said quietly.

Leo gave me an odd sort of smile. 'No, you're not.'

That was close to the bone. I didn't want them to break up or anything. I was just uncomfortable with a situation where your closest female friend starts sleeping with your emotionally distant half brother. That's normal, right? 'Sorry you're sad,' I elaborated.

Leo tapped me on the nose, because apparently he learned how to be a brother from 1950s movies. Actually, that would explain a lot. 'I'm not all that sad. I'm relieved, if anything.'

'Really?' I was startled he would admit something like that.

Leo looked immediately guilty. 'Is that bad?'

I shoved my hand into his pocket, because I didn't have gloves. Gloves meant admitting that it was winter. 'It's fifty percent bad,' I told him. 'But as you know, ninety-two percent of statistics are made up on the spot.'

He nudged me with his shoulder. 'I can live with that.'

I observed the teams—the collected staff of each of the contestants for *Café Wars*. Daisy, Dot, Zandra and Stewart. Maaka, with Bruce and the rest of his #Sconebros, the ones who weren't dead or already sodded off to New Zealand or whatever. A magnificent array of hipster barista beards. Some of them were decorated with glitter.

Tabitha had Jase, Lara and Yui in support. Even Nin was here, though she was on the sidelines knitting, scowling at Tom whenever the camera's line of sight swung too close to her.

Presiding over it all was Petula Parrish, effortlessly glamorous, with her dull children on one side, and a sharp conga line of Cameron Crewe's sous-clones in grey and green on the other. Earl, Lief and Grey. There was Fredde the new producer. There was Kari still doing the actual directing and most of the work (boy oh boy her assistant had worked overtime on the makeup to make her look fresh as a daisy instead of tequila-killed like the rest of us).

'I suppose it is,' I said finally.

'Is what?' Leo asked.

'A gathering of the suspects. They're all here.'

'What's Tabitha going to do, to put a firework under them?' Leo looked uncomfortable, like he always did when he made a random joke about something Tabitha might do, and realised before he even finished the sentence that it wasn't outside the bounds of possibility.

Being out of that relationship was going to do wonders for his stress levels.

'I have no idea. I'm going to watch and listen and not get involved, and I suggest you do the same.' I replaced my sunglasses on my face, and felt instantly better.

'Way ahead of you,' Leo said under his breath.

The second act of the Bikky Battle was indoors, at least, though also in a public place. Petula hired the town hall for a formal tea party, inviting all manner of local dignitaries and minor celebrities. This was a step up from all homemade bikkies being used as cannon fodder and comedy props. Also, I eventually got the feeling back in my ears.

Leo followed us for this second bout, lurking in the roped off spot for media. I stuck close to him until Tabitha pulled me in at the last minute to fill a table.

'I'm not taking my sunglasses off,' I warned her. 'Or my beanie.'

'Fine, I'll just tell everyone you're an ASIO observer, and they should ditch any drugs or terrorist paraphernalia they have on their persons.'

'Whatever you feel you have to do.'

LIVIA DAY

KARI NAGARRA: At long last it comes down to the final round of our epic Café Wars Bikky Battle. Each café nominated a single signature iced shortbread design to present to our esteemed host, the Saucy Chef herself, Petula Parrish! They need to have made forty separate bikkies for this spectacular challenge.

PETULA: I'm looking for charming designs and delicious crunch. Bonus points if you can surprise me.

DAISY: The Chocolate Teapot presents our classic tea cookie. These teabag-shaped shortbreads are infused with lavender and Earl Grey tea, then dipped in white chocolate—three pastel shades of blue, pink and violet, with gold sprinkles.

DOT: They're adorable, if I do say so myself.

DAISY: Yes, yes they are.

[Daisy and Dot hold hands and await the verdict]

MAAKA: Our #Sconebros hokey pokey shortbreads are shaped like kiwi birds, coated with dark chocolate. We call them Choice Bikkies, Bro.

KARI: They're not scones, I see.

MAAKA: If anyone could invent the shortbread scone, it would be me. But I didn't.

KARI: I don't blame you.

TABITHA: My La Femme Wombats are vanilla shortbreads, frosted with pink marshmallow fondant and homemade rose petal jam, then dusted with coconut. They're secretly Iced Vovos. Shaped like wombats.

KARI: I have no words.

TABITHA: I was going to add edible glitter and then I thought no, pull back. They're already more disco that any biscuits have a right to be.

PETULA PARRISH: Before the final points are tallied, we're going to test the structural integrity of the shortbreads—and the skills of their chefs—by seeing who can build the highest tower with their bikkies.

[Pause as this sinks in for the contestants]

DOT: Oh, you have got to be [expletive deleted] kidding me.

= **31** =

If Tabitha Builds It, They Will Come

It finally sinks in. If I need a sign that the last eight weeks were a complete waste of my time, this is it. They expect me to build a tower out of a batch of perfectly decent disco wombat shortbreads.

My only consolation is that my marshmallow fondant is thicker than usual, and makes an excellent secondary mortar. Also, wombats are better designed for stacking than kiwis, true fact.

We're back in the Teasperience kitchen for this final Bikky Battle, each at a different station. I'm horribly close to the spot where Cameron Crewe was killed and adorned with my toffee decorations.

No time to think about murder. There's a battle to be won.

Maaka and the #Sconebros lost heart days ago. They barely manage to glue four of their biscuits into a swaying curve. Doomed to failure.

Stewart offers the greatest challenge, cementing Daisy

and Dot's teabag cookies together with dark chocolate like his life depends on it.

I almost let my natural competitive nature take over at that point, because hell no, I'm not going to be beaten at gravity-defying baked goods by Scotsman-stealing aunties no matter how amazing their taste in vintage shoes.

But then I catch a look of contempt and triumph in Petula Parrish's eyes—when the camera isn't pointed anywhere near her—and I remember what I'm fighting for.

My tower teeters. There isn't enough rose petal jam in the world to keep it upright, not even with Yui and Jason leaping forward with support trowels.

I could save it. I don't. My wombats collapse, crumbling across the floor in a sticky mess of crumb and smear. Dessert, deconstructed.

I laugh and groan and make appropriately rueful faces for the camera. Tom and Kari and Petula swarm around Stewart and his winning superstructure. I take advantage of the distraction to amble toward the Sunglasses Siblings, AKA Xanthippe and Bishop, who have been hovering all day like someone might shoot the Prime Minister on their watch. 'You know,' I say, standing close enough that they can hear my undertone. 'I feel that a woman who makes human beings go through a challenge this cruel is definitely capable of murder.'

'Way ahead of you,' says Xanthippe, surveying the crowd

with a professional nod.

'Please tell me you have more evidence to go on than that,' says Bishop plaintively. He does not tell me I'm wrong.

'You watch,' I promise him. 'Doors, Zee?'

'Doors,' she agrees.

When I give the signal, Earl and Grey step in front of the door leading to the alley behind the kitchen, while Lief steps in front of the door leading to the main bar.

I talked to all three of them before the games began earlier today. Turns out, if you treat them like humans and not the matching sous-clone work unit Cameron Crewe transformed them into, they're pretty stand up blokes.

Earl is paying for his sister to go through law school. Grey spent a couple of years working in a circus. Lief two(or rather, Lief twelve based on the rate that Crewe chewed through his assistants) is hoping to be part of the Sydney-Hobart yacht race next year, in a team with his best friends from high school.

None of them will take Petula Parrish up on her offer to work on the next season of *The Saucy Chef*, or whatever she is calling her new show. Working as the underpaid whipping boys to an angry celebrity chef is one thing, but Petula—according to restaurant industry scuttlebutt—has an icy, vengeance based kind of anger that is far less predictable than all the bullshit Cameron Crewe put them through.

They know a bad deal when they see one, are happy to help with the final scene we need to film.

I draw Xanthippe a little way from her brother. 'Do we have a good reason for leaving Stewart and me awkwardly alone together this morning?'

'Hey I had stuff to do,' she retorts. 'Any awkwardness was all your own work.'

Okay, fine. Subject dropped, for now. 'Research?' I ask, raising my eyebrows.

'Research,' she confirms. 'I now have a comprehensive list of every kitchen assistant working for Cameron Crewe in the history of the Teasperience franchise. Every single Earl, Grey and Lief.'

'And?'

She nods reluctantly.

My heart sinks.

That's that, then.

I love people. I really do. If I didn't enjoy people, the service industry would be twelve kinds of hell for me, and I would have suffocated at least one customer with a tiramisu years ago.

Still. It sucks when people disappoint me. Every time.

'I can't even enjoy being right about this,' I lament.

Xanthippe elbows me. 'Who was right?'

'We were right. Teamwork yay.' I hate it when the murderer turns out to be someone I like.

'And that's a wrap for this season of *Café Wars*!' Kari calls from the middle of the kitchen.

We gather for hugging and grinning and general crowd footage. We're used to the routine by now. Tom hops up on one of the counters to get a swooping 'hero' shot of the group. 'Wrap' doesn't mean that you stop filming. Works for me.

'Thank you all for your help during this difficult time,' says Petula in the tone of a woman who knows every word that falls out of her mouth will be retweeted somewhere in the world. 'On behalf of Teasperience, and the *Café Wars* contestants, I invite you celebrate the culmination of this, my husband's final vanity project.'

Oh, *there* is the woman who married the Toffee Shark, all teeth behind her two hundred dollar lipstick.

Each of the cafés—because we hadn't donated enough free labour to *Café Wars*, apparently—was invited to donate a contribution to the wrap party. Maaka and Daisy, correctly guessing we'd be so over sugar by now, provide savouries: cheese scones, quiches, tiny pies and other mouthwatering delights.

Meanwhile, I unpack my own oh-so-subtle contribution: goth toffee apples.

Did you know it's possible to dye toffee jet black? And that it's therefore possible to turn an innocent childhood treat into something totally macabre? Oh, Pinterest, men come and go but you will always be my first love.

Stewart gives me the weirdest look as I arrange my delicious obsidian toffee death sticks on a tray. 'Too soon, Tabitha.'

'That's the idea,' I say brightly, my eyes flicking to the covered doors, and then to Xanthippe. She saunters over and helps herself to a toffee apple. Yes, it's terrifying to watch her bite into it. Even I flinch as the black toffee cracks under her teeth.

Up on the counter, I see Tom lower the camera—a rare move for him—and I mime that he should keep it rolling. He gets it, disappearing back behind the lens.

I clap my hands to get everyone's attention. 'As the owner-manager of Café La Femme, and a newly survived veteran of *Café Wars*, I think it's time we address the turducken in the room. Cameron Crewe was a twenty-four carat bastard, but he died in this kitchen. I believe that one of us killed him. We probably shouldn't leave until we figure it out, once and for all.'

'This is outrageous,' Petula Parrish fumes, her beautiful eyes flashing at me like I'm the paparazzi and she's been caught out in public wearing tracky-daks and ugg boots.

'Is it, though?' I ask. 'Seems to me a stunt like this can only increase viewing figures, and build interest in your public profile just in time for you to launch your new show. I think we can promise some interest from the Twitterverse.'

I give a small fingerwave to the McTabitha girls. They wave their phones at me enthusiastically.

Kari steps forward. 'Tabitha, do you really think—'

'Yes, I really think,' I say seriously. 'Come on, Nagarra. You want to be an investigative journalist, not a presenter of puff. This is going to make a way better final episode, don't you think?'

Kari glances hesitantly up at Tom, who gestures at his camera, in a silent question to her. 'Keep filming,' she decides finally. 'I'd better not regret this, Tabitha.'

Sadly, her regret is inevitable.

'On with the show!' I declare.

[Camera takes in the crowd shot of the party in the Teasperience kitchen]

[Close up on TABITHA DARLING]

TABITHA: So you all know that I was here the night Chef Cameron Crewe was murdered. You probably also know that my toffee knife was found sticking into his body. I don't have an alibi. I could have done it. But I didn't. So I called in a private investigator, my friend Xanthippe Carides, to find evidence that proved I was innocent. How are we going on that, Zee?

XANTHIPPE CARIDES: Got nothing.

TABITHA: Thanks for the update. She charges by the hour, people. Tell your friends. So let's run through the suspect list. It was hard at first because anyone who ever met or worked with Cameron Crewe had a motive to want him dead.

JASE: Co-signed.

[Jase offers Maaka a fistbump. Maaka does not leave him hanging.]

TABITHA: We got especially excited by those knife skills displayed by the sous-clones—sorry, Earl, no offence.

EARL: None taken, Tabs. Also, my name is Barrington.

TABITHA: Wow, is it? Anyway, suspects, moving on. Let's consider the incredibly stylish Dot from The Chocolate Teapot—seriously, Dot, are those vintage loafers? I love them—she can also throw a mean knife. But then we found out through perfectly legitimate means that the knife wasn't thrown—Chef Crewe was stabbed at close quarters, by someone shorter than him. Keep in mind, he was the size of a small mountain, so there aren't many people in this room taller than him.

[Camera scans the crowd.]

TABITHA: Let's talk alibis. Maaka, Bruce and Ani of #Sconebros were hanging out together at the time of the murder, and they vouched for each other along with a bloke called Nico who isn't involved in the business. That's relevant not only because Maaka had a history with Crewe—which means he had motive—but because it gave Ani an alibi. Xanthippe, tell us about Ani?

XANTHIPPE: Ani Wilson was a New Zealander who worked at #Sconebros. We're pretty sure she was the one behind a series of threatening anonymous texts to Tabitha, and may also have been the person who texted Tabitha on the night of Crewe's death, to lure her to enter the kitchen so she found his body—we haven't found the phone that message came from, but we have all the others. This fits with Crewe's history of using threats and other nasty tactics to force successful café businesses out of their prime locations so he could move in a Teasperience bar. His pop up store lease was nearly up, and we believe he wanted the Café La Femme building.

TABITHA: But Ani couldn't have killed Cameron, because she has that alibi with Maaka and Bruce. Assuming that holds up ... but we know she was involved in faking her own death in my building, and setting the fire, though she was probably not working alone.

XANTHIPPE: Definitely not, because whoever she was working

with, whoever took that picture of her faking her death, actually killed her a few days later, and dumped her in the Derwent.

TABITHA: The weird thing is that Ani kept her scare campaign going long after Crewe was dead. A communication malfunction of some kind? Did she believe he was still alive? Was she some kind of double agent...

XANTHIPPE: Or maybe she was never working for Crewe in the first place. Tabitha thought he was behind the offer to buy her building because of his past patterns, but he hated Tasmania. He couldn't wait to get out of here. Who else would benefit from Teasperience getting a foothold in Hobart, if not Crewe?

[Camera shakes, then pans directly to Petula Parrish]

PETULA: Oh really, this is where I play the villain in your little pageant? I can't wait, darlings. Let's do this.

TABITHA: I guess that depends on how far you're prepared to go to pretend that you didn't set all this up. Teasperience was behind this murder, one way or another—and Teasperience is yours now. So it was you, or one of your kids.

PETULA: Leave my kids out of this.

TABITHA: You know, I really thought it was Otto. He had reason to resent his stepfather, and working in this kitchen had to have given him some confidence wielding a knife. Unlike his mother, he was right here in Hobart when the murder happened, and I'm pretty sure he doesn't have an alibi unless you can pinpoint his Skyrim participation for that day.

[Otto, standing near his mother, looks vaguely flattered]

TABITHA: And I'm pretty sure it's not Cherish, because she seems beastly careless about food or, well, everything. If she was going to put a knife in anyone, it would probably be the mother who thought naming a kid Cherish Parrish was a good idea.

[Cherish also looks vaguely flattered]

TABITHA: So no, it was totally you, Petula. No offence, but it was obvious from the start—custody battle, secret marriage, so much motive. I've spent enough time around real detectives—no offence to you either, Zee—

XANTHIPPE: All offence.

TABITHA: —to know that the spouse is always the most likely suspect. But Petula, that's exactly why you made sure you weren't here when it happened. I'm surprised you didn't ensure Otto was out of the state too. He must not be your favourite.

PETULA: I'm not sure you understand what the words 'no offence' actually mean.

TABITHA: But it wasn't only Ani working for you. You had someone else under your thumb—the person who eventually killed her. Not a professional hitman. This is way too messy for me to believe the people involved knew what they were doing. No, you found someone willing to kill for free, or for something else you had to offer. Someone who really needs one of those jobs you've been scattering like edible confetti, perhaps? If I didn't love and trust them so much, I could throw Jase and

Stewart, Lara and Yui into the mix as potential suspects. But let's not pretend I'm impartial. Who does that leave? Zandra, breaking away from the adorableness of her aunts? A #Sconebros conspiracy, with Maaka and Bruce backing up Ani? Kari Nagarra.

KARI NAGARRA: Me? I don't want a bar of Petula Parrish and her stupid show, you know that.

TABITHA: You did say that. But that's exactly the sort of thing you'd say if you had committed murder on Petula Parrish's behalf. You came down to Tasmania to put a stop to Cameron Crewe's reign of terror, after all.

KARI: You were in on that from the start. Are we absolutely sure it wasn't you, Tabitha?

TABITHA: You're forgetting someone. Someone who was here all along, part of everything. Someone who, my pet private detective confirmed today—

XANTHIPPE: Your what now?

TABITHA: He had every reason to hate the Toffee Shark, and even more reasons to hitch his wagon to the Saucy Chef. He's genuinely desperate to make it in showbiz.

[Camera trembles slightly]

[Tabitha tilts her head to look directly into the camera]

TABITHA: Congrats, Tom. You're going to be famous.

≡ **32** ≡

Xanthippe Admires the Show

For a minute, for a whole literal minute, I thought Tabitha wasn't going to get away with this.

Tom the cameraman lowered his camera and stared at Tabitha like he was in shock.

'What, you think I'm going to confess?' he sputtered. 'This is bullshit, Tabitha. You made all that crap up. There's no evidence.'

'You thought spending all that time behind that camera meant that people wouldn't notice what you were up to,' she said with confidence. 'Why didn't you tell anyone you were one of Cameron Crewe's Earls in the Sydney branch, four years ago?'

Tom shrugged. No one else in the room was looking at him like he was a threat. He'd done a good job of making himself part of the furniture, for all of us. 'It didn't matter. He didn't even remember who I was.'

'Ah,' said Tabitha, nodding sagely. 'I can see how that

would be annoying.'

I sidled up to my brother. 'Going to arrest him yet?'

Leo shook his head. 'She's got nothing. It's all conjecture so far. This is a waste of everyone's time.'

'You think she's wrong?'

Leo shrugged a shoulder, observing the scene. Kari had joined Tabitha to accuse Tom now. She was shaking with anger. She at least believed Tabitha. 'Oh, I have no doubt you two found your man. Chances are likely we can back it up with DNA too.'

I stared at him. 'I'm sorry, what?'

'Whoever killed Ani Wilson did a sloppy job of covering their tracks. We've got hair and skin samples at the lab—they're due to come back some time this week. We can hurry things along if we swab your camera bloke today, but we were always going to test all this lot.'

Petula Parrish snapped. She was waving her arms at Tom now. His camera fell by the wayside, and he gave up all pretence. Within a minute, Tom started angrily listing all the communications they had shared, including an entire electronic paper trail of Petula convincing him to murder her husband.

'Huh,' I said. 'So, proper police work then.'

'It takes time, but we get there in the end.' Leo winced as Petula tried to punch Tabitha, and her daughter caught her in a headlock from behind. 'Confessions are nice, assuming they stick to the same story once we arrest them.'

'I'm still not seeing any arresting going on,' I noted.

'Not my case. I texted Inspector Fitzgerald about fifteen minutes ago, I'm sure he'll be along shortly.'

Stewart stood protectively in front of Tabitha while Daisy and Dot advanced on Petula Parrish with their handbags ready to strike if necessary.

'What are the odds Fitzgerald's going to arrest Tabitha?' I wondered aloud.

'Pretty fucking high,' said Leo. 'He's had about fourteen different senior police officers inform him to pull his head in when it comes to the Darling family, and the stubborn arse is about ready to press charges against her to prove a point. But he's not a complete idiot, he'll do it by the books.'

'We got her a good lawyer.'

'It's amazing she hasn't needed one before this year, really.' He sounded oddly removed from the situation.

'Go figure.'

I could hear the siren. Blue and red lights gleamed through the kitchen windows at the chaotic party.

'I've been thinking,' I said, wincing as the elegant, sweet and adorable Daisy punched Tom the cameraman directly in the eye, and was hauled off him by her punk niece Zandra. 'Maybe I should learn to cook.'

Leo winced. 'God, really?'

'Nothing dramatic, maybe learn a few of Nonna's recipes,

while she's still with us.'

'Huh.' He considered this. 'Maybe we should ask her together. Family bonding all around.'

'You think you'll be better at cooking than me,' I accused.

Leo grinned, and shook his head. 'Not everything is a competition, Xanthippe.'

Tabitha Ties Up Loose Ends

This time around, I spend six hours in a police station, being interrogated.

Totally worth it.

After I'm released, I find out that Tom has finally been charged with the murders of Ani Wilson, and Cameron Crewe.

The trial of Petula Parrish for being an accessory before the fact and conspiracy to murder lasts for seven days. She wears so many amazing dresses, hires so many pretty lawyers, weeps on the stand and plays every trick from the musical *Chicago*. She still gets eighteen months inside.

Petula and Cameron's adorable baby twins (shown off at every opportunity during the trial, to build sympathy with the media) are being cared for by their siblings Cherish and Otto, far from the media spotlight.

None of my friends will watch cooking shows with me any more.

Kari Nagarra got a job with *SBS News*, as a roving reporter. She and Xanthippe have a regular Skype date, but I'm classy enough not to ask for details.

Maaka never went back to New Zealand. He and Bruce got an offer for their own show on Netflix, *Search For A #Sconebro*, in which they tour Britain on a tandem bike, learning about the history of tea and scones in various counties and making fun of other people's accents. It's pretty popular.

It's been six months, and Stewart still hasn't kissed me. I have high hopes for New Year's Eve. No one can resist kisses on New Year's, right? All I need is the perfect frock, the perfect cocktail and the perfect scheme. He won't stand a chance.

Xanthippe Ties Up Loose Ends

A few weeks after the *Café Wars* chaos ended with the arrest of Tom the camera operator, Tabitha found me in the courtyard of her (still closed) café, looking over the renovation plans for the building on a tablet. This time around, Darrow was going to let me have input in my new and improved office. I was in a long-running chat thread with him, arguing that bathroom and kitchen fittings really didn't have to fit the film noir aesthetic.

Also, I wanted a hot tub.

'It's not too late, you know,' I teased Tabitha. 'We can order a new business name for the glass panel in the door. How does Carides and Darling, Private Detectives sound?'

Tabitha got the oddest look on her face, like she didn't know whether to smile or smack me in the face. 'Maybe as a retirement plan,' she conceded. 'I have a lot of mirror glaze and butter cream to whip up between now and then. Selling panini and espresso brings in a more reliable income than locating runaway pet turtles.'

'That was one turtle,' I protested, but not with any heat. I hadn't expected her to accept the offer. Or to stop making fun of the runaway pet turtle.

Tabitha smirked at me. 'You can't seduce me into the life of a private detective. I already know it won't be celebrity chefs and murderous desserts every day of the week.'

'It's mostly sitting around in cars and spying on people's love lives,' I agreed. 'I can see why it appeals to you as a hobby.'

Tabitha rolled her eyes at me. 'Whereas you're positively bored by it all.'

'Last week I spent four hours on a classic cars forum to find out if some bloke was cheating on his wife. Turns out he was buying a really expensive car. I think she'd have preferred the affair.'

Tabitha leaned over the tablet. Darrow was threatening to replace the gutted first floor office with a roller rink, or possibly a paintball studio. My only request was that he offered it to a business that didn't regularly attract dead bodies, to balance out the magnetic combination of Café La Femme and the Xanthippe Carides Detective Agency.

'I do plan to be Miss Marple one day,' Tabitha admitted finally. 'I mean, I'll probably be hardened to the whole murder thing by then. I like the idea of growing up to be a little old lady detective who defends the world via knitting needles, gossip, and whatever hipster cooking trend is hot that decade. Artisan gummies. Deconstructed protein goo.'

'That sounds like you now, except for the knitting,' I observed.

Tabitha laughed at me. 'Call me in as a people skills consultant now and then if you like. I won't work boring cases, though, none of this security-adultery-missing pets crap. I will join in only when you are faced with elaborate puzzles that belong in a Dorothy Sayers novel, or when your flirting for clues hits a brick wall.'

'How often do you think that kind of case is going to come along, Tish?' I wondered.

She stuck her tongue out at me. 'Witness my life.'

Well, yes. She wasn't wrong.

'Silent partner?' I suggested. I didn't actually want to share my pretty glass door with anyone else's name.

'Slightly silent partner,' Tabitha conceded. 'With an option for extreme chattiness if and when the situation calls for it.'

I smiled warmly at her. 'Sounds about right.'

We sat there for a moment, basking in the knowledge that Tabitha could never be a silent anything.

'Cake?' she suggested after a long, thoughtful moment.

'Cake,' I agreed.

Cake hardly ever gets you murdered.

Book 1 in The Café La Femme series

LIVIA DAY

Availiable in paperback and ebook

Tabitha Darling has always had a dab hand for pastry and a knack for getting into trouble. Which was fine when she was a tearaway teen, but not so useful now she's trying to run a hipster urban cafe, invent the perfect trendy dessert, and stop feeding the many (oh so unfashionable) policemen in her life.

When a dead muso is found in the flat upstairs, Tabitha does her best (honestly) not to interfere with the investigation, despite the cute Scottish blogger who keeps angling for her help. Her superpower is gossip, not solving murder mysteries, and those are totally not the same thing, right?

But as that strange death turns into a string of random crimes across the city of Hobart, Tabitha can't shake the unsettling feeling that maybe, for once, it really is ALL ABOUT HER.

And maybe she's figured out the deadly truth a trifle late...

Shortlisted for Best Debut Book, Davitt Award
for Australian Women's Crime Writing

Killer Nashville Silver Falchion Finalist

Merry Happy Valkyrie

TANSY RAYNER ROBERTS

ebook format only

'A sparkling holiday fantasy story full of deliciously fun characters and fabulous magic.' – Stephanie Burgis

Norse myth and magic collides with a small town Tasmanian Christmas in this festive romantic fantasy!

Lief Fraser has mixed feelings about returning home to Matilda, the only Australian town where it always snows at Christmas. As a TV weather presenter, it's her job to report on the strange holiday phenomenon … but as a local, it's her duty to preserve Matilda's many magical secrets.

Then pretty Audrey Astor rolls into town to shoot the ultimate romantic Australian Christmas movie with her film crew. Sparks fly, secrets unravel … and soon everyone will know exactly how Mt Valkyrie got its name.

Marry Me Mischa McPhee

KATE GORDON

ebook format only

When Maddy discovers a love note scrawled on the toilet cubicle wall at work, she decides to go on a quest to find out who wrote it and to see if, just maybe, it was intended for her.

This sweet Christmas holiday romance set in Hobart, Tasmania, is just the thing you need to ease into the festive season this year. BYO cup of hot chocolate and slice of cake!